MW01257050

SleepyEye Publishing Presents:

THE ORGANIZATION

By T. Freeman Jr.

THE ORGANIZATION

ISBN 978-0-615-21033-9

This book is dedicated to my wife Sherrel and my 4 children.
Also to my mother and father who told me to keep chasing
My dreams, when everyone else told me to live reality.
Now my dreams are reality!

Acknowledgments

Mike Freeman - Cover Art Concept
Vedic Design - Book Cover Design
Stacey Diventi - Book Editor
Self-Pub.net - Book Formatting
Taino De La Ghetto - Co-author of Sons of Sin
Rhonda Crowder - for the helpful advice

Table of Contents

1

Camden, NJ 08013

It's hard to believe, but in 1925, Camden, New Jersey was a beautiful place to live. The city was very much segregated, with the distinct ethnic neighborhoods. Each neighborhood had their own shops and delis and was very different from the others. The Whitman Park Section of the city was labeled Pollack Town because the majority of its residents were of Polish descent. The area was made up of row homes on small tree lined streets. Parkside, a predominantly Jewish neighborhood, bordered Pollack Town. East Camden and Cramer Hill were mixtures of the Irish, German and English residents who once dominated the city. The diversity in these neighborhoods caused for constant rivalry about almost everything. This lead to attacks on one another, and as a result, Cramer Hill and East Camden had a much higher crime rate than Camden's more ethnic neighborhoods. East Camden is Second only to South Camden in size, but has much bigger houses and yards than South Camden. In 1925, East Camden was actually more suburban than urban. The Italian neighborhoods of North and South Camden were filled with bakeries and shops that attracted all ethnicities and even served blacks. The Italians occupied all of North Camden, from The Delaware River on the north side to Tenth Street on the south, and from the newly constructed Benjamin Franklin Bridge on the east, to Cooper River on the west. The Italians also controlled a large section of South Camden, from Benjamin Franklin Bridge on the west, to Morgan Blvd. on the East, and from 10th Street on the north, to Broadway on the South. The Section of South Camden from 4th Street to the river was known as Froggy Bottom, and was home to the city's black population. Where as, the Italians, Jews and Polish had shops that attracted all ethnicities, the blacks owned speakeasy's and sold dinners out of their kitchens, catering mainly to blacks, although Italian men would come to the neighborhood to eat. The Italians and blacks maintained a good relationship in the city, especially in the area between 4th Street and Broadway, known as, The Center. It was located in The Center of South Camden, between the Italian district and Froggy Bottom. The area was about 3 blocks wide and 15 blocks long. It was also one of the most diverse in the city. The majority of residents there were well-to-do blacks that could afford to leave Froggy Bottom, and poor Italians who couldn't afford North Camden or South Camden's all Italian neighborhoods. It was there, on August 23, 1926, that my grandfather, Sonny Robinson, was born.

Sonny's mother Emily Robinson was a beautiful, fair-skinned woman with curly, brown hair to the middle of her back. She was 5'7 and weighed about 140 with what I've heard described as "dangerous curves". She was a showgirl who danced and sung with some of the great performers of her time. She was born in Macon, Georgia and was trying to escape an abusive father and a look-the-other-way mother, when she met a promoter who toured all the major theaters that allowed blacks at the time. After seeing Emily, and hearing her sing, the promoter offered her a contract. Emily signed with him and hit the road, singing on the chitterling circuit at 15, after lying about her age.

In December of 1925, somewhere between the Regal Theatre in Chicago and the Howard Theatre in Washington, D.C. she became pregnant and moved to Camden, New Jersey with her father's Sister, Ola. Ola, like the rest of Emily's family, hadn't heard from the now 17 year old, in nearly 2 years. Emily loved her Aunt Ola and believed she could tell her anything, even about her father. It was a cold March evening as Ola approached her 5th and Line Street home, hand in purse, searching for her keys. It was a long winter that couldn't seem to end fast enough. The snow illuminated the streets and Ola could see a young lady sitting on her porch.

"Excuse me, young lady I believe you're…"

"Aunt Ola!" a voice interrupted.

"Emily, is that you?"

"Yes, Aunt Ola. It's me, Emily."

"Thank you, Jesus! Emily, come give me some sugar!" Ola said, gripping Emily in a bear hug.

Ola looked into Emily's eyes and could see herself, a beautiful woman with hair to her shoulders,

Ola was still turning heads at 43, but no longer had the coke bottle figure she once enjoyed.

"Where have you been? We've been worried sick." Ola paused, feeling Emily pull back and slightly turn when pressed for answers. "Well, let's just get inside. It's freezing out here."

Emily nodded and the two walked into the house together. Ola walked Emily through her dimly lit living room. *It was a small, 2-bedroom house, but it was a major accomplishment for a black woman to own one. The living room walls were lined with pictures. On the wall in front of her, Emily saw Walter and Joseph, Aunt Ola's two sons', graduation photos, a picture of Emily and a service picture of her father.*

"He'll be so happy to know you're okay." Ola said, noticing Emily stare at the picture of her father.

"What's wrong?" Aunt Ola continued, as Emily was now crying.

"I don't want nothin' to do with that man. He raped me, and his wife, *my mother*, let him".

Ola, though stunned consoled Emily, made her a cup of hot chocolate and the two talked each other to sleep.

Ola woke up at 5:00 am as usual. She thought about her brother as she watched Emily sleep. She then thought about her own father molesting her. She wiped away her tears, went back to her bedroom and said her morning prayers:

Lord, I pray you forgive my brother the same way I prayed you would forgive my father. I ask that you would help my niece Emily to become a God fearing, respectable woman, and to have her do what she was called to do. I ask that you would mend her heart, and that one day she could find it in herself to forgive her father and mother, as I know they both miss and love her. Lord, I also ask that you would keep my sons safe and help their families stay rooted in Your Word. In Jesus name Amen.

Emily smiled and shut the door. She had awakened and walked in on her Auntie's prayers. She knew that, although her Aunt gave her word that she wouldn't tell her brother of Emily's whereabouts, the mother in her would never let her keep it a secret. Furthermore, Emily had no intentions to forgive. She never wanted to see her parents again. At that moment, she decided she was going to have to leave Camden, but at 4 months pregnant, she had no clue how.

Ola knew Emily was pregnant, but planned to wait for Emily to reveal the news. However, by lunch, Ola was growing impatient with her niece and bluntly asked her, "Girl, you pregnant?"

"Yes, Auntie." answered Emily.

"Un huh, I don't see no ring on your finger and no man here wit you, so I'm guessing he ran off. Was it that promoter fellow you told me about who stole all your money?"

"No." answered Emily. "I never had sex with him. That's why he dropped me when he found out I was pregnant. Cuz I had told *him* I was saving myself for marriage."

"Well if not him, who?" Ola snapped back. "You don't know." Ola said, answering her own question. She paused from doing the dishes as Emily, feeling ashamed, leaned back in her chair. "I suppose it aint your fault. As young as you are and bein' you was raped an' all. Well, we gone just have to do the best we can do now aint we?"

"Yes, Auntie." Emily answered, later revealing either a trumpet player from Chicago or a drummer from D.C. could be the father of what she just knew was her baby boy.

"Sonny."

"What you say, nah?" Ola whispered.

"Sonny" Emily returned "If It's a boy like I know it is I'm a name him Sonny after Sonny Greer the best drummer in all the chitterling circuit."

"He wouldn't happen to be from D.C.; would he?"

"No." Emily laughed. "That's not his daddy. He's just the best. He makes the drums talk to you, Auntie."

Ola laughed. "Right now the only thing talking to me is my stomach. How 'bout some fried chicken?"

Emily smiled "It's good to see family, Auntie."

Over the next couple of months Emily would renew some contacts with bands, promoters and club owners to plot her return to the night scene. She had led her Aunt Ola to believe she would talk to her parents after she safely delivered her baby. Aunt Ola was excited and couldn't wait until her niece gave birth. Meanwhile, across the bridge in Philadelphia, Emily was meeting with Nino Caridi. He was a short, Italian man with a slim build who owned The Uptown Theater. Nino blew smoke from a cigar as he inspected Emily like a new purchase." I saw you in Baltimore at the Douglas over there on Pennsylvania Ave. You were something else. If you can still sing I can use you Labor Day weekend. $10 for the week take

6

it or leave it." Nino said spitting and puffing smoke with every word. Emily looked around the theater, the stage, and the seats. She could see her fans; hear the band play and she couldn't wait.

"I'll take it!" She said, smiling from ear to ear.

"Good, if things work out you can play The Earl, too."

"You own The Earl, too?" Emily said, astonished.

"Let's just say, it's in the family." Nino said with a laugh.

Emily signed the contract and it was set. Emily Robinson at the Uptown Theater in Philadelphia, August 31-September 3.

(Screaming sounds) It was August 23, 1926 and Emily Robinson gave birth to her son William Sonny Robinson in her Aunt's Line Street home. He was a big baby, brown in complexion, with a head full of curly hair. Aunt Ola, along with Dr. Miles, cut the cord and washed the baby. Dr. Miles was one of the few black doctors in Camden. As he checked baby Sonny, Emily fell fast asleep. She awoke hours later to two familiar faces, Aunt Ola and the face of a trumpet player she had met in Chicago. The mystery was over. She knew who the father was, although she would take that secret to the grave.

"Here he is." Aunt Ola said, handing Sonny to his mother.

"He's precious! He's so little. I don't want to..." Emily said, before being cut off.

"Now hush up and take this boy. He's yours!" Ola said smiling.

"He's mine too, but he's yours" (laughing).

That night Emily lay in the bed quietly crying herself to sleep because she knew what she had to do. It would only be a matter of time before Aunt Ola would tell her brother of his daughter's whereabouts. The next day Emily surprised Ola when she walked in her room and proclaimed, "I'm ready to speak with my father and mother. It's not going to be easy, but I'm ready."

Aunt Ola was excited. "I'll call them now; they'll love to talk to you."

"No!" Emily screamed.

"I mean, no." She said, lowering her voice to almost a whisper. "I'd rather talk face to face. You can call and tell them I'm here and tell them I'm okay, but I won't talk until I see their faces."

As the days went on, Emily seemed depressed and Ola thought it was a result of her mother and father's pending visit. Now Sonny I want you to promise your mommy you will always respect women and mind your Auntie. You never gone end up like your granddaddy. You hear me?" she said to the infant, as if waiting for a response. It was August 29th, and her parents would be there in the morning, but Emily had no plans on greeting them. Instead, she was headed for the ferry station for a trip to Philadelphia.

It was 5:00 am, prayer time for Aunt Ola, when she heard the baby cry. She figured Emily was asleep and went into her room to check on Sonny. The baby lay in the crib crying. Emily's bed was made with a letter on the pillow. Aunt Ola hesitated, and then picked up the letter, already knowing what it said.

Dear Aunt Ola,

Thank you for everything. I know how much you love me and my father and wanted this reunion to work, but it's just not what I want. I'm sorry. Sonny loves you and you can raise him better than me. May he bring much joy to your life? Love,

Emily

P.S. I got a new gig. I'm back on the circuit doing what I love doing. What I'm called to do.

Ola smiled, and then paused. She had to get the baby out of there before her brother Lester and his wife Anita arrived and began to question who's baby and maybe worse, try to take Sonny away. Ola rushed with just the baby and a diaper to her oldest son Walter's house. Walter was a worker at the Campbell Soup Company and was married with two small kids. He knew of his cousin's situation and despised her father for what he had done, although Ola had urged him to keep all knowledge of the incident to himself. (Boom, boom, boom)

"Mom what's, is everything okay?" Walter said as he answered the door just at the crack of dawn.

"It's Emily; she's run away and wants me to keep the baby and I can't let your uncle Lester know she had a baby or else…"

"He'll want the baby." Walter interjected, taking Sonny from his mother's hands as his wife Thelma came to the door.

"Mrs. Davies?" Thelma said, "Is everything alright?"

"Yea, everything's okay honey. Take the baby; I'll explain later." Walter said, handing his wife the baby. Thelma took the baby and left for the bedroom allowing for Walter and his mother to talk.

"I got a mind to come kick that man's ass. Trying to."

"Now, you hush cussin' In front ya momma like that? And that's still your uncle so you respect him."

"I'll handle this. You just keep the baby until they leave for Georgia, after the holiday."

"Yes ma'am." Walter answered, before kissing his mother and shutting the door.

"My boy, Sonny!" Marco "Small Man" Reginelli yelled from across Broadway. Sonny came running across the street. Blacks were not allowed on the Italian side of Broadway, but when the boss of South Jersey's La Cosa Nostra calls, you come running. This is Sonny, my number one numbers runner. Marco said, introducing Sonny to members of his family.

"Sonny Robinson, you're starting to look just like your mother."

"My mother?" Sonny whipped back after hearing a short Italian man refer to a woman Sonny had seen maybe a half dozen times in all his 17 years.

"Yes, your mother Emily, a beautiful woman and great singer."

"Hi, I'm Nino Caridi," announced the pint sized Italian with his hand stretched out. Sonny shook Nino's hand, standing at 6'4; Sonny towered over Marco, Nino and two other associates who did not give their names.

"So, you know my mother?" Sonny asked.

"Sure. She used to sing in my club all the time. I used to own the Club Uptown in Philly."

"Right. I've heard stories about my mother being a great singer." Sonny said.

"Not to mention a great looker." Nino added with his associates laughing.

Sonny shot Nino a look that could've killed and Marco quickly defused the tension.

"I don't usually deal with kids, but since the war started, what are you going to do?" Marco reasoned.

Sonny was in charge of the numbers game in Froggy Bottom and The Center. He answered only to Marco. It was June of 1942, and William Sonny Robinson had just graduated from Camden High School. At the edge of The Center, new neighborhoods full of affordable apartments were built. The apartments were called Roosevelt Manor after the current President Franklin Roosevelt who approved the federal aid to fund the housing. Brach Village and other projects were built adjacent to Roosevelt Manor forming the new area called Centerville.

Centerville was all black unlike The Center, and even a mob boss could have problems trying to collect in that neighborhood. Marco respected Sonny and didn't tolerate others disrespecting him. He not only used Sonny as an entrance into the black community, but he valued his opinion and viewed Sonny as a valuable asset. The city was booming with industry from the shipyards, DuPont chemical plant, RCA, Campbell Soup and of course the numbers racket.

2

Dominicans Come to the City

It was late in 1942. The draft had sent a lot of young Camden men to war and the cities industries were feeling the strain. Campbell Soup had begun to go to the Dominican Republic to find replacement workers, while 40% of their full time employees went to serve their country. Campbell's brought thousands of Dominicans to Camden to live in barracks they made behind their warehouse, and to work in the factory. The majority of workers were men, while some wives, cooks and women workers were permitted to make the trip. A lot of city residents were not pleased with the arrival of the Dominicans. Sonny was not one of these residents. Sonny immediately saw this as an opportunity to control another part of organized crime in the city. Every ethnicity had their own underworld and controlled their own gambling and drug dealing operations. With the Dominicans being the newest ethnic group to the city, Sonny saw a chance to become the overseer of the whole Dominican underworld. All he needed was an entrance man into the community, similar to how Marco had recruited

Sonny. There was one easy way to make this happen, and that was to get a job at Campbell Soup, which wouldn't be hard.

"Sonny, what a pleasant surprise. How have you been? Have you found a job, yet?"

"No, cousin Thelma. That's why I'm here."

"Oh, Walter will be thrilled! They can use the help you know. With the war an' all. Plus those Dominicans will be coming next week, and half of them don't speak English" she interjected.

"So? Some of them do" Sonny fired back.

"Yes, the real educated ones learned English in School. They're going to be supervisors for the non-English speaking workers," Thelma answered.

Sonny nodded and Thelma promised that Walter would be in contact.

Sonny didn't tell Walter or Marco of his master plan. He just waited.

The next day Aunt Ola woke Sonny up at 6:00 am and told him to get dressed. Walter got him the job. "That was fast", thought Sonny, as he showered and dressed for his first day at the job. Sonny was a well-built, brown-skinned, young man with a full beard and mustache. He was now 18, standing 6'4, weighing 215 and was a real lady-killer. Although, Sonny was more concerned with making money than making love.

Sonny went to work and reported to his cousin Walter, who was now finally a supervisor, after being with the company for 20 years. The work was easy to Sonny who was strong as an ox. He also heard Walter tell so many stories of his job that he felt like he knew all the workers and exactly how the job was done. Sonny was a humble man despite his stature and was liked by everybody. That, he got from his mother.

It was 10 days after Sonny was hired that the Dominican workers arrived. Sonny had never seen a Dominican and was shocked at what he saw.

"They're black people that speak Spanish."

"No, they're Dominicans", Walter responded.

"Man, say what you will, but that brother is darker than me. Aint no way he anything but black," Sonny said seriously while Walter, a chubby light-skinned man, now in his 40's, shook his head and chuckled.

"Let me introduce you to the foreman. I mean, forewoman", Sonny said.

"Yea, most of the women are better educated, so they were brought over as translators/supervisors.

"Damn, it takes a nigga 20 years and a war to be supervisor! And a Spanish woman nigger gets the job immediately", Sonny said laughing.

But, seeing Walter was uncomfortable with the remark, he apologized.

"Hey, I didn't mean to insult you."

"No, the sad part is you're right cuz; you're right", Walter said, now in a more somber tone.

"Sonny, I'd like you to meet Delilah Hernandez. Delilah, this is my cousin Sonny. He knows this factory inside out and can give you the grand tour", Walter said noticing Sonny's obvious attraction to Delilah.

"Hi...Hi...Hi. I'm Sonny", the usually confident Sonny said to the drop dead gorgeous woman.

Delilah was a 5'4 with long, black hair and she was darker than Sonny but with a reddish tint. She was in a factory shirt that couldn't conceal her perfectly round breasts and her butt was perfectly round too. She was the prettiest girl in Camden and Sonny was going to make her his, one way or another.

"Hello I'm Delilah," she said, in a seductive, thick, Spanish accent. Sonny was star struck and began to smile. This was going to be better than he thought.

Sonny showed Delilah around the plant and then took her to get a Donkey steak. Donkey's was a famous Polish sandwich store on Haddon Ave. The two laughed and ate. After work when most of the Dominicans went to the barracks Delilah would go spend the night on the town with Sonny who was now even higher in the chain of command at work and with Marco Sonny was falling in love making money and finding an in into the Dominican community. Things couldn't be better. Over dinner, Delilah explained how Dominicans were a mixture of African slaves, indigenous people and the Spanish. They were actually more of the African descent than of Spanish.

"I knew it! I knew you were black when I first saw you", Sonny said laughing with Delilah joining him. Delilah told Sonny that her brother was worried about her dating Sonny.

"Does he speak English? I'll talk to him and reassure him I only have good intentions", Sonny said smiling.

"Yea, he speaks English. When I would come home from school, I would teach him what I learned.

"Oh well, here it is. There's more to me than you know. I run numbers. It's gambling. It's illegal. And I make a lot of money doing it. I want to bring it to your community, but I need an in."

"I'm listening", She replied, to Sonny's surprise.

"I want to bring your brother in", He would control all numbers for the Dominicans. He reports to me, and I report to an Italian guy named Marco.

"What's the split?" she asked.

"What was it you said you did in the D.R.", a stunned Sonny asked, as they stared at each other, before they laughed and exchanged a kiss.

That kiss led them to the Walt Whitman Hotel at Second and Cooper Streets. When they got in the room, they immediately began kissing. Sonny slid Delilah's belt off and her pants fell to the floor. He then unbuttoned her shirt as she took of her panties and bra stood before him butt naked. She laid him on the bed and began to remove his shoes, then belt, then pants and underwear. She took off his shirt, so he then lay naked in front of her. He reached over and turned off the lights and then began to massage her inner thigh. He then began to kiss her up and down her spine until he reached her ass. Then he gently slid his tongue down between her cheeks. She shook as he lowered his tongue behind her knees and around the front up her leg to her inner thigh where he first started. He then moved to her navel, up her stomach, to her breasts gently gliding towards her nipples. Once there, he licked her nipples in a circular motion before finally sucking away as she laid and quietly moaned and began to rub his hair. The moans got stronger as he worked his way back to the vagina. Then without hesitation he covered her whole vagina with his mouth and began lightly sucking while simultaneously licking her clitoris. Within no time she exploded and cum filled his mouth and ran down her legs as she trembled and begged for more. Sonny shifted upward and placed his already rock hard penis inside the vagina, which was now swimming pool wet. The feeling was great. The two thrust in a slow motion until Sonny felt the best feeling in the world as he released all inside of Delilah. The two laid next to each other for the remainder of the night without putting clothes on.

Within two weeks Sonny's operation boomed. Delilah and her brother would receive 40% of the profit, as would Sonny; Marco got 20% of the top. The business flourished and Sonny and Delilah bought a house in The Center, 2 blocks from Walter. Aunt Ola was supportive, and really liked Delilah, but wished they would get married. Delilah's brother Ramos was now a close confident of Sonny; he was even introduced to Marco. Ramos eventually moved out of the barracks to Sonny and Delilah's house on Spruce Street. Sonny now controlled a major stake in numbers running and out grew his job at Campbell's Soup. Walter was happy for Sonny and even played the numbers himself. But, he continued to hide from his mother, the fact that Sonny quit his job.

It was now 1945. The war was over. Soldiers returned home to their jobs, and Campbell's Soup gave the Dominicans three options. They could either go back to the D.R. at Campbell's expense or take a payout and leave the barracks, continuing to work part time, or do what the majority of the Dominicans chose to do and stay in Camden and make a home for themselves, with no help from Campbell's, of course. This bothered Sonny and Delilah although they were powerless.

Ramos who had moved out and got his own apartment in Froggy Bottom was just concerned with making money, and the more Dominicans in the city, the more money he could make. With the returning soldiers taking more and more jobs, the Dominicans and blacks found themselves out of work. Another change to the city was the increased population of Asians. As a result, Camden became crowded and the boundaries of the once ethnic neighborhoods started to blur. By 1954, Sonny and Delilah were married and planning to start a family. Their first child, my mother, Tasha Marie, was born on Christmas Eve 1955. Then on April 9, 1957 Marc was born. By this time, Marco was like family, the numbers game was treating everybody right and Sonny and Ramos were looking to expand.

Atlantic City was always a tourist destination, so when Sonny came to Marco with the idea, it was a no brainier.

"You're a fucking genius, I tell you!" Marco said, while patting Sonny on the back.

This joint venture would take a lot of trust. Sonny couldn't own anything in Atlantic City. He would have to have the business completely in Marco's name and trust that he would be compensated properly as a silent partner, with no paper work to prove anything. Sonny trusted Marco and the 500 club was created. Ramos was not an investor, as he wouldn't put his money anywhere his name couldn't be.

The club was a success, capitalizing off the popularity of baseball; the club was themed after greats such as Jackie Robinson, Babe Ruth and Josh Gibson. Allowing Negro League pictures proved to Sonny he was equal partner, and although all the locals didn't agree with Marco's decision to put Negro league pictures up who could question a mob boss. Over the years Sonny learned things about the mob no other black man had known. The main thing Marco stressed to Sonny was to never go into business with the mob, and if something were to happen to Marco, he should let the mob have the club because another mobster would surely kill Sonny. In fact Marco reasoned, "You would've been dead long ago if you weren't my good friend. Yea, they'd have whacked you for sure. You did a lot in this city and a lot of people don't like it, but I love it. Save your money because when my time is up, so is yours my friend". Sonny understood perfectly that the hand of protection, which had been around Sonny all these years, would not always be there and he needed to get all he could get now.

Over the next few years Sonny distanced himself from the everyday business of the 500 club and started aligning himself more with Ramos who was running the city's growing heroin trade. By 1958, Sonny was rich and had moved to East Camden. Ramos was sentenced to 5 years in '59 and in '60 Marco died while awaiting trial on federal racketeering charges. Angelo Bruno, Marco's successor extended an offer to Sonny to continue doing business but Sonny declined opting to sell the club to Bruno for a modest $30,000. The next few years were quiet Delilah ran a Dominican restaurant on Broadway and Sonny spent most of his time with his children or fishing.

The family owned a 3-bedroom house on Baird Boulevard and sent their kids to private middle schools and Camden Catholic High School. Tasha Marie was a free spirit. Sonny said she reminded him of his mother and that worried him, although he was nothing like his father. Emily was now frequenting the city, staying with Sonny or Aunt Ola. Walter was also still in the city, still working for Campbell's.

Tasha Marie proved to be more like her grandmother than Sonny could imagine and on June 17th, 1973, one year after graduating from Camden Catholic, she gave birth to me Simon Hector Gonzales Jr., in Cooper hospital. My father was going to be a good father, or so I was told. But after cutting the cord and taking his first and last pictures with me, he celebrated with a friend and tried some heroin for the first time. That proved to be fatal. My mother fell into a deep depression and tried to kill herself when she found out. After the unsuccessful attempt on her own life, she began to indulge in the same thing that killed my father.

Between 1975 and 1980 Sonny lost his mother Emily, Aunt Ola, his cousin Walter and his cousin Joseph. Walter had 2 children but both lived in California and rarely came back to

Camden. Ramos now ran a boxing gym in east Camden and ran a job-training program for ex-addicts and offenders. Sonny and Delilah passed on their restaurant to their son Marc. The couple was still relatively young and wanted to enjoy life and raise me, their only grandchild. My mother had finished rehab and stayed in L.A. where the rehab was located. She got a job at a Hollywood restaurant. It was nothing fancy, but it paid the bills and kept her away from Camden, heroin and the memory of my father, but most of all, her son.

3

1985

"Make sure that room is clean boy!" "Yes, Abuela". Abuela is Spanish for grandma and that's what I called my grandma Delilah. It was the day before my birthday and my mother Tasha Marie was coming to town for the first time since 1982. She frequently called and sent gifts but this would be the first time she saw me or her parents, who had been raising me, in nearly 3 years. The smell of fried chicken, collard greens and home fries filled the air. Sonny sat on the porch reading the Courier Post as he did everyday. He was real close to his daughter and was anxiously awaiting her visit.

My mother was so pretty. I hoped I would get a woman like her when I got older. I sat at the top of the steps, half watching The Transformers and half watching my Pop Pop on the porch.

"Daddy." a sweat voice said, sounding like a 12-year old child.

"Tasha's here! Delilah, Simon, Tasha's here!"

"My baby!" Abuela said running to meet her only daughter, who was already being embraced by her father. Although I had been waiting for this moment for years, I was nervous and slid like a slinky down the steps. I slowly walked to the front door as my mother walked in.

"Simon, baby!" my mother said as she hugged my head and then gave me a kiss on the check. How are you? Have you been listening to Abuela and Sonny? She never called her dad, "Dad".

Of course that boy is fine. He's a lot of help around here. He's a blessing. Sonny's words made mom and I smile. As much as Sonny loved his daughter, he knew the feeling of not having a mother around and he protected me at all costs. "Get your mother's bags and put them in her room".

"Yes, Abuela." I answered, while taking the two suitcases upstairs, one at a time.

"So, where's Marc?" Tasha asked about her brother, and as If on cue the door opened and Marc entered.

"Sis." Marc said barely poking his head around the kitchen wall.

"Marc!" Tasha said, in a horrified voice.

The last time Tasha came for a visit Marc had his own apartment and car, ran the family restaurant and weighed a good 200 pounds. How things change. He was now 160 pounds on a good day, his face was sunk in and his mouth had a twitch. His clothes were old and dirty and he smelled as If he hadn't showered in years.

"Marc, what happened to you? What are you doing?" Delilah began to cry and walked out of the kitchen followed by Sonny, as Marc tried to smile and change the subject.

"Just working hard, but how's California? How are you, Sis?" Realizing Tasha was in shock, and the embarrassment on his parents' face, Marc quickly backed out of the room and the house.

"I guess I'll see you later!" he hollered to his sister on his way out the door.

Tasha stood in the kitchen with a blank stare; while she was on drugs her brother was her rock, but he too had fallen to the pressures of the city and America's new epidemic. Crack.

Crack was like nothing Camden, or America for that matter, had ever seen before. Heroin was bad and everybody knew it. Cocaine was expensive and was a high status drug. So, when crack, the cheaper, smoke able form was introduced, it wasn't seen as "the new heroin", but as "the cheaper cocaine". Many people were lured in by the attraction of paying $5 for cocaine, and crack caught on like cable T.V. This was still a whole year before President Ronald Regan would even mention crack or admit America had a drug problem. Camden had experienced white flight and by '85 the city was 53% black and 39% Hispanic. The neighborhoods were all mixed, with the majority of the Hispanics located in North and East Camden. The ethnic shops and the factories had moved from the city, leaving Campbell's Soup, the hospitals, and the Board of Education as the only major employers in the city. The drug trade would begin to fill the job void for young black and Hispanic males.

My uncle Ramos was still very much connected to the streets. Whether or not he still sold drugs was up for debate. But, one thing was for sure, he knew all the dealers and users and they all respected him. My mom knew she could get the

24

answers to her questions about Marc from Uncle Ramos, so after dinner she confronted him about the situation.

"Uncle Ramos, can I speak to you for a minute?"

"Sure, Tasha. What's on your mind?" he asked as the two headed for the porch. Since my bedroom window was directly over the porch, I ran to my room to listen to the conversation.

"So, what's on your mind, California girl?" Ramos asked with a smile.

"What's going on with Marc?" she asked bluntly.

"He's on crack." Ramos answered.

"Crack? "I've never heard of it." she responded.

"Well, it's like a solid rock form of cocaine. It's like buying freebase already prepared." he responded. "It's bad; its...it's tearing the city apart. The murder rate is up. There's a lot of violence that surrounds it. The heroin dealers let the young guys get control of it. They don't know the rules. They shoot first, think second. Now there's guy's 16, 17 with a million dollars."

If Uncle Ramos would've known I was in the window he would've never made that statement, and that statement changed my life. I knew at that moment what I would do with my life. The only profession where a 16 year old could make a million dollars...selling crack!

The next week was the best time of my life. My mother was clean, financially stable and I was enjoying the benefits. We went to Clementon Park and rode every roller coaster there. We went to Atlantic City, the Philadelphia Zoo, and Baltimore Harbor and even drove to see my Aunt Linda and my cousin Manny. My Aunt Linda was my dad's only sister and she and my mother remained close.

My mother let me take my best friend Ace with me on all of our outings. Ace Young was a brown-skinned, half black, half Dominican who lived next-door to me with his mother and his grandparents. Ace's grandparents Mr. and Mrs. Young were very religious people and his mother was a hard working single parent who I admired greatly. Through the hard times she stuck it out, worked 2 jobs and did whatever she had to do to make sure Ace didn't go without. Ace hadn't seen his father since 1st grade and knew little about his Dominican heritage. He would come to my house and my Abuela would teach him Spanish and tell him stories of the D.R. I had no siblings and the only cousins my age were on my dad's side. Although I knew Manny, and he was cool, we didn't see each other much. Ace filled that void. We were inseparable, like brothers.

I had been dreading Sunday all week; It was the day my mother was to leave Camden for sunny California.

"Maybe next year you can come see me. We can go to Disneyland and Sea World. Hey, don't cry Simon! You going to make me cry." my mother said as tears filled her eyes.

Sonny patted me on the back "He'll be alright." he said looking me straight in the eye, instantly stopping my tears. As Abuela, Pop Pop, Uncle Ramos, Ace and I watched my mother bid her farewells, she announced she had a surprise. "Marc is coming with me," she said smiling ear to ear.

"What, when, how did this happen?" everyone seemed to ask simultaneously. "She told me about the program...what it did for her, and I think I need a new start." Marc said enthusiastically.

Everyone celebrated. No one was happier than Sonny. He saw how a change in environment helped his daughter and hoped it could do the same for his son. It wasn't that I didn't want my uncle to get help but I was 12 years old and I had never been to California and here he was about to get rewarded for smoking crack. Sonny and Ace were the only ones to notice my discontentment, although neither said a word.

It was almost 2 months before I told Ace what I planned to be when I grew up. We were in an alley behind our house on Boyd Street smoking a cigarette Ace stole from his mother. The alley was really adjacent yards facing each other with no fences meaning you could look out the back windows of houses on 2 different streets and see the same alley. "A drug dealer? Are you serious? I know plenty of drug dealers," he boasted, exhaling smoke like a professional. "You know Darren Johnson" he asked me.

"No".

"Yes, you do. They call him D.J. I've seen him with your Uncle Marc before." he responded.

"Oh, D.J.! Of course, I know D.J.

"Yea, well then you know a drug dealer too."

"Wow, D.J. was a dealer? No wonder my uncle Marc always went to see him; he was buying drugs." "But what about Uncle Ramos", I thought. I saw them talk plenty of times. About what, I intended to find out. Like Mrs. Young always said patients is a virtue.

"Yo, yo. You all right? What you over there thinking 'bout?" Ace said breaking my train of thought, and almost burning me.

"Selling crack, getting paid!" I answered while taking the last puffs from the cigarette.

"Man you can't sell crack. You too young. You would have to work on a set, and who around here is going to let Ramos nephew work they set?" Ace barked. "What's a set?" I wondered.

"You don't even know what a set is, do you? Do you?"

"No." I answered almost ashamed.

"You got a lot to learn. Saturday we can ride bikes to Cramer Hill to see my uncle. He'll explain everything." Ace assured me before leaving to go home.

I always walked the long way home after smoking, scared of the reaction of Abuela if she smelled smoke on me. As I walked across the street from McGuire Projects, I saw people park their cars, run to the building, exchange money and run back to the car. The flow was non-stop. To the left, on a wall, spray-painted was "crack kills". I wondered what kind of uncle Ace had that would tell his 12-year old nephew about a set. I would surely find out and couldn't wait to.

As I turned the corner to my house, I noticed Uncle Ramos out front of his house talking to D.J. I stopped behind a tree and listened.

"Why would we do that now? Every set is making $15,000 a shift, at least. To rock the boat now..."

"Listen," D.J. said, interrupting Uncle Ramos. "In the heroin days you had to follow the chain of command. Now I can go direct! Fuck New York! It's a new way of hustling, a new wave of hustler." D.J. continued, hopping in the car. I now quickly walked up to cut the dead air. "Hey, D.J. Nice car! That's the E28, 5 series right?"

"Little man knows his cars." D.J. laughed. Here's a couple of dollars for the corner store he said sliding me a $20 bill as casual as Ramos would slide me a dollar. "Thanks, D.J.", I said as he drove off with a head nod.

"Look, Uncle Ramos." I said turning around, but he was already closing the door to his house.

Ramos lived 3 doors down from us on Baird Boulevard. He also had an apartment on top of the gym he still owned and operated on Federal Street. It was there he spent most of his days, so I would have to wait until night to sneak in and find out what, exactly, he was doing.

It took what seamed like 40 days and 40 nights for Saturday to come. I had already set it up for Ace to stay the weekend (which was a normal occurrence. We usually rotated houses on the weekends.) So, we left first thing in the morning.

"He probably won't be out until like 12 on a Saturday. You know, he probably was getting some pussy last night." Ace said, half jokingly.

"Yea, well, I know somebody who's up and I have an idea." I said grabbing 2 buckets, soap, a bottle of turtle wax, and some rags. We filled both buckets with warm water put them on the handle bars and headed for McGuire. On the way,

Ace revealed his mother had warned him to stay away from his uncle, and that in fact, Bingo wasn't his uncle at all, just a friend of his father. Not only that, he was a *bad* friend, whom Ace was to stay clear from. For his part, Bingo would swear to be Ace's blood uncle whenever Ace asked. "E28, this is the dopest car in East Camden. Damn, and he paid you to wash it? How much he give you? I want half if you think I'm helping." Ace said dead seriously as we arrived in the projects. "He didn't pay me." I said crushing his dreams.

"Yea right, well, why the hell you washing' it for free? I don't care how fresh this car is, I aint washing shit for free!" Ace said.

"Look, your mom said."

"My mom?" Ace interrupted, lightly slapping my face, before squaring up to slap box "Don't talk 'bout my mom Simon. I'll bust ya shit.

"Stop playing'. I'm serious." I said raising my voice.

Ace sensing my anger, lowered his hands and moved closer to listen.

"Remember, your mom said drug dealers like for people to pump up their ego? Well, that's what I'm doin'. I complimented his car. Now Im gonna wash it."

"And where that's gone get you. He jus gone think you a little dick rider and I'm starting to think so too.

"Fuck it! I'll do it myself!" I said.

Unlike Ace, I rarely cursed. I began washing the car while Ace stood there laughing and teasing me, calling me Kunta Kinta.

"What's yaw name boy? Simon?" Ace said laughing, refer-ring to the mini series Roots we watched last Christmas break at the Afro-Male Institute. I began to wonder. Was I dick riding? Was this all pointless?

The ride to Cramer Hill was fast. We rode down High Street to avoid the Federal Street traffic and crossed the 27th Street Bridge. Then we went to a bodega on 26th and River Road.

"Hey, is that my nephew? Ace? One of 3 men out in front of the bodega said.

"Yea, it's me Uncle Bingo", Ace answered.

"You got a nephew out here."

"Why didn't you tell me?" the shortest of the three said.

Bingo was only about 5'9 himself with a low cut of coarse hair and the skin complexion of Don Johnson. He was a smooth dressed dude who could've past for black before he spoke. One of his associates was definitely black. He was dressed like Run DMC on the Krush Groove poster. Adidas suit with sneakers to match and a Kangol with one of those gold chains that where so big, "they must be fake", according to Abuela. The third one, the short one who asked about Ace, was obviously the leader of the bunch. The way he carried himself and the way people greeted him over the course of our 2-minute introduction told me all I needed to know. He was the man.

"Take them in the back." the short man who I later found to be Pedro Montoya instructed. "Let them pick out some chips and soda and shit" Pedro told Bingo. "So nephew, what brings you over here? Do you need something?"

"Yea, my friend wants to know what a set is." Ace asked, straight forward. Shouldn't you guys be asking 'bout maybe bikes or somethin'? Bingo asked in a thick Dominican accent.

"We already know about bikes." Simon answered.

Bingo was a slick talker himself and liked Simon's quick wit.

"Good point. So, I answer you questions. A set is an organized drug corner. There's someone who owns the corner. He gets a certain quantity of drugs from a supplier. Think of the owner as the superintendent of schools. His supplier is the board of education. He then bags the drugs in these".

"Those are caps; they are all over the street." Ace added.

"Right, nephew. Well, the caps are then given to the block manager. The block manager runs the block everyday and should only contact the owner for more drugs or an emergency, but he runs the show.

"Like the principal." I added not to be out done by Ace.

"Right, my nephew's friend." Bingo said, laughing.

"The block manager gives a certain amount of capsules to a trapper or worker. The worker works shifts. From 9-4, 4-12 and graveyard 12-8. You get paid per shift like $500 a shift, no matter what you sell. It's like a job. You get paid every week. Sundays you have off and the block manager gives everybody a half-ounce to sell freelance. You can buy more caps from the manager and sell them only on Sundays but If you have enough caps you can make $3,000-$4,000 on Sunday alone.

"A piece?" I asked.

"That's right my friend." Bingo answered.

"Do you know Ramos?" I asked.

"Yea, Ramos and Sonny were old-school gangsters. They were mobbed up. They also got that dope money. Sonny retired. Ramos kept his foot in the water. That's smart you never know when you might need a quick link back in."

"Do you know D.J.?" Ace asked his uncle.

"Of course." Bingo responded.

"Does he have a set?" I continued.

"Yes, 3 or 4 of them."

"Is he the Superintendent or Principal?"

"He's a superintendent and even the board of education for some."

"How can you be the board of education for some?" Ace wondered out loud.

"He supplies a lot of the sets on less busy drug corners". Bingo concluded before giving Ace a $10 bill and excusing himself.

Ace looked at me, I smiled It wasn't pointless after all.

On the ride back to East Camden I thought about uncle Ramos and Pop Pop. Mobbed up? I knew Uncle Ramos did a stretch. He told me, but he never said why. He just said he used to be a knucklehead. Pop Pop? I thought he worked at Campbell's Soup. Did Abuela know? What about Uncle Marc and my mom. Did they know? I thought Italians didn't like black people. I now had an icebreaker for the conversation I had been waiting to have with my Uncle Ramos.

Once back in East Camden Ace and I went to the alley to smoke some of the cigarettes we took from the bodega. While smoking I wondered what life was like in the 50's being an old-school gangster, as Bingo put it.

"That's crazy right? About you're Pop Pop. Makes you wonder what your dad was like. I mean they say women marry men like their fathers. Ace continued, while I dwelled on the thought.

What *was* my dad really like? Not the sugar coated version, but the real Simon Gonzales?

"My dad was a hustler, Bingo said my father killed a man and hasn't been back to Camden since. I don't know where he is, but last time I asked, Uncle Bingo said he was safe", Ace said. "Well, I'm going to talk to my uncle Ramos tonight and I'm finally going to get some real answers".

It was the 2nd Sunday in October and like every year we were ready to pass out pamphlets for the Democratic Party and city council candidate Jorge Lopez. We finished the cigarette and headed the long way to my house.

The next day we went to Marlton Pike to the Democratic headquarters to get our pamphlets and our voucher for $10. As we walked back toward Baird Boulevard, we ran into D.J. It was the first time I'd seen him since I washed his car, but I'm sure somebody told him it was me by now.

"What's up, D.J.!"

"Simon what's happening? What you doing?"

"Just handing out these pamphlets." I answered.

"What you got here? Oh, my boy Jorge Lopez." D.J. said while checking out the pamphlet.

"You know him?" I asked thinking he was playing.

"Yea, we grew up together in North Camden. He'll be good for the city. Real good for the city".

"Yea, well they are paying us $10 so we got to get going."

"How did you like the wash job?"

"Simon that was you? "How much do I owe you?"

'It's on the house D.J. You owe me a ride; that's it."

"You got it; I'll come get you from school one day next week."

As I walked away I saw Flaco get into the car with D.J. Flaco was a stocky man built like an out of shape body builder. He had a goatee with a curly 'fro. He was Puerto Rican and he was from Federal Street. I usually saw him when I was going to visit Uncle Ramos at the gym. This was the first time I saw him and D.J. together but my instincts told me he was a principal in other words a block manager.

The very next day when I came out of school D.J. and Flaco were out front in a Mercedes Benz 190 with temporary tags. Flaco was driving and D.J. riding shotgun. Ace and I walked home from school together about 3 times a week, the other two days one of us usually had detention, today was Ace's turn. "What's up, lil' man? Hop in", Flaco said, as D.J. just looked on with a sly grin.

"We going shopping. We headed to Broadway Eddie's to get some sneakers. Pick what you want."

"How about some Air Jordan's", D.J. said referring to the new Nike's worn by second year Bulls star Michael Jordan.

"Wow the Air Jordan's? They cost $100!"

"You let me worry about the price tag lil' man.'

"Well," I reasoned, can I get 2 pair of Dr. J's? They only cost $40. Cause I don't want to have fresh sneaks and my boy Ace still has those worn out Adidas." "Damn, now that's loyalty!" D.J. said to Flaco before motioning for 2 pairs of Air Jordan's size 6 and 7 for me and Ace.

"Tell your homeboy he's lucky to have a friend like you. Most people would have taken the Jordan's and not thought about their friends."

"That's why I got you 2 pairs of Jordan's instead of the Dr. J's. Loyalty is important, especially in my business," said D.J.

When Flaco took me home, I had him drop me off in the alley where Ace was already waiting. As I walked up Ace looked mad I didn't understand why and I intended to ask but I pulled out the sneakers instead.

"Look the new Air Jordan's", and before Ace could respond negatively I pulled out the second pair.

"You know I got a pair for my homeboy".

"Oh snap D.J. bought these for you," asked Ace.

"For us. I told him we were like brothers and we needed to be fresh together."

"I was going to settle for two pairs of Dr. J's but he sprung for the Air Jordan's", I said enthusiastically. "So you turned down Jordan's so I could have new sneaks?" Ace asked.

"Yea, don't go getting girly on me." I said joking, but it was at that moment that I knew what loyalty was. It was the look in Ace's face, at that moment I knew he would do anything for me and I would do the same for him.

Over the next few months I spent more and more time with D.J. and Flaco. I brought Ace in as much as I could.

Flaco would say, "Ace follows your lead. You're a natural." like I knew what that meant. It was a couple days before New Years, when me Ace and Manny stood in the alley across from the projects. Manny was a couple of years older than me, and by the time he and my Aunt Linda moved to East Camden, he was already hustling. Getting back and forth to Pollack Town was no easy task. Manny had a squatter, but driving all the way from East to Pollack was risky business.

I wanted to play big shot, so I told Manny, "I probably could get you a job over there in the projects."

"For real? You know them nigga's?" Manny asked.

"Yea, we know them nigga's." Ace responded.

"See what's up, McGuire man. My nigga's would never believe I was slingin' over here", Manny said with hunger in his eyes.

"What's the difference between slinging in Pollack and slinging out East?" Ace asked sounding slightly confused.

"Man, East nigga's is gettin' it! If you hustle out East, you gettin' that bank." Manny stated, quite frankly.

I knew I would see D.J. later and I would ask him then.

Instead of waiting I walked over to Flaco who had been hanging in the projects more lately. Word on the street was that Rico, who was block manager in the projects, got locked up and Flaco moved up since the projects brought in more money than Federal Street.

"Simon. What's up, Simon? Simon we gone have to find you a nickname." he said laughing "But anyway, what can I do for you, brother?"

"Well, my cousin Manny, he from Pollack and he was trapping out there but now he lives on Rand Street and."

"Say no more. Tell him to come see me. Is that him over there with Ace?" Flaco said.

"Yea." I responded.

"Well call him over here."

"Manny come here." I called out.

He came across the street with Ace right behind him.

"Manny this is Flaco, Flaco this is Manny."

"So, Manny, you say you worked in Pollack. Who you work for?" Flaco questioned as if conducting an interview.

"Blockz." Manny replied. Blockz is connected to my team. You not lying', is you?"

"Nah. The reason I ask is because Blockz is from Parkside." Flaco said as if he caught Manny in a lie.

"Yea, but him and some nigga from downtown run a small set down on Thurman and Louis. I was trapping out there until 3 days ago." Manny responded.

"Solid. Welcome to the organization. Since you young and you Simon's cousin I'll let you pick your shift".

"I can work 9-4" Manny answered like school was no longer an option.

"See you tomorrow don't be late." Flaco said smiling.

"Simon, when you ready you let me know."

4

I Think I'm In Love

It was summertime 1987. I was 14 years old and I was in love, or at least I thought I was. Manny had been trapping in McGuire for close to a year and got an apartment, courtesy of Flaco. It was a two bedroom and my Aunt Linda, who little to my knowledge had been hip to the game, lived there for a short time before relocating to Pennsauken. Manny had a two bedroom but was never home as he now hung more with the older dudes and less with me and Ace. To me and Ace, we had our own apartment. We were getting good weed in Cramer Hill from Bingo for $200 a quarter pound. Ace and I bought it with a loan from Manny. We would bag up 120 nicks and sell that in the projects since nobody sold weed there. By the end '86 we both had nearly $10,000. I knew how to save. I don't even think Manny saved that much by that point, although he drove an Audi 5000.

The ten thousand we made last summer seemed like nothing compared to how '87 summer started. My Pop Pop and Abuela thought my Aunt Linda still lived in McGuire and she was even willing to lie for, me so staying the night wasn't a problem either. The real reason I stayed in the projects so much was Jasmine. She was a dark skinned, with long track star legs. Her butt stuck out almost like it didn't belong on such a petite frame. Her hair was long to the point everybody said she had Indian in her family. She had a model face and had breast like a grown woman she was 16 and she liked me as much as I did her. By summer of '87, I was 5'8 with a medium build and a light mustache plus I was seen with some of the biggest dealers in the city and that always helped. I met her coming out of Manny's crib. I think she would've liked Manny but saw him with one too many females over the months. Her mom worked nights and that was perfect.

It wasn't my first time, just my first time with a real girl. Well not a real girl, but Manny had schooled me to what a crack head would do for a hit. But this is the first time where there was no trade off just two people with the same motive. It was at her house, she was more comfortable there. Plus, there was a no chance of getting interrupted since Jasmine's mom worked nights. After smoking a joint, we went inside where Jasmine told me she was so high she had to take a shower. She came out in a towel and asked me to lotion her. She sat on the couch with her back to me and dropped the towel. I started at her neck and went down the center of her back, getting almost to her ass before returning up to the shoulders on the left side of her back. I then worked back down on the right side, this time continuing to her ass. She sat up with her ass now perched in the air as If she wanted me to hit it doggy style. I lotioned her butt amongst small moans I went down the back of her leg to the ankles and slowly turned her on her back as I began to suck her toes. As I came back up the front of her legs, I skipped the lotion and used my tongue. Once I got to the inner thighs she was already pulling me up so I could enter her, but I made her wait instead, spending more time caressing her thighs with my lips and tongue while she began to beg for me to be inside her. I then began to lick her lips below like I saw in a movie once before. Minutes later I was hit in the face with what I thought was hot pee until I felt her nails in my back and heard her scream, "I'm coming!"

By now I was totally relaxed and comfortable with entering. I penetrated what felt like a wet cave. I stroked until she moaned then I stroked in the same spot again and again, harder each time. She began to scream, "Oh shit, I'm cumin, Oh shit! I'm cumin!" at that moment I felt the best feeling ever. When we fucked the crack heads we wore condoms. This was a whole new feeling. I came in her and then laid there for a second before my relaxation was interrupted.

"Did you come in me"?

"Oh, my God! Get up! Get off me! Did you come in me?" she repeated while running to the bathroom. "You aint never heard of pulling out," she snapped at me. "I'm 'bout to get back in the shower, I'll see you later." she said giving me my hint it was time to go.

Jasmine couldn't rain on my parade and I left the happiest dude in Camden. That night I went home to Pop Pop and Abuela's house. Pop Pop was asleep on the couch with the T.V. watching him.

42

"Wake up!" I yelled out startling him. He looked at me and smiled walking upstairs to his room without saying a word. That night I thought about Jasmine and the $16,000 I was now sitting on. Most of the hustling in the projects was done on the strip near the alley behind my house. I sold weed on the corner in the back near Manny's apartment. This location was easily accessible from Admiral Wilson Boulevard, a key highway in the city.

It was my second summer selling weed and I planned on doing it better. I created a set with myself being the owner and Ace the block manager. We used kids our age from the projects as trappers. We had about 3 or 4 different workers and paid them $100-$150 a day. We were now selling between 300 and 400 nicks a day bringing in between $1,500 and $2,000, with about $900-$1200 of that being profit. As Ace and I grew, so did Manny, and soon he gave us the apartment in the projects and he moved to a townhouse in Fairview. Jasmine got over me not pulling out and her and her friend Star began bagging weed for us. Jasmine liked me even more once she found out how much money I was making, and of course Ace started fucking Star.

Star was an, "aint no shame, in my game" kind of chic. She had no problem being 16 fucking a 14 year old. Ace was known more as a fighter than me and even beat up Star's old boyfriend Jimill, who was 16. He had respect as the muscle, and I was more of the brains. Star was a gold digger with a capital G. It was bad enough they clipped us for a few bags every time they bagged up. Now she was juicin' my boy and still fucking Jimill.

Star was a light skinned chic who minus 20 pounds would've been the thickest chic in the world but instead was thick wit a gut. She had a pretty face but not as pretty as she thought. She lived in Westfield Acres, which were projects on the other side of East Camden. She kept a weave and never came out unless she was dressed. She was a gold digger not a hood rat. She was fly and older nigga's always tried to impress her with money. She had a pay to play philosophy she was a lot different from Jasmine but they were also a lot alike. I began to spend more time with Jasmine. We would sit on the steps late night and watch the fiend's shuffle from the back of the projects to the strip where they could get caps.

One night a fiend called International walked by. They called him International because he could be found in any hood copping on any given night. This night International was walking bare foot from Admiral Wilson toward the strip. As he passed Jasmine and I, he said, "Damn you only sell weed you could make some real money if you got some caps and cut all this traffic off late night."

That was the best advice I ever got from a fiend. I immediately went to Manny with the idea. Manny liked the plan and at that point was the block manager, but still had to run it by Flaco. D.J. had begun to be less and less visible on the streets, so for all intents and purposes, Flaco was the boss. While talking to Manny, he pulled out a gun and handed it to me.

"What's this for", I asked.

"For you. It's dangerous out here and if Flaco lets you get your own setup you're going to need it," he replied.

Later that night, Flaco came by our apartment. He brought with him 1,000 caps, which were to be sold for $10 a piece and told us to bring him back $5,000. After all the weed was sold we never got fronted, and even though we were cool with Flaco, we didn't feel comfortable with taking the consignment. That night we decided to take $2,500 a piece and pay Flaco the next day. After the caps were paid for we set up our operation. We kept our weed set running from 10 A.M. to 10 P.M. We would start selling caps at 10 P.M and shut down early the next morning. We kept the weed trappers but sold the caps ourselves. Neither Ace nor I really knew how fast the caps would go, but by 6:00 the next morning we had sold all 1,000 caps. That morning as we sat in the apartment counting our money while talking and smoking. We had finally made it. "Remember a couple years ago you told me you wanted to be a hustler? Well, your dreams came true." Ace said coughing while exhaling at the same time.

"Yea it's crazy, that crack money. Man its crazy I said, as we both laughed and fell asleep.

Later that afternoon, I walked to Pop Pops and Abuela's house. I still officially lived there and kept my clothes and money there. When I walked in Ramos was on the couch. "So you graduated; you sell crack now" he asked. "What?" I asked.

"You heard him? You sell crack now." I recognized Pop Pop's voice behind me, but I couldn't bring myself to turn around. He put his hand on my shoulder and said, "It's time to talk."

We went on the front porch me, Pop Pop, and Uncle Ramos. They began to tell me their story. From Marco, and running numbers, to heroin. They told me the importance of saving money and trusting no one. What I thought was going to be a lecture, turned out to be the some of the best advice of my life. "Pop Pop."

"Call me Sonny now. You a man, right? Well, call me Sonny now"; he said cutting me off in mid sentence. He told me he never wanted this route for me, but if I was to do it, I was going to do it right and by the rules. I'd heard stories of Sonny but I'd never heard him talk like that before.

"One last question. How did y'all know I was selling crack?" I asked. (Laughing) "You got a lot to learn kid!"

"Black Beauty. That's what I'll call you".

"How I'm gonna have a nickname and you don't", Jasmine said responding to me calling her Black Beauty. I finally felt like I wasn't sneaking. It was out in the open. I was a hustler with a fly girl to match, and I loved it.

"I'm just Simon the hustler."

"Oh, God. Here you go." she said, laughing. We were spending more and more time together and I was starting to believe she really liked me for me. I mean we went out, I gave her money, but she could've got a lot more from others. We were spending all of our free time together. Ace was spending more and more time in the Westfield Acres with Star and her cousins, Ace was a cannon so I didn't need to worry about him much. We now had trappers for a late night shift so our days were spent overseeing the bagging, dropping off bundles and collecting money. Ace was making moves on the other side of town and forming relationships with hustlers I didn't even know. Ace put some weed on 33rd Street. I met the 2 trappers, Star's cousins, who were both older than us, but the word was out whom we ran with, so nobody played with our money. All our dealings were 50/50, so I was eating over there. One of Star's cousins was named Rim the other one was T- Money, over time Ace and T-Money would become good friends.

It was an early Saturday morning. Well, early by hustler's standards, which is about 10:30, 11:00 am. (Door opening)

"Yo, you up nigga?" the voice was Ace's. I was in our crib in the projects laid up with Jasmine. Ace still had a key and kept work here but he was staying over on 29th and High with Star, who was expecting.

At 14, he had almost totally moved out of his grandparents crib.

"What you get me?" Ace said walking into the room where Jasmine and I lay.

"Oh, shit! What's today? November 11th, already?" I said.

"Yea, nigga. Yo boy is 15." Ace replied.

"Happy birthday, Ace!" Jasmine said voice still cracked.

"Thank you. Think I can have my boy back for today?" Ace inquired.

"As long as Star can come out." Jasmine replied sarcastically.

"Come out? I don't know; but I will allow her to have visitors today."

"Boy, you crazy!" she said with a laugh, while walking out of the room in a robe. Last year she would've walked out in her T-shirt and boxers, but she had more respect now. I was noticing a change.

"So what's up?" I asked him,

"Nothing. I got my man out there. We ready to talk business".

"Out where?" I asked while putting on my jeans.

"Out there, in the living room."

I peaked around the corner and saw Jasmine say something to T-Money as she came back toward the bedroom. I instantly didn't like him.

"What's going on?" I asked in my most threatening voice.

"Nothing. I know him. That's Star's cousin," she said flatly.

"No disrespect. Just saying hello."

"He knows that's your girl. Aint nothing." Ace reassured. I put on a shirt and the three of us hoped in the Audi that Ace bought from Manny. T-money drove because he had a license and Ace rode shotgun. I sat in the backseat.

"Listen before you interrupt, just let me tell you everything, and then you ask questions." Ace asked. I nodded in agreement.

"T- Money got a connect in Florida $10,000 a key. We got a flight attendant can get the coke on the plane. The only risk we have is getting the coke out the airport." "No, the risk we have is selling coke we didn't get from Flaco in the projects." I said cutting Ace off.

"I knew you weren't going to let me talk." He said annoyed.

"Okay go head".

"We can bring D.J. in." Ace continued, "Skip Flaco; straight to D.J." Now that was a thought. For the past 6 months, D.J. had been opening up legitimate businesses such as an Auto Parts store, and a full service gas station. He was also financing drug spots all over Camden, not just east.

"We make a test run with our money, and then we bring in D.J. Plus, I got another spot we can sell." Ace said confidently.

"Where?" I asked.

"24th and Howell" T-Money answered.

"It's my grandma's block and there's no coke. Their fiends got to walk to McGuire or the other side of Federal St".

"What's the potential?" I asked,

"We think we can do about 500 caps a day to start" Ace replied.

"I gotta think about it. I'll let you know by tomorrow. Drop me off at my unc's gym on Federal."

"What you doing for your born day." I asked Ace.

"Shit, whatever. Page me nigga. I'll be around," he said. I closed the door and started walking towards the gym.

I walked past the first of three boxing rings on my way to the office in the back. The man jumping rope next to the ring looked like he could beat Mike Tyson.

"Hey, Uncle. Who's that jumping rope over there?" I asked motioning to the first ring. That's Jose Martinez. He's from Glassboro. He used to be Mr. Universe. He's a body builder.

"Damn, I can see why. But the reason I came is. Well, is coke a lot cheaper in Miami than here? I asked naively.

"Of course, that's an entry point. An entry point is any-where drugs come into the country like Florida, California, Texas, Arizona drugs all drugs will be cheaper in these states than anywhere else in the U.S. There's always an exception but that's a general rule."

"Thanks, Unc."

"Hey, that's it. Want to go 3 rounds or something don't let the age fool you I'm sharp." he said.

"Maybe next time." I laughed, while walking out. Next was to holler at D.J.

As I walked up towards the projects, I saw Flaco and Man-ny and a couple other dudes who I've never seen in the PJ's standing in the alley where Ace and I used to smoke cigarettes. I walked up on Manny.

"What y'all doing over here in my cut", I asked.

"This *was* your cut. It's about to be the new powder spot." Manny responded. "What?" I laughed "A spot in a wide ass alley?"

"We got cribs on this side and this side." he said pointing to both sides of the alley. We pay the rent. They look out, stash drugs, bag up, whatever. It's more accessible than the PJ's, to the powder customers coming from Cherry Hill and Merchant-ville. One-person traps, one takes the money and one shuffles bundles and money back and forth from the stash house to the alley. Its gravy. We still going to sell our crack in the projects. Just powder over here baby $20. We're just looking for a better connect.

"Ding! The magic word."

"Connect." I said, well, check this out."

I then explained in detail what Ace and T-Money told me Manny was wit it. I didn't like T-Money but I was no fool. This was a good idea about money and I was in. I paged Ace and put in 777, which meant come to the crib. Manny and I smoked a joint and waited for Ace and T-Money to come through.

Ace walked through the door 10 minutes later with T-Money. I told them the plan was in affect. Manny, T-Money and Ace would go with $120,000 and get 12 kilo's. Everyone was a little nervous. T-Money had to come back with the coke and Ace, Manny, and I were putting up $40,000 a piece of our own money. This would be the first time we ever bought weight of cocaine. Up till this point we were buying caps.

Selling caps had earned me a little over $140,000 to date, which I had spread between Pop Pop's house, my apartment and Jasmine's house, in a safe, of course. I would stay home In case something happened. Manny had to go because he knew T-Money and Ace were going. He didn't trust them with his $40,000. I would have to handle 33rd Street, so I got to know Rim better over the next week. We set up a drop off/ pick up destination and exchanged pager numbers. The day before they left, Manny told me that D.J. had started aligning some of the biggest dealers in the city, like Flaco, Blockz from Parkside, Louis Noel from downtown and Pedro Montoya from Cramer Hill. "Pedro Montoya. I know him, or at least I met him. We get our weed from somebody that works for him", I said excitedly.

"Yea, this drug world is small. You stay around long enough, you meet everyone." Manny answered.

"We got a cop that's down with us, and even got a man on city council."

"I know. Jorge Lopez." I said remembering the pamphlets and the conversation with Flaco.

"How'd you know?" Manny asked.

"I'm in the street too, nigga." I said laughing. Manny laughed

"Well, it's 'bout to get better for us with everybody under D.J. He'll be the godfather of the city. The only person not willing to team up is Kalic from North. But, other than that, the city's ours. I hope this Miami thing works. It could put us in a whole new tax bracket. Imagine how many keys D.J. would buy at $11,000 a piece." Manny said smiling about the extra thousand he added on."

"Flight 256 to Miami," the loud speaker announced.

"Well, that's y'all." I said to Manny and Ace, more so than T- Money. I shook hands with all of them and wished them good luck. I rode back from the airport with Rim. We stopped at Geon's in South Philly and then crossed the Ben Franklin Bridge back into Camden. The conversation turned to his cousin Star and how without her, we would've never known each other.

"Yea, her friend Jasmine lives in McGuire. That's how we met her." I said, as if I only knew her casually.

"Oh yea, T-Money used to hit that." he said sending a dagger through my heart. I didn't say a word. I didn't talk too much for the rest of the ride. He dropped me off in McGuire and I walked the long way home. Right before I walked through the door something stopped me and I turned and walked back to the projects. I got to Jasmine's and knocked on the door like police. She answered and saw in my eyes something was wrong.

"What's the matter baby?" she asked. Tell me how you really know T-Money and don't say from Star.

Without hesitation she answered, "We had sex 3 times like two years ago. It meant nothing. I was scared to tell you, I'm sorry," she said almost in tears laying her head on my shoulder. It was the honesty and the sincerity that moved me. I didn't think anymore. I *knew* I was in Love.

5

Rise to Power

I sent Rapid Rover to get Manny, Ace and T-Money from the airport. With 12 kilo's of coke, I didn't want to send anybody else to get them. I had International light the grill and cook burgers and steaks. I waited for about 45 minutes before they walked through the door with two suitcases. We immediately got up and walked into the kitchen. T-Money opened the first suitcase and pulled out literally, "bricks", of cocaine. As much crack as I sold, this was the first time I saw powder. Ace immediately opened one of the bricks and got a coffee pot from the cabinet. "What you doing?" I asked.

"'Bout to cook up, nigga." Ace answered. It never occurred to me that Ace knew how to cook up and I didn't even know the process.

"Where you learn to do that," I asked.

"You need to get out more," he said as T-Money and Manny joined him in a good laugh. Within the next hour Ace cooked a kilo of cocaine into 1400 grams. That was 400 grams extra. Manny chose to take his 3 keys in powder. I took the 1 Ace cooked and 2, more in powder Ace kept the remaining 3.

Ace and I agreed to take 2 bricks a piece and use them to supply our late nightspot in the projects.

Ace decided not to put any work on 33rd Street where our other weed spot was located. Ace wasn't from around there and there were already crack spots on Tres Duce (32nd Street) and in the Westfield Acres. Plus, T- Money didn't have the clout to put work out there.

Manny went to Flaco and told him about the bricks. Flaco allowed Manny to bag up the coke as $20's and let the trappers test it out in the alley. They sold a brick bagged up as $20's in 16 hours. That's 2 shifts. $42,000 is what I made off that brick, that's before I paid the trappers.

Manny always told me, "You gotta go get it cousin." I shook my head at the thought and hopped a cab down to 24th and Howell. It was a back block that I could tell got real dark at night. It was 2 blocks away from Federal Street by the Crown Fried Chicken and the liquor store, which both kept a lot of late night traffic. I met Ace and T-Money who had been bosom buddies the last 2 months.

"So, where the packs gone be stashed?" I asked.

Ace told me that T-Money's Grandma's house would be home base. They planned on moving her to a new apartment, and her house would be our Howell Street headquarters. The first day we sat out there together for a whole shift we sold about 200 caps. It wasn't bad for the first day of work, it was no alley but it could definitely make us some money.

The first worker we hired for the new location was Raoul.

Raoul was from Centerville but his grandma lived on Carmen Street two blocks from DJ's sister. He had just come home on parole. He was a hustler and he was about his business. Plus, that was DJ's man, so we put him down eventually. We hoped to make him a manager. He brought a 14 year-old named Butter with him.

Meanwhile, in the alley, things were going great. A guy named Eduardo was brought in to manage the alley. He's one of the dudes I saw with Flaco and Manny when I first heard about the alley. Manny told me that Eduardo was a hit man in Santo Domingo, Dominican Republic. He came to America with his wife and 2 other killers but none of them knew each other. The second gunman was named Cuba and he was short and fat. The wildest of the three was named Manuel Vargas, and they called him Muscleclo. The wild cowboys gang in New York used him in a hit and his reputation preceded him. I guess if you sell a brick in 2 shifts you need to keep a couple of killers around. With Manny, Eduardo, Cuba and Muscleclo the alley was in good hands and nobody wanted any problems.

Raoul had only been home for two weeks when he ran into Tito at the Chinese store on 8th Street in Centerville. Tito supposedly robbed one of Raoul's workers while he was locked up. Raoul confronted Tito about the situation. Tito denied it and left in a borrowed red Cadillac. Tito double parked in front of his friend Nico's house, the owner of the Cadillac, and went in to eat his Chinese food. After finishing the food Nico came out to move his car and was ambushed by machine gun fire. Police found 77 .223 shells and 5 nine millimeter shells at the scene along with a shot up caddy and the bullet riddled body of Nico Sanchez. It was Christmas Eve. His wife and 3 children were in the house. Raoul was never questioned, but Jorge Lopez was. An eyewitness got the license plate number to a blue pick up truck that fled the scene; the truck was registered to Jorge Lopez. A M-16 fires .223 shells and while Jorge was in the army he was trained with an M-16. He was questioned and even volunteered for a polygraph, which he passed. No one was charged.

After hearing the news I was starting to think Raoul was the wrong person for our new set. You always need goons, don't get me wrong, but they can't be managers. Everyone has a position in the food chain we call the streets. Nobody likes cops or stickup kids but without them there would be a million dealers. Without fiends there would be no dealers. Without dealers Camden could fire 75% of their police so everybody needs each other...but the fiends can't be millionaires the millionaires can't be fiends and the dealers can't be the cops. The cops can't be the dealers, or can they? During the next couple of months my perception of cops would change dramatically.

While Raoul chilled for a week or two I got real cool with Butter, the kid Raoul brought with him. Butter lived at 25th and Howell and both of his parents were on drugs. He would work shifts and even come chill on the set while he wasn't working. He was a chubby round face kid with no traces of facial hair. He was like Cheech and Chong when it came to the weed. He always came and smoked with me when he went to 7th and Clearfield Streets in North Philly to get weed. He would roll up a nick in 3 joints and smoke them back to back to back. Plenty of nights I closed down the set early all-high from smoking with him. T-Money and Ace had started coming around more and we were schooling Butter on the ins and outs of the game. Butter was smart and I could tell he was a natural.

T-Money and Ace started to feel the heat from the nigga's on 32nd Street. At first they gave them the go ahead to sell weed on 33rd, but now I guess they were making too much money and they nigga's didn't like it. T-Money and Ace were now making the Florida run monthly, and even brought back coke for D.J. a couple times. As we all sat around talking, Manny dropped some knowledge on Ace.

"You're too visible around there. See, you not from they block so when they see you everyday eating in they neighborhood they get mad, get jealous. Now if you were to not go there and let some nigga's from over their trap for you they wouldn't even be concerned". In the middle of his sermon Manny's pager went off with Flaco's number 911. Manny called him back and told me he had to go meet with Flaco; he'd see me later.

When Manny got to one of the designated stash houses over-looking the alley, Flaco, Eduardo and Muscleclo were there and they were looking out the window at Cuba.

"See that nigga right there?" Flaco asked Manny. "He try-ing, to take over the alley. You gone let that happen?"

"Hell, no!" Manny answered half way scared.

"That's what I want to hear!" Flaco said, handing Manny a 357.

"Go handle y'all business!" he instructed like a general giv-ing his soldiers orders. Manny, Eduardo and Muscleclo headed downstairs to handle their business. Apparently, Flaco got word that Cuba was planning to take over the alley. Eduardo's name wasn't mentioned in the plot but telling him to kill Cuba was one way to find out if he was involved or not. Before Manny got downstairs, Flaco told him to keep an eye on Eduardo. They wasted no time. They saw Cuba and another man about 30 feet directly in front of them and began firing. Pop, pop, pop...the sound of gunfire filled the air as all 3 shooters emptied revolvers; although, Manny saw Eduardo intentionally miss. Manny hit Cuba in the neck but he would survive. The other dude got away unharmed. The three then hopped in a waiting car and spun off. They dropped Manny and Muscleclo off on Federal Street where Flaco had his Camden apartment. The driver then took Eduardo home where he overheard Eduardo's wife telling him he should kill Flaco and Muscleclo and control the alley himself. The driver came back to the Federal Street apartment and told Flaco what he had heard. Flaco and Muscleclo flipped a coin to see who would kill Eduardo and Muscleclo won. Before leaving, they got word an innocent bystander was killed in the gunfire.

Flaco, Manny and Muscleclo went to the stash house where they first met. They lured Eduardo there and told him the police were out, so he should leave his gun home. When Eduardo walked in, Manny grabbed his arms. Instinctually, Eduardo tried to reach for his hip but had no gun. Muscleclo came from behind the closet door and bang! One to the face, and Eduardo slid to the floor where Flaco kicked him in the face and yelled,

"You wanted to kill me! That's what you get now!"

Minutes after Eduardo was murdered, Manny and the unidentified driver went to Eduardo's house to kill his wife. Manny went in and put the gun to her head but the gun jammed and Eduardo's wife ran out of the house screaming, so Manny and the driver left. Eduardo's wife was never seen again.

Eduardo's body was stuffed in the trunk of the getaway car, which had been stolen, in Collingswood the night before. It was then driven to North Philly where the car was burnt. The car and body wouldn't be recovered until nearly 3 months later.

With the murder of an innocent bystander, the Projects were hotter than ever. We shut down all operations in the projects for a week. 24th and Howell made a lot of money during those 7 days. With a portion of the project money coming to Howell Street, Raoul started coming back around and T-Money was making runs to Miami, while Ace handled their business affairs.

"It's 6:00 and I still aint heard from T-Money", Ace said, sounding worried.

"Man, planes are late all the time. That's regular shit." I said trying to be optimistic. The truth is I was more worried than Ace because I had money involved and I had less faith in T-Money.

The 911 page from Rim came at about 8:30pm, 4 and half hours after the plane was due in to Philly. Ace called back

"Yo, what up?" Ace asked with panic in his voice.

"They got 'em. They got T-Money coming through the airport with 12 kilos." Ace hung up. We got in the Audi and went straight to Westfield Acres where the call came from.

Once there, Rim explained, "He didn't say much, but I know he needs $250,000 for bail. He's being held at FDC in Philly". With all the prior trips T-Money made for D.J. it shouldn't be hard to get $250,000.

I lost over $50,000 in that trip. I had just bought 1988 money-green Honda Accord with the flip lights. The projects had shut down and I was still keeping Jasmine fresh for her senior year at Woodrow Wilson High School. I had maybe $80,000 or $90,000. Ace was spending a lot more money and paying a lot more bills, not to mention the Audi he had, and the Regal he bought Star. I wasn't sure, but I figured he was in that $20,000 -$30,000 range. Manny was rolling with the big dogs, so I was sure he was caked up. But, he was tight and no way was he giving up any kind of bread for T-Money. I asked Manny to go to D.J. for the money.

He replied, "Ace already went to D.J. and asked. D.J. told him his best bet was to leave T-Money alone; he's probably snitching. He told him to let those dudes in the Acres take care off that. I felt bad for T-Money but what could I do? I knew Ace was probably mad, I just didn't no how mad."

I hung with Manny the rest of the day. We went to their hang out on Federal Street where they counted money from the set they still operated there. Flaco was there and he was happy to see me. "What's up Simon? You still haven't found a nick name?" he said jokingly.

"Nah". It's no good to have people on the streets call you by your government name.

"You remind me of me, Simon. A young hustler and a good one. A natural." This was the second time he called me a natural, but this time I understood why, I thought to myself.

"See, I started out hustling in North Camden on 5th and Grant. I was a young trapper and my bosses Jorge Lopez and Julio Quivoures were some greedy muthafuckas. So, I moved to 5th and State Streets. I hustled over there. North Camden gets hot from the dope traffic, so I move out here to McGuire. In McGuire I run into D.J. who was supplying Jorge Lopez back when I worked for him."

"There's that name again", I thought,

I had to ask. "Jorge Lopez the city councilman"?

"Yea that one." he said without a second thought. He continued, "D.J. started fronting' me half kilo's and from there we started the first set on Federal. We chose Federal because of its access to the highway. Plus, McGuire was filled with hustlers. But, you know only the strong survive, and in a year or two we controlled the projects too. D.J. showed me the importance of owning legal businesses, so in '86 I bought a bar in Cramer

Hill and named it Euphoria. It's already paid itself off and '88 is just getting started. This summer I plan to open a used car lot right here on Federal St." Flaco said smiling. He gave everybody a pound and left. I was enjoying the history lesson. I liked hearing those types of stories. After Flaco left, Manny and I went to Popeye's and then to the projects.

When we walked through the door, we saw that the apartment was a mess. Jasmine and I were already planning to get a spot together when she finished school, and since the shootings, I had been staying at Pop Pop's house. Ace was sitting on the couch smoking a joint. He was steaming.

"I know this nigga told you, right," Ace said referring to Manny.

"I know he told you what your boy D.J. said."

"Man, listen. That's the game. When you fall you aint got no friends." Manny said nonchalantly. Ace knew Manny was right, but wasn't trying to hear it.

"Fuck that! That's some foul shit!" Ace screamed.

"So, what you gone do? Kill him? Then where you gonna live?" Manny said sarcastically.

"Look, you're out your league. There's nothing you can do but forget about it." Manny was right. The best thing Ace could do was to send him some money and have something for him when he came home.

I enjoyed hanging with Manny. It had been a long time since we kicked it all day together. I told Manny that 24th and Howell was running low on product. He assured me he would have it by the morning.

"You got it… from where?" I asked.

"I could tell you, but then I'd have to kill you." he joked. Before walking out the door he let me know he would explain the details when it was done. He didn't want to jinx himself.

Ace and I got a chance to talk when Manny left. I wasn't sure what was going on with my best friend but he was going through some things. Whatever it was, he didn't want to talk to me about it. He brushed off every attempt I made to make the conversation go in that direction. Instead, he brought up our early childhood and my mother, who we had a ball with, almost 3 years prior. The stress of selling drugs was catching up with Ace way too early in the game. He had a newborn and a girlfriend who was a handful to say the least. The conversation stayed light and we laughed and joked about old times while smoking joint after joint.

Around 10:30 Jasmine came home from work at Macy's in the Cherry Hill Mall. Since she lived across the hall she heard my voice and knocked on the door. When she came in, Ace left. After exchanging hugs and kisses she looked me straight in the eyes and told me she loved me before pushing me on the couch. Without hesitation she went in my pants, whipped it out and began sucking. It was the best feeling in the world and it lasted 7 or 8 minutes before I shot all in her mouth. She sucked every drop before spitting it out in the bathroom. She then wanted to have sex but I was dead tired. I slept like a baby until the next morning.

When I woke up, Manny had paged me 3 times. I called back and told him I was still in the projects. He came a half an hour later and told me he had kilos for $16,000 and I didn't have to travel.

Manny said, "Last night I picked up two scuba divers from the airport and drove them to Delaware, just past the Memorial Bridge. Yo, you aint gonna believe it, but they dove in and got two oil drums. Each one had 50 keys in it."

"And you drove back from Delaware with all that coke?" I asked, stunned.

Luis Noel rented me his Lincoln Town Car for $1,500; it has two stash spots that can hold 50 kilo's each. Whatever you need we got it", he assured.

"I need 3. Meet me back here in an hour."

I went to Pop Pop's and cleared the safe. I had $50,000 in there so I took out $2,000 and gave the rest to Manny in exchange for 3000 grams of some raw coke. I sold one kilo to Ace at cost and we re-opened our spot in the projects.

I took a half a key already cooked and bottled in capsules to Howell Street. There was a lot of movement on Howell Street when I pulled up. I had to be cautious because I had 2,100 capsules in a book bag in my trunk. I got out with the .38 revolver Manny gave to me. As I walked toward the stash house I heard a click when I turned I saw fire and heard screams. I felt hands running through my pockets and could hear voices, but I couldn't see. I heard sirens and I felt my body being put on a stretcher.

The next morning I woke up to my mother's face. It was great seeing her; I just wish it wasn't at Cooper Hospital. She had tears in her eyes and was apologizing for not being there for me. I tried to speak but tears were filling my eyes and my voice was cracking so I remained silent. I regained composure and we had a needed heart to heart. She explained why she left and, more importantly, why she hadn't come back.

I now understood how you could run from your own life, but I wasn't ready to run from mine, and moving to California was not an option for me. She respected my wishes and we vowed to stay in closer contact with more frequent visits and phone calls. The funny thing was that Abuela and my mom already knew I sold drugs. I guess they had been around enough in their life to recognize a hustler when they saw one. Now I was fully relieved. All the cards were on the table. Everybody knew what I did. They didn't like it, but they accepted it.

The doctor came in. He said I had been shot 8 times in the neck, chest and both arms. "You're lucky to be alive Mr. Gonzales." The doctor left and told me to get some rest.

The next time I woke up it was Camden detectives I saw. They came to question me about the shooting. This was the first real contact I ever had with the police. They began with the basic questions like, "Do you know who shot you?" "No", I answered, "It was dark. I heard a click, saw fire and woke up here", which was true.

"Do you know Chris Johnson or Raoul Quivoures?"

"Not by name, maybe by face." I answered so I didn't paint myself in a corner. "Why? Do they have something to do with this?" I asked.

The detective informed me that the porch I was shot on was Chris' house. Chris and Raoul were in the house at the time of the shooting. Police produced a search warrant and found guns and drugs in the house. They also impounded a green Honda with bullet holes in it. The keys in my pocket matched the Honda and 2,100 capsules were found in the trunk.

"The car was registered to Jasmine Irvin. We have two officers on their way to pick her up from Woodrow Wilson High School."

"Do you have anything to tell us?" The Detective asked. I was stunned. Let me tell you what else I know the detective added, "I know that the house that 14 year old, Chris, or Butter that's what you call him, right? Butter?" he said without pausing for me to answer, "The house he owns, he bought from a Mrs. Ellis. Mrs. Ellis has a grandson named Thomas excuse me, T-Money, right? And stop me if I mess up. Thomas Ellis was arrested two weeks ago while de-boarding a plane from Miami Florida and charged with intent to distribute 12 kilo's of cocaine. Now, I know you and Butter are pawns. T-Money was even a pawn. Give me the brothers; I want Raoul and Julio Quivoures."

I told the police I had no dealings with Raoul, Julio, Butter or T-Money, although I knew them. I also said Jasmine let me use the car and the 2,100 capsules were mine. They immediately cuffed me to the bed.

Over the next couple of days I would have multiple visits from Jasmine, Abuela, Pop Pop, Uncle Ramos, Ace, Manny, Aunt Linda, and my mother. Uncle Marc stayed in California but sent his regards. The one visit I got that surprised me most was D.J. and Flaco. They came in late at night, well after visiting hours.

"Hey little man." They said while walking in. "Looks like you finally got a nickname." Flaco said with a smile.

"What?" I replied curious to his response.

"Gato."

"Cat", I responded, sounding confused. Yea, anybody that survives 8 shots must have nine lives." He said with a laugh. In the hood, when you get shot and survive, you're somewhat of a hero. The whole projects would be talking about me. They asked me what happened and what the police had asked me. I showed them my cuffs and told them the story; they respected me even more for being a real nigga. D.J. didn't say much but assured me I'd be good when I came home.

6

New Jersey Training School for Boys

The prosecutor never believed that all those drugs were mine. He recommended a 1-year sentence to the judge saying that I failed to cooperate, probably out of fear. I should have hired the prosecutor as my lawyer. Maybe I would've got probation.

After spending a month in Camden County Detention Center in Lakewood I was off to The New Jersey Training School for Boys also known as Jamesburg. Jamesburg was a lot different than the detention center. In the detention Center 90% of the population was from Camden. I had a cell that looked more like a college dorm room than a jail. Everybody had heard of me because my case made all the local papers and news stations. The word was, down "the burg", Newark nigga's and Camden nigga's stayed at war. Those were the two deepest cities in the NJ prison system juvenile or adult, and they were always bumping heads. I didn't care; I had 11 months to go and I was ready to get it over with. I worried about Jasmine. I hadn't seen her in 3 weeks. The rest of the money I had was at a safe in her house with the exception of a couple thousand and a kilo I had left in the apartment.

On the way to Jamesburg I found out why NJ is the garden state. Nothing but farm land, trees and spaced out houses for miles. When we arrived at Jamesburg, there were 7 cottages where inmates were housed. All the inmates were outside watching the buses come in from the different counties around New Jersey. This was state prison for kids. Besides the cottages, there were a school, a rec center and a vocational school for kids who already had a diploma or G.E.D.

I planned on getting my G.E.D in the summer when I turned 16 so going to school was going to be a good thing for me, a blessing in disguise. When I got in my cottage it was mostly Camden nigga's. I knew a couple of people, a couple people knew me, so I was cool. I stayed to myself as much as possible in a dorm. There were 50 beds in my cottage. 50 attitudes, 50 personalities. This was going to be an adjustment.

During my first week there, I wrote Jasmine everyday. I missed her so much, more than anybody else. When I finally got a letter from her she said I had embarrassed her at school, got the car taken and this wasn't the life for her. She would be starting school in Delaware State this September and wanted to leave this part of her life behind her.

Somebody's fucking my girl. That was my first thought. My second was, the safe and the roughly $35,000 that was in it were gone. My third thought was "How the fuck you going to talk shit about my car that I paid for just because it was in your name?" And last but not least, "I got to get the fuck out of here and back on the streets."

While in the burg, I thought about Julio and Raoul Quivoures. Julio was Jorge Lopez's old partner, the one Flaco use to work for in North Camden. If Julio was Jorge's best friend that would explain Jorge's truck being at the scene of a murder linked to Julio's little brother Raoul. He had either lent Raoul the car, or was with him during the shooting. I wasn't sure of the details, but that made sense. I had no idea who shot me. I didn't think it was Raoul because he knew I was bringing caps and he would have surely taken them if it were a robbery. I couldn't think of who would want to kill me, so robbery I thought was the only motive.

Also, while there, I made some new acquaintances and renewed some old ones. I ran into a nigga named Akmed I knew from 27th Street. He was from Bangladesh and I went to elementary school with him. Everybody teased him when his family first came here, except me; I was always cool with Akmed. He went on to embrace the streets, and was now just another nigga in the hood. He was in for selling guns and was 17 months into his two- year sentence. Akmed was Muslim and cool with all the AK's. He had also gained some weight since school, so he was holding his own in the burg. Besides guns, Akmed had connections to heroin at great prices. Even though I didn't sell dope, I knew Akmed would one day come in handy.

For the next 11 months I did nothing but exercise, play spades and plot my takeover. I stayed to myself with the exception of Akmed, a nigga named George from Newark and two cousins from Centerville. I also got cool with a nigga named Fox from Burlington. He was a hustler like me, but he was sent to another facility after my first month in Jamesburg. Nigga's knew we were all getting money in the streets, so everyone tried to be our friends. The ones that didn't try to be our friends didn't like us, but we never had any real problems. We promised to stay in contact with each other, however, with the exception of Fox; I never saw any of them again.

7

I'm Home

It was February 2, 1989 and I was a free man for the first time in almost 13 months. Pop Pop and Uncle Ramos came to get me. On the ride to Camden I thought about Jasmine and how she was so shitty to me. When I walked in the house I heard, "Welcome home!" I scanned the room. It seemed like the whole projects was there. I couldn't believe my Abuela let all these drug dealers into her home.

We had a good time and laughed and ate. Everybody left, but I stayed home with my grandparents. We stayed up and talked all night. I told them my jail stories and my Abuela told me how it was dating a numbers runner in the '40's. It was the first time I heard her talk like that. Pop Pop told me stories of mobsters and how his mom left him. I learned everything about my grandparents that night and they learned everything about me. From that point on, we had a better understanding of each other and a more open relationship.

I felt so comfortable sleeping in my own bed. I woke up at 6:00 a.m. and couldn't get back to sleep. Manny got my coke out of the apartment and sold it for me, so I had $24,000 to my name. Ace let the apartment go and my car was impounded. Raoul was now running Howell Street with Butter as his worker. They both still had cases pending. I could have gone to Howell Street, but I came back to home base. The projects. It was hard trying to re establish the set, and for a time, I worked in the alley as a trapper for Manny. Sometimes I earned as much as $3,000 a shift. I grinded all winter and spent money on nothing. It was like the old days. I lived at home and I stacked my money.

Ace was struggling. Star had left him and got pregnant by a nigga from Burlington, a town 15 minutes north of Camden. Someone broke into his house and he was forced to move back with his grandparents where he couldn't run wild. T-money had just been released from FDC after waiting on bail for more than a year. Ace started hanging with T-money again, and they were always coming up with a get rich quick scheme.

Flaco was about to open a bar on 24th and Federal called Oasis. He also had that used car lot up and running. D.J. was opening a car customization store. He also co-owned a furniture store with Luis Noel and a construction company with Jorge Lopez. Even Raoul owned a liquor store on Kaighn Avenue. Everybody was making moves and it was my turn. I approached D.J. about starting a car wash.

"I see Jamesburg has made you grow up some, Gato. Life's not all about selling drugs. You have to make your money work for you or you'll be dealing drugs the rest of your life", he said.

I figured D.J. to be about 30 years old and Flaco to be 25, 26 although, I didn't no for sure. I wanted that type of money at that age so I listened to his blueprint.

"Give me half your profits and I'll save them for you like an underground bank." I'll then open businesses in both our names and clean the rest of your money. I'll do all that for 5% of whatever you give me."

Those numbers were great, Manny had been doing it the whole time I was gone and had $250,000 in the bank. I told D.J. I needed some time to get my money right, but I would definitely be interested in starting this summer.

It had been 3 days since I saw or heard from T-Money or Ace. I was worried they had done something stupid and gotten themselves killed. On the fourth day I got a page from a 305 area code. When I called back, Ace answered. I recognized the voice immediately. He asked me what's new in a voice that let me know he did something.

Over the phone he told me that him and T-Money had found DJ's Cherry Hill home, broke in and stole over $100,000. They were now laying low in Miami, where they would remain until things cooled off. I was speechless. I told him to stay up, and banged the phone.

Later that day, Manny confronted me with the news. I told him they were in Florida and weren't coming back and that I had no prior knowledge of their plan. This wasn't the mob and I knew D.J. was not going to Miami to chase someone down over $100,000.

It was late May when I first heard Jasmine was home from Del State. I had the '89 Pathfinder and lived in Washington Apartments on Benson Street. I was back on top. I had a drivers permit and ran the same block in the projects where Jasmine's mom lived. I had stopped selling caps and was selling $5 rocks in bags. I was getting my coke from Manny and Flaco. By this time, D.J. was never seen with or around drugs. He still financed and received profits from drug operations, but he was far removed from the daily dealings of the drug business. I had a two-bedroom apartment and one room was for my Akita, a Japanese fighting dog I paid five grand for. I also kept a couple Pit Bulls at Uncle Ramos house.

I also started traveling. Uncle Ramos and I went to the providence of Dajabon in the D.R. I met some family members and possible connects. I also went to Universal Studios the same weekend as the Woodrow Wilson Senior trip. I took Butter and Rim with me and paid for the whole trip. I fucked three different chicks that weekend; we had weed, liquor and a rental car I blew $14,000 in Orlando.

Stack all winter. Play all summer. That was my motto, and I was living it. When I finally saw Jasmine in the projects during the Memorial Day block party I didn't know what to say. I didn't know whether to ask her why she did what she did, not say a word or choke the shit outta her for stealing my $35,000. Before I could decide she spoke to me, "When'd you come home"?

"I been home a minute, like four months or something." I said while noticeably eyeballing her friend.

"That's you?" her friend asked pointing to my Path.

"Yea that's my shit," I answered with a grin.

"You would've thought a college girl would have more manners," I said referring to Jasmine not introducing us.

"Hi I'm Simon but my friends call me Gato."

"Gato? When they start calling you that?" Jasmine asked with a hint of jealousy in her voice.

"When I got shot 8 times and survived they said I must have 9 lives so they started calling me Gato. That's cat in Spanish".

"You got shot 8 times..."

"You asking a lot of questions, and I still don't know your name." I said cutting her off in mid sentence.

"I'm Keisha",

"Keisha huh, where you from Keisha?" I asked?

"Willingboro. You know where that's at?" she asked?

"Yea, I been up there. My Aunt Linda used to work up there in the Willingboro Plaza, back in the day." I said pulling out my papers.

"Ooh, can I smoke?" she asked?

"Yea you can smoke. I was 'bout to take a ride though".

"Come on, Jasmine. You coming?" Keisha asked. Jasmine didn't want to come, but definitely didn't want Keisha alone with me.

Keisha was lighter than I usually preferred but there was no denying her beauty. She was about 5'6, 160. She was thicker than Jasmine with more gut and definitely more ass. Her hair was pulled back with the baby hairs brushed on her forehead.

She had a tattoo that said Jersey's Finest on her leg. I rolled up 3 joints, like my nigga Ace used to, and hopped in the truck. I told Keisha to get in the front because I didn't want anybody thinking I fucked wit Jasmine. I rode them through the whole East Camden pointing out to Keisha different spots where I had sold drugs. After our tour of East I went across the 36th Street Bridge to Cramer Hill.

I rode by the bodega where Ace and I use to get weed from his uncle Bingo and saw Flaco's car. I pulled over and saw Flaco with Bingo's boss Pedro. I walked over and greeted the two.

"What's up?" I said.

"There he is. Gato! The best fucking drug dealer under 18 ever," the two laughed. "I see you got Jasmine back, and her friend that's my little.... I mean Gato," he said almost forgetting the nickname he gave me. Business is good and it's about to get much better Flaco said as the most beautiful woman I ever saw in person walked up."

Pedro introduced her as his wife Carmen. She was perfect. Olive skin, model height, big titties and fat ass with not even an inch of fat. Her hair was long and shinny. We exchanged handshakes and I hopped back in the jeep.

"That's my man, and shit he runs the projects," I said giving Keisha more information than I should have.

We headed back out east. Keisha and I were chatting while Jasmine sat in the back seat on mute. Every once in a while Keisha would try to include Jasmine in the conversation, or ask her if she was okay. Jasmine would just say, "Yea, I'm good."

After about an hour of riding I stopped by my house and Keisha asked if she could use the bathroom. I left Jasmine in the running truck while Keisha and I went in the house.

"Damn, that thing big!" I said walking behind Keisha admiring her assets.

"Boy, you better not let Jasmine hear that." she said smiling.

"Straight back to the left." I said pointing to the bathroom door".

"You got a dog?" she asked, hearing my Akita, Kujo begin to bark,

"Yea, but he in the other room. You good. I won't let him get you." I answered with a laugh.

"This is a nice place. You live here alone." she asked through the bathroom door, which wasn't completely closed.

"Yea, just me and the dog. "Why? You going to keep me company?" I asked her. She flushed the toilet and washed her hands before coming out of the bathroom and answering, "If you go in the car and tell Jasmine I'm staying, then I'll stay the night."

"OKAY!" I answered.

"Sike, sike! I'm just playin'." she said grabbing my arm. As I turned around we caught eyes and I stole a kiss.

"You crazy. And I'm staying at Jasmine house tonight anyway." she said before leaving the apartment. I waited about 30 seconds and then went back to the truck. Everything seemed normal, so I knew Keisha didn't tell Jasmine.

The next day I caught up with Manny in the Projects and we rode to Lee Street in Philly to get a $30 of weed. On the way I told him about Keisha and Carmen, Pedro's beautiful wife. Manny told me Carmen was Columbian and her brother Enrique had been supplying Pedro and Flaco for more than a year now.

"That's how I be givin' it to you so cheap.", Manny explained. Manny got his normal 2 $30's and I bought one I rolled up on the way back since Manny was driving his black '89 Iroc Z.

After the weed spot, Manny drove to 7th and Race streets in China Town. There we got a massage with the happy ending for $150 a piece. It was my first time there. I picked a green-eyed beauty named Miao Yin. She put me in the shower, washed me all over, then dried me off and laid me on the table where she began a deep tissue massage. By the time she rolled me on my back I was half asleep. She then massaged my legs and again had me relaxed until she started sucking my dick like her life depended on it. She rubbed my balls at the same time and made me cum in what seemed like seconds. My day was going great, and it was only 12:00.

It was Memorial Day weekend and the hood was Jumping. It was still early, so I went to Westfield Acres to pick up Rim. In the Acres nigga's hustled in front of the building entrance, which they called archways. Each archway was a different set, ran by a different nigga and all of them were eating. 32nd Street ran next to the Acres and was one of the busiest drug spots in Camden. There was definitely a lot going on over here.

Since I had been home and hanging with Rim more, I found out a lot of things about T-Money. He told me T-Money was not really his cousin, but they both were Star's cousins and had grown up together in the Acres. I met a lot of nigga's who had clout out there, and I began to see why Ace opened a block on 33rd Street. I also saw why he couldn't keep it running. T-Money was cool but he wasn't thorough enough to run a drug spot here, let alone bring in an outside nigga to do it. I still wasn't 100% comfortable in his projects, so Rim and I slid to my hood. He told me how stupid Ace and T-Money were for stealing that money from D.J. "Like it was a million dollars or somethin'." and that they would be "fucked up in a year or so." He was absolutely right. He was letting me know he didn't move like T-Money.

Once back in the projects, I was determined to *run* into Keisha. When we pulled up Butter was out there with his cousin Orlando who worked for Manny in the alley. They were already smoking, so I rolled up. It was 2:00 p.m. and the smell of barbeque and weed filled the air. We ate burgers and shot dice while talking shit to the chicks that walked by.

More than an hour went by before I saw Jasmine walking up. The first thing I noticed about her was that she was by herself.

"Where's old girl?", I asked casually.

"She went home. I just walked her to the bus stop", Jasmine said without stopping. Without hesitation I hopped in the truck.

"Yo. Where you going?"

"I'll be back." I hollered answering Rim, before pulling off.

I figured Keisha's bus had already left, so I drove straight to the Willingboro Plaza. The Plaza had been closed down for some time but was still the main bus stop for the 409 (the Camden to Trenton line). I usually didn't drive this far without a licensed driver but I didn't need a third wheel with me. I pulled up and checked the bus schedule. The bus from Camden was due to arrive at 4:07. It was 3:53. I had made it with time to spare. I did what I always did to kill time. I rolled up and turned on my tape deck. I leaned back my seat and dosed off.

You Know Jack of Spades is now down wit the BDP posse (music playing) (knock, knock) the sound of someone tapping my window woke me out of my light sleep.

"Turn that music down! This aint Camden, nigga!" Keisha said. I smiled and sat up while rolling down the window. "What? You followed me?" Keisha asked smiling.

"Nah, I was just in the neighborhood and I was about to smoke this weed", I said holding up the joint.

"A joint? That's all you think it takes?" Keisha said laughing. "You a young boy you aint ready for me."

"I got a car, a crib and enough money to feed an African Village for the winter. I'm a grown-ass man. Now get in!" I said lighting the weed and rolling up the window."

When she walked to the passenger side and got in, I knew I had her. We rode around Willingboro smoking and talking. The town was like a maze; she told me "Just ride all the streets look the same here." It was fun to get out the hood and see black people living good. Willingboro was the suburbs but it was almost all black. After a couple more hours and a couple more joints we stopped at Cramps liquors and ended up at Seafood Shanty, a nice little spot on Rt. 130.

There are 3 towns between Willingboro and Camden. Delran, Cinnaminson and Pennsauken. All 3 towns' police were notorious on the highway at night so I let Keisha drive. The whole ride she complained about going to my house and the possibility of seeing Jasmine, so we stopped at Garden State Motel in Cinnaminson. When we got there I gave Keisha a $100 bill to go pay for the $30 room, she came out and *forgot* to give me my change. I had exact change. I t was just a test, and she failed miserably.

She passed the next test with flying colors. A joint wouldn't cut it but I guess 4 joints and a shrimp dinner did the trick, because as soon as we got in the room she got busy. The door was stuck so we had to get the manager to let us in. She sucked on my neck in front of the manager and pushed me on the bed while he was still in the room. The Indian manager stood astonished and watched her jump on me and begin to take my clothes off.

"Close the door on your way out.", she mumbled snapping the manager out of his trance. She continued and sucked me all the way from forehead to balls. She sucked my dick for about 3 minutes so good that I couldn't take it and I stopped her. I began to take off her shirt and she pulled her skirt up and didn't have panties on. She licked her fingers and started rubbing her clit a mile a minute. She was acting like she just came home from a 10-year bid.

"Yes, yes, oh shit!" She said while making herself cum.

She then hopped on my dick and began to ride; I had a condom in my hand but never had the chance to open it, much less put it on. She kept saying "Tell me when you 'bout to cum.", so I figured she didn't want to get pregnant. When I was about to nut I told her and she hopped up and began sucking the cum out of my dick, straight out of the pussy.

I dozed off and woke up to more head. This time she stopped and said "Hit it from the back.", while turning her ass to me. I hit it from the back as fast and hard as I could. She came twice before I finally came in her. This time I passed out for the night. When I woke up I climbed on top off her and hit it one more time before getting dressed. We left around 9 a.m. and I dropped her off in Willingboro, gave her my beeper number and told her to page me before returning to Camden.

When I got home, I decided to take my Abuela and Pop Pop to the movies. We went to the Pennsauken Mart to see Spike Lee's, *Do the Right Thing.* My grandparents loved the movie. On the way home they told me about Camden in the 40's and how they met. That night I stayed in the house listening to old stories before falling asleep on the living room couch. I woke up at 2:00 am and went out front to smoke a joint and think. I was making money but I needed a plan, a plan for my life after hustling. But what? I sat on the porch smoking and brainstorming of legal business' that could make me drug dealer money! My brainstorming ended with my joint and I went back to sleep for the remainder of the night.

The holiday was over and it was back to business. I got 3 keys from Manny for $51,000. I had already learned to cook and usually cooked just enough crack for 2 days. There was a harsher sentence for crack than there was for cocaine so keeping your product in powder form was the smarter thing to do. The projects were doing about $7,500 a shift and after paying workers I was still doubling my money. I was eating, but I started to realize I really didn't have a team. I fucked with Rim and Butter, but if I wasn't under the umbrella of such a powerful *Organization* I would have definitely felt the pressure from the wolves. For the first time, I began to miss Ace. Ace was sometimes reckless but he was a cannon and a force, a force I needed back!

As I pulled up to Cramer Hill I saw Bingo talking to a young Spanish girl. He immediately waived her off and greeted me. My pager was going off but I ignored it and walked over toward Bingo. After exchanging greetings, I told Bingo straight out, why I was there. He told me he heard about what Ace did and that he could straighten it out. By the end of our conversation Bingo told me to get in touch with Ace and tell him to come home, and that he was safe.

He also told me that I could come see him direct and save about $3,000 per key. Flaco and Manny wouldn't have a problem with me going direct but I would then have to rent the block. I could rent the block for $10,000 a week, but to pay $17,000 per kilo and not pay a fee for the block was cheaper than it would be to rent the block and pay $14,000. The only way it would make sense is if I could sell 4 or more keys per week, but at the time I was only selling 3. Plus, that would eliminate my muscle, as I would be no longer making them money. It was a great offer and I told Bingo I would keep that in mind and get back to him.

After leaving Cramer Hill I went straight to Westfield Acres to find Star. She was the one person who might know how to reach Ace. Star had 2 kids one by Ace and one by some nigga from Burlington who was now doing a 5-year bid for armed robbery. She had gained at least 100 pounds and was living back in the projects with her mother who was a crack head. Star was smoking wocky (wet) and drinking a Natural Ice when I pulled up. There were two other nigga's sitting with her and I got the feeling I had made a mistake by going there alone.

It wasn't quite dark yet and I could see the two nigga's making a lot of movement, so I rolled the window down and told Star to hop in. She gave me a funny look before getting in the truck. I asked how Lil' Ace was doing and gave her $300. Then, I asked if she knew how to get in touch with her Baby Dad. She looked at the three one hundred dollar bills I handed her and gave me the pager number without even asking why I wanted it.

"Thanks", she said before getting out of the car and rejoining the two nigga's she was with. I looked at her and thought the streets can get the best of anyone including fe-males!

I finally checked my pager, which had been beeping for the last 20 minutes on and off. It was Keisha! I went to my apartment and called. She wanted to see me and I wanted to see her. I told her I didn't feel like driving to Willingboro so I arranged for a taxi to pick her up and bring her to my house. She was still skeptical about coming to my house, but realizing that was the only option, she agreed.

It was nearly 10:30 when she arrived in a peak coat with only silk pajamas underneath. When she walked in, we got right to it. We sat on the couch and began undressing. She got on top and began to ride me. It was so wet; I loved it. We continued for 20 minutes and then both fell asleep. When I woke up around 6:00 am to use the bathroom I noticed blood all over my couch. I looked down and it was all over my boxers, too. She was on her period and didn't even tell me. I called a cab, then went to the bathroom and took a shower.

As I got out of the shower the cab was beeping out front. "Keisha, Keisha, Wake the fuck up, you nasty bitch"! I yelled nudging her with my foot.

"Nasty Bitch", she said while sitting up and noticing the bloody mess she left.

"Yea, Nasty Bitch. Your cab out front," I said handing her a $50 bill. Keisha was obviously embarrassed. She took the money and left screaming.

"Fuck you, you little dick nigga!" on her way out the door.

I went back to sleep and woke up around 12:00. I went straight to the projects and there had been an early morning shooting and everybody was outside. I ran into Jasmine, who saw me and frowned before saying,

"You fuckin' nasty muthafucka".

"Yea, an' you a thief. I guess we all got our problems.", I answered sarcastically. "A thief? I aint never stole nothin'!", Jasmine replied with attitude.

"Yea, I would believe that if I weren't missing $35,000, I answered.

"I got your safe with every dollar in it upstairs, so come get your shit before I put it out with the trash." she said walking upstairs to her apartment.

I began to follow her, and before I got all the way up the steps I saw my safe tumble down the first four steps. I still remembered the combination it was 6 - 17 - 87 the day we met.

Once I opened the safe I saw 35 stacks of money wrapped in rubber bands just like I left it over a year ago. I was shocked. I never asked her about the money, but why hadn't she mentioned it? I was speechless, and she just shook her head with tears in her eyes.

"My friend!! I can't believe you fucked my friend!" she said before slamming the door. I banged on the door, she wouldn't answer. I looked at the safe and began stuffing all 35 stacks of money in her mail slot with a short letter that said, *"This is for you, use it for school. I love you."* I wasn't sure if it would work but I was desperate, I fucked up a good one.

But to this day I still don't know how she found out.

8.

Can't Knock the Hustle

It was early January 1990, during a cocaine drought, that I had my first run in with Officer Jeremy Harris. I was suppose to be getting 5 keys for $110,000 but was only able to get 2. On my way back from Federal Street, with 2 kilos in the trunk and $66,000 in a duffel bag in the back seat, Rim and I noticed police behind us. I got my license the previous June, but had it suspended around Christmas for letting an unlicensed driver drive my truck.

"You see the boys behind you, right?" Rim asked.

"Yea, I see 'em." I answered while turning left onto 28th Street.

"He's on us." Rim said noticing the police car had also turned left.

"Calm down, nigga." I said, as I made the right onto Washington. *(Sirens)*

"Shit he pullin' us; don't worry I got this." I said grabbing the duffel bag out the backseat. The officer walked to the car and before he could say a word a handed him the opened duffel bag and said, "I aint got no license, take this and let me go". I started the car back up before he answered and pulled off, while the officer stood staring at the money amazed. I read his nametag, *"Officer Jeremy Harris."* "That was close. Gato. I guess you do got nine lives?" Rim said laughing.

"Guess I do." I answered with a smile. I was scared to take the drugs into my house, so I drove to my grandmothers and stashed them there. Then I headed for the gym. Uncle Ramos ran one of only 2 gyms in Camden. The other, *Heavy Metal,* was frequented by a lot of cops, and the two gyms would have boxing matches against each other. I wanted to see If Uncle Ramos knew Jeremy Harris through these matches.

When I got to the gym Uncle Ramos was helping a young fighter train, so I stood and watched for about 15 minutes while they finished up. Jose Martinez, the former Mr. Universe, was there as were a couple of police officers and other regulars whom I recognized.

"Simon, to what do I owe this visit?" Uncle Ramos asked while walking towards his office.

"I know a lot of cops work out here, plus you have the exhibitions against *Heavy Metal,* so I was wondering if you knew Jeremy Harris?"

"Of course, he owns Heavy Metal. Why?" Uncle Ramos asked

I explained the situation, which had taken place a few minutes prior.

"Who said money can't buy freedom?", Uncle Ramos responded. Then he called D.J., who walked into the gym soon after. Uncle Ramos and D.J. talked for a couple of minutes,

D.J. called me over and explained that I would have to take the $66,000 as a loss but said I would not have to worry about Jeremy bothering me anymore. The money wasn't the issue to me, I just wanted to make sure Officer Harris didn't have it out for me, and now I was reassured.

The incident with Officer Harris didn't stop my hustle. The next day I cooked and bagged a quarter key. It would take me selling both kilo's to make back most of the money I lost to the Police the night before. I avoided jail, was in good health, and was sitting on about $700,000 between my stash and the money I had saved with DJ so fuck it!

That day I was feeling cocky and went out and bought a black Mercedes Benz 300 E. It was the hottest Benz on the market and at 17; I was one of the first dudes to own one. I kept the Path and parked the Benz at Abuela and Pop Pop's house under a car cover. It was a crazy 24 hours. I was beginning to realize I needed more spots to sell my product. I had too much money to only be getting 5 keys, but I had nowhere else to sell my shit.

That day I paged Ace; it was nearly 7 months after Star gave me his number. I'm not sure why I waited so long to try and contact him again but it was only the second time I paged him since I got the number. I waited at the crib for over an hour but he never called.

The next time I saw Officer Harris was even crazier than the first. I called Flaco for 3 kilo's and he said one of his workers would bring them to my apartment on Benson Street.

Twenty minutes later, Officer Harris knocked on my door in uniform with a gym bag in his hands. He said he was there to drop off and not pick up and I should give the money to Flaco. He laughed before saying, "Have a nice day", and walking back out to his cop car. I couldn't believe what just happened I was stunned, not only was he making drops but in uniform! I checked the bag and there was 3,000 grams. The Organization had at least one cop on payroll. I wondered If Manny knew about this?

"For real? 3 cops got shot?" I asked International, the crack head standing in front of the projects. It was 2:00 pm and there had been another shooting. An undercover buy and bust went wrong. A man was shot and killed and three cops also got hit. The shooting happened around 12:30 and the alley was almost back to normal when I got there.

Manny had just pulled up, so we decided to go to China-town. On the ride, Manny told me about how much money they were making in the alley. He said Flaco was making $70,000 a week profit. I was sure Manny had a million dollars by now, but I didn't ask him. He owned a couple of small businesses including a bodega in Pollack, which was run by one of our cousins. He also bought a house in Cherry Hill for him and his girlfriend Veronica.

Muscleclo was doing more of the day-to-day dirty work in the alley and Manny was handling all the drugs behind the scenes. Manny told me Muscleclo was a beast and that he would fly in hit men from the D.R. to kill someone and fly them back to the D.R. the same night.

Manny also had begun to sell weight in Pollack Town where he grew up He was making thousands daily. I told Manny of my run-in with Officer Jeremy Harris. I explained how Flaco sent him to my crib with 3 keys.

"I don't like fucking wit cops no matter who they grew up with or who they know. They will turn on you at anytime. It's never a good situation." he explained.

"How do you know Officer Harris?" I asked Manny.

Manny explained that a few months back, Chris, a friend of DJ's from North Camden, introduced Harris to D.J. as a cop who could provide service to him. Greg even let Harris stash 33 kilo's at his Heavy Metal Gym. 2 weeks after Greg gave Jeremy the coke to stash, 2 men in black fatigues shot him dead on his porch.

"So he got a body?" I asked about Jeremy. "I don't know about a body but I know what he did get and that's 33 keys."

"Does D.J. know?" I asked.

"Shit, D.J. probably bought the coke from him. (Laughing) That's a grimy nigga", he said, as we pulled up at the massage parlor.

We got back to Camden around 4:00. The alley way was once again chaotic.

"What the fuck happened out here now?" Manny said as we parked next to some cop cars and yellow tape.

"Somebody else got capped?" I wondered.

International was still wandering around and couldn't wait to tell us the scoop. "Some young boy and another cop got shot...it's crazy out here today." International said.

"Damn, 4 cops shot on one Street in one day. Looks like we'll be shut down for a little while." Manny said annoyed. A while proved to be less than 24 hours as the alley was back open by the morning shift.

The day was so crazy; I decided to spend the night at home. Jasmine still hadn't spoken to me since I gave her that $35,000 back and I hadn't seen or heard from Keisha since I kicked her out. I had no steady pussy but I was starting to realize my value. Girls like to be with a nigga who got money even If the nigga don't give them shit. It's just the status of saying, "I fuck wit Gato and he got that bread." Realizing this, I began to fuck everything moving, but no one could fill the void Jasmine left. I thought about jasmine a lot, even though I tried to block her out of my mind. I walked out front to smoke a joint.

Washington apartments were filled with bitches so I knew smoking out front would attract some of the local hood rats that were walking by. It was a cool night, but not cold. The street was quiet, although there was a steady flow of traffic coming through. I walked to the corner and saw a dice game around the block on Dudley. I checked my pockets and only had $200 on me, so I decided to go try my luck. As I approached the dice game, I saw a man in a hoodie running toward the game from the opposite direction. Before I could turn back toward my house, I heard the first shots (Bang, bang.... bang...bang...bang. bang...bang) I kept running toward my house, and I kept hearing shots. As I got to my house, I noticed I was hit in my upper left shoulder. I figured whoever got shot at the dice game would be taken to Cooper, so I drove myself to Our Lady of Lords Hospital.

As I sat on the hospital bed, I wondered why me? "Wrong place, wrong time." I thought. At least I was conscious and able to drive myself. A few stitches and I should be out of here. The doctor had other ideas. He said the bullet had to be removed or it could cause nerve damage in my neck and back. He wanted to immediately prep me for surgery.

"Do I have time to make a phone call", I asked.

"Yes, you have about 10 minutes before we get started", the doctor said. I immediately called Uncle Ramos at the gym. He was the best person to relay the message to my nigga's on the street and Abuela and Pop Pop.

I told him that a stray bullet hit me and I was okay.

"They gotta do surgery to remove the bullet, but I'll be okay."

When the doctor and nurse got back in the room they began to explain the process I was about to go through. They said I wouldn't feel a thing and put me under sedation.

The next morning I woke up to the sight of Ace and D.J. The last two people I expected to see together.

"What's up nigga, everything good?" I said. I was asking Ace but really checking with D.J. The smile on DJ's face let me know things were good.

"Yea, I'm back and the doctor said you good, so it's on.",
Ace answered. I smiled and D.J. told me to get some rest. I
wanted to ask Ace what happened when he saw DJ? How'd he
hear I was shot? So many questions but my eyes were getting
heavier and I didn't want to ask in front of D.J. Within seconds
I was asleep again.

Within 3 days I was back on the streets. My apartment had
been ransacked and I lost everything in there, from 2 kilo's to
my dog. Ace was back and I didn't care about losing those
things. I had money and I had my boy back. It was time to go
hard. My first day home, I met with Ace and D.J. D.J. was now
controlling most of East Camden and he allowed me and Ace
to set up shop in the Woodrow Wilson Arms Apartments on
33rd and Westfield Ave. These apartments were right next to
the Acres the projects that Star, T-Money and Rim were from.

T-Money was in federal prison sentenced to 6 years for the
kilos he got caught with at the airport so it was just Ace, Rim
and I. The apartments had 3 Buildings: A, B and C. We decided to sell $5 bags of weed in Building A, $20 bags of
powder in Building B and $5 bags of crack in Building C. D.J.
would provide the start up money, $112,000, which was to be
used to buy 6 kilo's of cocaine and 20 pounds of weed.

I decided to get Rim to run the set and I was leaning toward
using Butter as one of my trappers. Although Butter was
working for Raoul on the set, we started at 24th and Howell.
We had grown close and I was sure I could persuade him to go
to work for us. T-Money did do some good before he turned

himself in. He plugged Ace in with his Florida connect, who had a brother in N.Y. The brother had bricks right in N.Y. for $14,000, about $3,000 more than they cost in Florida. Having a connect that cheap and that close put us back in a winning position. D.J. got us an apartment to use in all 3 buildings. That was where we could cut, cook, bag and stash the drugs. I still had a spot in my projects and I let Ace eat with me. I even gave him $75,000 to get a car and apartment. We both got one bedrooms in the nearby Penn Gardens Apartments in Pennsauken. Everything was set. The only thing left to do was go to N.Y. to get the work.

The first trip to N.Y. Ace, Rim, Star and I went in 2 cars. The plan was that Rim and I would ride back clean and Ace and Star would bring back the drugs. I took my Benz and Ace drove a Lincoln. We rented from Manny's boy Luis Noel. The Lincoln had a stash box so we were good. The trip from Camden to N.Y. took about 2 hours.

When we crossed the GWB I began to get nervous. What If Ace and Star made a run for it with all the drugs? What If they get pulled over? What If we get robbed? I needed to relax. I began to split a phillie, (a cigar that was quickly replacing zigzags as the preferred method of smoking weed) and spread my weed around. Just as I finished rolling we pulled in front of a steakhouse on 175th and Broadway.

When I got out, I thought I was in Santo Domingo everybody everywhere was Dominican. We walked into the restaurant and were greeted by a man named Sheppy. Sheppy told us to order some food, so I got a Roasted Chicken and Shrimp with rice and beans. Rim and Ace both ordered chicken and rice while Star just drank water. I was beginning to feel more comfortable until Sheppy came back with 12 keys in a duffel bag.

"This is 12. You gave me $84,000 now you owe me $84,000 see you in 2 weeks." he said before walking out of the restaurant.

"What the fuck? He just giving us shit? He didn't even ask if we wanted it?" Rim barked.

I saw it another way. This was the start of something real big for us.

When we got back, we started selling everything from nicks to bricks right out of Building C. We started supplying a lot of smaller, local dealers, mostly quarter and half ounces of crack. The powder brought another clientele that never would have come to my projects otherwise. We were also selling a pound of weed per day, all nicks, which was bringing in $1,500 a day profit. The set took off like no one would have imagined.

Rim got some nigga's from his hood to be trappers along with Butter and a nigga named Vic who was from my projects. Managing Building C was always the most hectic, so Ace, Rim and I would alternate buildings weekly. Manny lent me a money counter and the money was coming faster than I had ever seen. After 9 days we were out of coke, so it was time for another N.Y. run. I was still buying coke from Flaco to supply my spot in the projects, but the coke we sold on 33rd was fish scale, the best quality cocaine available.

We used our same routine for the second trip to N.Y. Rim and I had the same duffel bag the bricks came in filled with $168,000. We arrived at the restaurant and Sheppy was so excited to see us almost like he expected us to try and beat him. "You made it", he said. "You thought we wouldn't," I answered in a half funny half sarcastic tone. I handed him the money and he again told us to eat. This time Star was less shy ordering broiled shrimp and lobster tails over rice. The wait was a little longer this time but it was worth it when Sheppy came back with another Dominican man each holding a bag. "This is double from last time", Sheppy said. "24 keys", I replied. "Good you can count" Sheppy answered seizing on his opportunity to get me back for my earlier smart remark. "$252,000 see you soon", Sheppy smiled and said. A deal for a quarter million, we had reached the big time. When we got back to Camden we followed the same format everything for sale. Word spread that we had the best product around and soon hustlers from all parts of the city were coming to 33rd for that raw.

I was hanging in the projects less and hanging on 33rd more and my spot in the projects was suffering. Manny had his hands full running the alley so I turned to Butter. Butter was a reliable worker who had no dreams of being boss. He played his role and was happy with it and he didn't blow his money. Butter had trapped for us on 24th, the projects and 33rd and I knew he knew the ends and outs, so I stepped to him about running the PJ's. Butter surprised me by turning down the offer saying he didn't want the responsibility or the headache. I knew one more nigga named Roberto who was thorough plus he was fly wit Butter so I offered him the job. Roberto jumped on the opportunity so I put him in charge and Butter worked for him.

By the third trip to N.Y. we didn't know what to expect. We got there and it was business as usual we gave Sheppy $336,000 the $252,000 we owed him plus the $84,000 we had been spending. This time Sheppy didn't return 2 females and an older man returned with 5 black duffel bags it was 100 keys. The old man also gave me the $84,000 back and said we didn't have to put up any upfront money and we were to bring back 1.4 million dollars. This was the first deal I couldn't personally cover the money we owed Sheppy. That alone made me nervous but the big picture was we would profit more than a million dollars on this deal. We had been paying back D.J. weekly with interest so I took him the $84,000 to make the clean break. D.J. had no idea how much coke we had been getting and was surprised to get paid in full in less than 2 months. I also took Flaco $10,000 for the first month rent in the projects, as I no longer needed his coke.

It was amazing the customers we were attracting in our 3 buildings. We started selling pounds of weed and we were getting hustlers from Burlington, Beverly, Mt. Holly and Pemberton coming through. Jorge Lopez the city councilman was even a customer and bought several ounces of powder on plenty of occasions. During the time we were selling our 100 bricks we even sold 4 to Flaco when his connect was out. We were supplying Blockz, which was the guy from Parkside who Manny use to work for. He was just coming home from a bid and getting check stubs from D.J for his parole officer. When he opened his drug spots back up D.J. recommended us as a supplier and he started copping bricks from us. Within 3 months of coming home Blockz had a mansion in Parkside. He took two row homes and gutted the walls he installed marble floors and 3 hot tubs. He added a chandelier and brass statues on the outside there was still 2 doors and it looked like two normal row homes. He had a mansion in the middle of the hood and nobody knew. Jorge Lopez's construction company did the renovations, which cost around $200,000. Blockz was way flashier than D.J. or Flaco.

Everyone tied into our Organization was getting money. I had touched a million for the first time and I was still 2 months shy of my 18th birthday. I had an apartment in Pennsauken, a Mercedes Benz 300E, and a Pathfinder. I had been stacking all winter and had about $500,000 saved with D.J., besides a mill in cash and assets. The N.Y. trips had continued and we were now getting a steady 30 keys every 2 weeks. Things couldn't be better, and to top it off Jasmine was due in the city in about 3 weeks. Star had lost weight and was looking good again. Ace was getting money and he fucked with Star, but kept a stable of bitches to entertain him. Rim was eating like never before and had 2 cars. Things were going well in the projects to; Roberto and Butter were taking care of business, so money was coming from everywhere.

In early May, things in Camden began to change. "You remember I told you about Kalic", Manny asked as we talked in the projects.

"Kalic, Kalic? Where do I know that name from?", I thought.

"Remember, I told you he's from North Camden and he didn't want to get down with us a while back?", Manny asked?

"Oh, yea. That nigga.", I said recalling the exact conversation.

"Yea. Well, he was fucking wit the nigga's on 32nd but something happened and now they at war." Kalic was a killer, no doubt about it, and having him at war with our neighbors was not good for our business.

Manny explained, the beef started when a nigga named Little Mark, from 32nd Street, beat up Vern. Vern's older brother, Poncho, was one of Kalic's soldier 's. Poncho and Art (another one of Kalic's soldiers) murdered Little Mark and the chic he was wit.

"Now it's all out war and you a block away, so watch yourself!"

That worried me. I stayed strapped since the first time I was shot but this was a reason to be nervous. It was going to be a crazy summer.

9

Verano Loco (Crazy Summer)

The summer season began on Memorial Day, as usual. On Friday, I came to the projects after getting a page with code 777. When I arrived, I got word that police had been in the projects looking for Butter. After further investigation, I learned that the prosecutors were looking for Butter to testify against Raoul in the case they had pending. I was sure Butter wouldn't testify. I knew him, and he wasn't a rat. On the other hand, Raoul should take the charge, because the drugs and guns were his. It was a tough situation, but we had lawyer money for Butter, and the only option for him was to keep quiet.

I decided to go holler at Raoul to see if there was a solution. When I got to 24th Street there were police there. A little boy I knew told me Butter was in a shootout and that he and Roberto went to Philly. Nobody was shot in the shootout, and the boy didn't know the other shooter. Things were definitely heating up. I paged Butter but got no response.

I went by Butter's house to see if his mother had heard from him. She said she hadn't seen him today, but that the day before he told her a rival dealer put a hit out on him. When she said that, I knew who put the contract out and why Butter had been in a shootout. I left and went home and told Ace the news, he immediately wanted to go see Raoul. We decided to wait and see what Butter had to say about the situation.

Meanwhile, we played Lakers vs. Celtics and smoked a couple blunts. I fell asleep on Ace's couch and woke up at 4:00 when my pager went off. I called back, "Who this?" I asked half asleep.

"Butter, man, Butter! They found his body on 7th and Clearfield!"

"What?" I yelled, waking Ace.

"What, what happened?" Ace asked. I handed him the phone and didn't say a word. Rim repeated the same thing to Ace and he went straight to get his gun. It took me 25 minutes to calm him and to make him put his gun down.

The next morning, we went outside and put our ears to the street. Roberto was in Temple Hospital with a gunshot wound to the thigh and he was the only one who knew what really happened. When Ace and I arrived at the hospital Roberto was treating us like we were police. He wouldn't tell us any details on the shooting on 24th or how Butter got killed in Philly. It was no coincidence that Butter was killed at his favorite weed spot. Somebody had either followed him or set him up. Roberto was not giving us any information, just saying," I don't know" and "I didn't see."

Since it was a Jersey murder that occurred in Philly, there was no real investigation, and the case was closed quickly. The case against Raoul was also dropped, since the prosecution had no witnesses and the house where the drugs and guns were found was in Butter's name.

The first person I saw when I got back to the projects was Jasmine. She was home from school and had heard the news. She came right over to me and gave me a hug. She was thick as ever, although I couldn't bring myself to tell her at such a time.

"I just heard. I'm so sorry. Is there anything I can do?" she asked. I just stared at her with a blank stare. I was 17 years old and emotionless.

"It's fucked up", I was able to respond.

"Do they know who did it", she asked.

"Nah. So, What's up wit you? I'd like to see you later." She paused for what seemed like a lifetime before agreeing.

"Good, I'll come get you at 8."

On my ride home, I thought about Butter being dead. Gone forever. By the time I parked in front of my apartment, my face was filled with tears. I went in the house and rolled a blunt and then got in the shower for about 30 minutes. I sat around in my boxers watching T.V. and smoking until about 7 when I got up and got dressed.

I picked up Jasmine in the Benz. It was the first time she saw it. She was amazed, but she tried to front. She was wearing a black denim skirt with a white polo shirt.

"This is nice. What Flaco let you use it?" Jasmine said with a serious face. (Laughing)

"Nah. This mines. You know how I do. Remember?" I asked.

"I remember a Honda Accord", she answered and we both bust out laughing. As much as I wanted to just forget about Keisha and that whole situation, I knew I couldn't avoid the topic. I felt she had just as much explaining for breaking up with me in a letter without even a hospital or jail visit.

"So you want to talk about this now or…"

She cut me off, "Talk about what why you aint getting' no pussy tonight".

"Here you go. I wasn't even talking 'bout that. I was talking 'bout…"

"Keisha. You was talking 'bout you fuckin' Keisha. Which, again, is the reason why you aint getting' none of this good pussy."

"You know how I do. Remember?" She said.

"Let's just go have a good time. We can argue tomorrow", I said.

"Where you taking' me", she asked.

"Atlantic City." I answered.

"What we doin' in A.C", she asked? "We can't gamble

"Chill. Just relax." I told her.

Camden was a half hour drive from Atlantic City. When we arrived in A.C we went to the Taj Mahal, the new casino Donald Trump had just opened in April. Besides going to the beach as kids, neither of us had been to A.C. The Taj was fresh. It looked like a castle. Our room was the size of some apartments in the projects. We ate at Doc's *Oyster House* on

Atlantic Avenue. It was an old restaurant that had been there since 1897. Pop Pop told me before that they were one of the only restaurants in A.C that served blacks, back in the day.

I got some tickets to see Evander Holyfield vs. Seamus McDonough at Boardwalk Hall, so come on", I said. At the time, Holyfield was the number 1 contender to fight Buster Douglas, who had just knocked out Mike Tyson for the heavyweight title. Jasmine wasn't too impressed with going to a boxing match until she got there and saw the atmosphere. Everybody was there from Eddie Murphy to Denzel Washington. She was star struck. We sat in the 11th row, which were great seats that cost me $2,400 a piece. Jasmine let her guard down and we had a great time. The night was going better than I planned.

Holyfield won by TKO in the 4th round. The night was young. Jasmine started drinking in college, and had no problem playing slots and drinking Hennessy and Coke on the casino floor.

"Wow I'm feeling it right now", Jasmine laughed as she won 200 quarters on a slot.

"Yea, I need to smoke some weed". I answered.

"Try this", she said passing me her cup. I wasn't a drinker but no way was I going to refuse this drink. It was like drinking fire. I wondered where the soda was. It was strong but I had to front.

"It's pretty good", I said with a bitter face.

"Give me that before you throw up", she said with a smile.

"Nah, get your own I'm keeping this." I said drinking the remainder of the Hennessey. Jasmine stepped off and came back with two cups.

"2 Henny and Cokes", She said. I took the cup and quickly finished it.

"Damn, you better slow down. That shit creeps up on you", Jasmine explained. She was sipping on her cup threw a straw, and I was seeing double.

"Come on, let's go upstairs", she said.

When we got in the room I was fucked up. I stripped to my boxers, rolled a blunt and got in the bed, while Jasmine used the bathroom. When she came out she was in a matching white lace panty and bra set. Her smooth black skin against the white lace got me hard instantly. Jasmine was thick as hell and when she got in the bed with me I started rubbing and trying to kiss on her. "You still aint getting no pussy nigga, thanks for dinner and all that but you aint getting' none of this." Jasmine said crushing my dreams.

"You serious", I asked?

"Goodnight, Simon", she said turning her back and that fat ass towards me. As I lay in the bed drunk, I thought about all the great sex I had with Jasmine and began to doze off.

"Ooh, Shit!" I said sitting up.

"What", Jasmine asked? I had fallen asleep with the blunt and burnt a golf ball sized hole in my t-shirt; I sat up and took a pull.

"Let me hit that", Jasmine asked?

"Yea that's what I'm talking 'bout", I answered jokingly but dead serious. Jasmine took two pulls off the blunt, coughed and past it back. She stood up.

"Do I look fat?" she asked standing up looking perfect. Jasmine and I both knew she didn't have an inch of fat, at that moment I knew she wanted to have sex with me; she was just playing hard to get.

"Yea a little right here and here." I said pointing to her titties and ass. This is fat she said while grabbing her ass and sitting on my dick. I was rock hard.

"Yo Jasmine, stop playin'..." Before I could finish, Jasmine had slid her panties to the side and pulled my manhood out of the pee hole of my boxers. She began riding me. Her pussy was so wet. My boxers were soaked, but it felt too good to stop her, just to take them off.

"You like that", Jasmine asked as I came all in her.

"Hell, yea", I answered getting up and walking to the bathroom. I turned on the shower and summoned Jasmine. We got in the shower and washed each other before having sex again. It was the first time I ever had sex in the shower. I made Jasmine bend over and I hit it from the back for about 15 minutes. Jasmine told me to tell her before I came. I did, and she turned and swallowed everything I dished out.

We got out of the shower and dried off before getting back in the bed. Now it was my turn to return the favor. I started eating as soon as we got in the bed. I saw a porno were the guy made a girl squirt out cum. I found out this was a vaginal orgasm as opposed to the regular clitoral orgasm. To reach the vaginal orgasm I licked Jasmine's g-spot. Approximately 10 minutes later she squirted directly in my face. It shot out like a water gun with a hard steady stream, hitting me for about 10 real seconds.

I didn't stop there; I began licking her clitoris for another 10 minutes or so. This time she experienced a regular orgasm before I slid back in her with my rock hard dick. This time I was able to last for half an hour. When we finished, we went to an all night buffet and had a few more drinks before returning to the room. I smoked another blunt and we had sex a final time. It was sun up when we finished making love and we both fell asleep until checkout time.

The ride home was quiet and smokey. Jasmine slept all the way back to the projects and when we got there I woke here up

"Jasmine, Jasmine, go get your clothes."

"What clothes", she asked confused?

"All your clothes you aint staying here no more. You mo-vin' to Pennsauken with me", I answered.

"Oh really? First of all, you aint got it like that. Second of all, you don't bring the old into the new. So, If I *were* to move wit you, I wouldn't be bringing any old clothes", she respond-ed.

"You right." I said handing her the rest of the money in my pocket, which was probably about $6,500. "Take this and go to Philly and get some things. Just drop me off at my Pop Pop's house so I can get the truck. Jasmine smiled and hesitated for a few seconds before taking the money. I drove to my grandpa-rents and told Jasmine to page me when she got back to Jersey.

With all the fun I had in A.C I almost forgot about Butter's murder. I was reminded by a mural on 24th Street that showed him shooting dice with a blunt in his mouth. I drove to 33rd to check on the spot. When I got there it was business as usual, and all three buildings were pumpin'. I stopped by Popeye's before heading home to wait for Jasmine.

Once home, I paged Ace and Rim and told them both to come by. Ace was home, so he walked right over. Rim got there about 15 minutes later. "What's up with the set?" I asked.

"Nigga you been gone for a night, not a year. Aint shit changed", Ace answered while Rim laughed. (Laughing)

"Got to check on ya'll nigga's. You know how ya'll do", I said.

"Wonder what this nigga Sheppy gone give us this time?" Ace asked. (Sighing) "Who knows? This nigga just keep giving us more", Rim responded.

"And we keep selling it faster, so fuck it", I interjected. "Yea, you keep thinking shit's a game until these N.Y. nigga's get mad or we fuck some money up", Rim said. "If you scared, get a dog Rim, shit, this is a drug dealers dream. I'm trying to get NBA money. I don't know 'bout you. I aint scared. Plus, we aint gone fuck no money up", I said.

"He's right. This is our chance. We can be retired by 20. Well, not Rim. Aint you like 30?" Ace said with a laugh. (Laughing)

"Fuck you, nigga. 22. Get it right. I'm wit whatever. Fuck it!" Rim shouted.

I got the page around 4:30 from Jasmine's house. I called back and gave her my address, 42 Penn Garden Apartments and she let me know she was on her way. By the time she got there, Ace and Rim had already left. Jasmine was pleasantly surprised by the furnishing job I had done in my apartment.

"Some bitch probably helped you pick it out", she snapped.

"If you don't like something you can redecorate. This is our house now." I told her. She smiled and gave me a hug, and for the first time that I can remember, she told me she loved me and I responded, "I love you, too". It was early evening and already I wanted to crawl in the bed with my girl, Jasmine.

However, Jasmine decided she was going to cook dinner and invite my grandparents and Uncle Ramos over. I thought that was a good idea. I was close to my family and wanted them to know Jasmine. This would also be the first time Pop Pop and Abuela had been to any of my apartments. Jasmine made fried chicken, corn, mashed potatoes and string beans. The food was delicious. This was the first time I tasted her cooking and I was surprised she could burn like that. Uncle Ramos, Abuela and Pop Pop also enjoyed the food and Abuela told me to, "Treat Jasmine good because she was a keeper."

The night went well, but after dinner, Jasmine began to question my employment for the first time. "So, how long are you going to sell drugs?" she asked.

"Until I make 10 million", I answered dead serious.

Jasmine looked puzzled for a moment before asking, "Are you close?"

Jasmine knew I had money but she had no idea how much money I really had. Plus a million dollars often seems unreachable to nigga's in the hood.

"Nah, I aint close yet, but I got a million".

"You have a million dollars?" Jasmine asked obviously not believing me.

"Yea, I got a little over a million", I answered.

"So what are you going to do? I mean are you going to open a business? Don't you want to travel the world? Um...um...what I would do with a million dollars!" "They always give money to the wrong people", Jasmine said.

I sat back and thought about what Jasmine said for a minute before changing the conversation.

Later that night, Jasmine and I talked about everything from my mother to her family and the ins and outs of how I make my money. We talked all night and didn't get to sleep until early the next morning.

The next afternoon when I got up, I left Jasmine a few thousand dollars to pick up some things for the house. Then I went to see D.J. It was getting closer to my 18th birthday and I was ready to start opening some businesses. We talked for a little over an hour and decided a car wash and detail spot would be the best thing for me to venture into. It was going to be named *FastWash* and would be located on Marlton Pike close to Route 130. D.J. already owned a building there, so I paid him $130,000 cash for it and he kept it in his name. The business itself went go in my name with D.J. named as the financier. The terms were set and the renovations to the building were to start immediately.

The next thing I did was book a trip to Paradise Islands in the Bahamas. I scheduled us to leave 2 days after Butter's funeral. When I got home and told Jasmine the news of our trip she immediately gave me head right on the living room couch.

The funeral was on a Saturday, there had to be 300 people crammed into a small funeral home in Centerville. I wore a three-piece, all black suit as did Rim and Ace. I tried to talk Jasmine into staying home but she wanted to go support me, so she came with Star. Both of them wore black, appropriate looking dresses. Raoul showed up, but there was some tension with him and some of Butter's uncles, so he left. Just when things started to settle down, Roberto came in, still sporting a cast on his right arm from the shooting.

All hell broke lose. Butter's mom attacked him shouting "You know what happened to my son, and you're supposed to be his friend! You're a coward!" Roberto tried to defend himself and was knocked out by one of Darnell's uncles. The commotion was quickly settled and Roberto was escorted out of the funeral home. When the funeral finally got under way, there was a lot of emotional outburst from family members.

He was buried in Arlington Cemetery on Cove Rd. in Pennsauken. After the funeral Ace, Star, Rim, Jasmine and I skipped the procession and went back to my place. We smoked a couple of blunts and discussed the trip to N.Y. we had planned for the next day. Jasmine was not happy to hear I was going to N.Y. the day before our scheduled trip to the Bahamas.

Jasmine was able to hide her anger, until our company left. Then the argument began.

"Why the fuck would you go to New York the day before our trip", she screamed.

"The world don't stop. I still got to eat", I answered.

"Oh you got to eat? Mr. Millionaire?"

"Yea, and I'm tryin' to keep it...and make a couple more. This is a business, and it's non-stop. I have partners, responsibilities", I shouted back.

"You sound dumb as hell. How you gonna have a million dollars and go to N.Y. yourself? How are all 3 partners taking the trip? If ya'll 3 get locked up, who's going to run the business?" Jasmine asked.

She stumped me. I was being stupid. "You right. I'm glad I thought of that", I said laughing. (Laughing)

"Yeah whatever, nigga. You better be glad you got me. Now call your boys and tell them you aint goin'." she replied.

I called Ace and told him that at least 1 of us should be staying home. My idea was, whoever went to N.Y. would be paid an extra $2,500. Ace called Rim and they agreed the plan made sense.

The next day I tried to sleep late but I couldn't. Ace and Rim left Camden around 9:00 am so I figured if I slept until 12 they would be on their way back. When I got up after being restless in the bed for over an hour, the clock read 9:19. Jasmine was making French toast and turkey bacon so I went in the kitchen with her.

"Good morning, doesn't it feel good to be here with me instead of on the turnpike worrying about state troopers?" she asked!

The truth was, I was more nervous now than I ever was riding to N.Y. On my trips to NY I was never in the car with drugs and I was there to make sure things went okay. Now that job was up to Ace and Rim.

But my answer was, "Hell yea, I aint never going back to N.Y."

The next 4 hours were like lockdown in Jamesburg, boring as hell. At 1:27 exactly, Ace called my house phone and told me to come to his apartment. I walked over and couldn't believe what I saw.

"Oh shit! How many...that's gotta be..."

"100 bricks, 100,000 grams, 3,600 ounces, nigga. 1.4 million dollars worth of fish scale!" Ace said, cutting me off. Ace was smiling ear to ear; I was usually excited about getting coke, but 100 keys? That even had *me* scared! Taking 100 keys to Woodrow Wilson Apartments was not an option so we all agreed to stash equal amounts.

Before I left for the Bahamas, I had to find somewhere to stash all that coke. Leaving 30 keys in my apartment while I was on vacation was not a smart move, so I took it where I knew it would be safe, Pop Pop's house. I still had my own room at my grandparent's house so stashing it there wouldn't be a problem. I put the keys in the chest where I use to store my winter clothes when I was younger. I didn't tell anyone about stashing the drugs at my grand parents house, not even Jasmine.

Before I got home I got a page from Manny, so I drove to the projects. Manny said Butter's cousin Orlando, who worked in the alley, was found dead in North Philly. That was crazy. Why had Orlando been killed? Did it have to do with Butter? What about Roberto? He was a witness; was he next? Manny told me he didn't know why Orlando had been killed, but it was definitely an inside job that shouldn't be questioned. It started to feel like a perfect time to take a vacation.

10

Keys to the City

When we got back from the Bahamas, it was 3 days from my 18th birthday. Jasmine was making a big deal of it but I just wanted to get back to the hood to check on the spot. I had no contact with anybody for the last 5 days and in Camden, that's a lifetime.

When we pulled up at home Ace was outside his apartment smoking a blunt.

"What's good, nigga? What's been going on?" I asked.

"What's going on is a war nigga," he answered.

"Fuck you talking 'bout", I replied.

"Man, Kalic and those boys come down 32nd or to the Acres on the regular. It's been 3 shootouts since you left, my nigga. Like, 2 nigga's got killed. It was crazy. Police everywhere. The whole time we 1 street over selling crack nonstop. "We getting that 32nd Street money and everything".

"So what's the problem?" I wondered out loud.

"The problem is sooner or later somebody going to realize we over their makin' a killin' while everybody else just killin'." Ace said. "Man, look. We don't need no problems wit

Kalic. We aint ready for no problems wit Kalic, neither is D.J. or Flaco!" Ace shouted.

"Where he from? Metropolis?" Nobody's untouchable!

"Listen, what you use to tell me, huh? That's not even our hood. We don't need to make no enemies", Ace said.

"Its Rim hood", I responded.

"Rim? Rim scared to death!" Man, you better ask around'. This nigga is a killer", Ace said.

"So, what? You want to shut down?" I asked sarcastically.

"We need to do something." Ace said throwing his roach and walking into the crib.

D.J. had just recently purchased Jeremy Harris' Gym, *Heavy Metal*, so I went there to talk to him. I told D.J. about the beef between Kalic and 32nd Street. DJ said,"Kalic is a animal. You stay away from him. If somebody from his crew comes and tries to start problems, you don't give them no hassle just let me know. You got guns?"

"Yea, we got some," I answered.

"Some? How many is some?" D.J. asked.

"Well, I got a 38, Ace got..."

"A .38" D.J. laughed. "You kidding me, right", he contin-ued.

D.J. motioned to a man who he identified only as a good cop and told him I needed some protection. The officer asked for a number where I could be reached. I hesitated but D.J. insisted, "He's one of the good ones", so I gave him my pager number. As I drove to my apartment, I thought about the difference between Kalic and D.J. They both sold drugs and killed people, but Kalic was viewed as an animal, and D.J. a businessman. Although they where equally dangerous and respected in the drug world. That's when I realized it's not what you do, but *how* you do it.

The next day I got a page and I called the number back. (609) 555-3244. *"Hello?"*

"Yea, this is Gato." Somebody paged me?" I asked.

"Oh, yea. It's me, "Good Cop. I got something for you. Meet me under the 36th Street Bridge in 10 minutes, and bring $5,000.

He hung up before I responded. I already had about $7,000 on me so I went to the old Conrail train yard under the 36th Street Bridge. I met the man I knew only as Good Cop, and he pulled out a gym bag with 2 tech nines, a tech twenty two, 2 .45's, a nine and a .380.

I handed him the cash and started to step into my car. "I don't just do guns, I do protection", the cop said.

"Protection?" I asked.

"Yea, I can let you know about raids, informants and can even help get rid of competition", he said.

"Okay. Well, when do we start this?" I asked.

"I'll page you in a week or so with details"; he said extending his hand for a shake. I looked down before shaking his hand.

The next day, when I woke up and went outside to get my newspaper, the front page was announcing a street raid on 32nd Street. Police hopped out on about 10 people and locked them up on various drug charges. They also were going to be posting squad cars on the street in an effort to curb street violence plaguing the area. Wow, what a headline. I thought about my conversation with the good cop. There was no way this was a coincidence. I still hadn't told anyone about the guns or my new alliance with Camden's finest.

Later that day I got a page (609) 555-3244 the number looked familiar. I called back and it was the good cop. *That one was free, but it will cost $5,000 a week to continue these services,* he said. \

"Okay but how'd you know".... he cut me off,

"*I'll be in touch.*", *he said,* before hanging up.

This was crazy it was a good thing, if controlled. I went to 33rd and met Ace and Rim to tell them what I thought was good news.

When I got there, I showed Ace and Rim the guns and we stashed a couple in each building. Ace wasn't too thrilled with dealing with crooked cops, but he went along with it. Rim, on the other hand, thought it would be great to fend of the wolves from the Acres, 32nd Street and North Camden. All 3 buildings were doing better than usual with the help of the street raid on 32nd. Kalic couldn't come through with the heavy police presence, so things were normal. The next day was my birthday, so I went to Philly and bought some Jordan's, a herring bone chain, a Camden baseball jersey and an overall set. And now I would be ready for the birthday dinner Jasmine had planned.

My birthday started off well, as Jasmine woke me up to a mean professional and decided not to spit. I tried to return the favor but she stopped me saying "This is your day."

I got dressed and smoked a blunt before going to IHOP with Ace, Jasmine and Star. After IHOP I went to the projects to go see Manny.

"Happy birthday cuz." Manny said, pulling out a cigar to roll.

"18! You old. You know what that means? You old enough to go to the county.", he said. As crazy as that sounds, Manny was just being real. At 18 I was eligible for the county jail, and in my profession, it was inevitable. Manny wasn't the only person to make that comment to me leading up to my birthday. Every time I heard it, I would just laugh and knock on wood.

Manny and I spent the whole day together going to China-town, Cherry Hill Mall and the Pennsauken Mart. I told Manny about my encounter with "Good Cop", and he identified him as, Matthew McDowell. He said McDowell was a county Sheriff with a lot of pull and connections, and that D.J. and Flaco relied on him heavily.

Manny told me, although McDowell was a good ally, it was dangerous for me to deal with him directly.

"When cops get caught, they tell automatically. They know they'll never make it in jail, and they have the first shot of getting a deal." Manny had me thinking I was in over my head, but I was only going to be hustling for another year or so.

"DJ's not the same street dude he use to be, and you can't take all his advice at face value. He's fucking wit steroids.

Steroids! That's some white-boy shit, fucking wit that body building nigga, Jose Martinez", Manny continued. "I got a couple dollars saved wit him but I'm washing my own money now. Fuck that!", Manny said.

At the time, I was giving D.J. anywhere from $15,000-$25,000 dollars a week to wash, and was living off the $1,600 a day profit from the weed in Building A. I asked Manny to stop by my grandparents' house, and I ran in to see Pop Pop and Abuela. When I went in Pop Pop was there by himself.

"Hey kid, I mean man. I guess you become a man today. Ah, shit! I guess you *been* a man!", Pop Pop said laughing.

"Hi Pop Pop."

"Pop Pop?" He interrupted, "Shit, what grown ass man call somebody Pop Pop? Call me Sonny.", he said.

"Hey, Sonny." I said, both of us laughing.

"I would give you some money, but you got more than me! Shit! Can I get a loan?" Sonny said jokingly. "The only thing I can give you for your birthday is advice. *Get yours while it's still here to get, because it won't always be. And save your money, and invest, because all good things come to an end.* I love you. Happy birthday, kid", Sonny said before hugging me and going upstairs to his room. I thought about Sonny's words for a minute, before remembering Manny was still waiting outside.

After leaving Sonny's I rode around the city for another hour with Manny just smoking and talking. "Yo, Kalic is putting together a strong crew of nigga's that didn't give a fuck".

"Yea them nigga's is reckless. They extorting nags, and all types of shit", I replied to Manny.

"North Camden is crazy right about now. I don't even ride through there like that anymore." Manny said.

"Hell no, especially by yourself, or late night, forget it! Them nigga's definitely will get at you. New Jersey Transit doesn't even ride through there after 4:30 know more. Now, *that's* crazy!", I said.

Manny talked about how people were beginning to call Flaco, Gordo, because he gained so much weight in the last couple of months. Manny finally parked, back by the projects. I got out of the car and went home to get dressed for dinner.

When I got home, Jasmine was already getting dressed, so I got in the shower. When I got out she was fully dressed and living up to the nickname Black Beauty, I had given her years before. Once I was dressed we left in the Bemmer, with Jasmine driving. We rode up Westfield Avenue, so I figured we were going to Philly, although Jasmine had already warned me not to ask her where we were going. When she pulled in front of Flaco's bar Oasis I was confused.

"What you stop here for?", I asked.

"Let's go have a drink before we go out", she replied. I thought, I guess I can get served in here so why not?

As we walked in, I noticed Jasmine had moved behind me and when I turned the bar was filled. Surprise! The crowd yelled out. I was truly shocked. I had no idea I was having a party, and everybody was there. From Manny to D.J., from Blockz to Pedro Montoya.

When I saw Pedro my eyes searched the room for his beautiful wife Carmen. I saw her across the room and she waved and smiled. I wasn't the only one who saw her.

"Aint that the bitch we seen in Cramer Hill? "What the fuck is she waving at you for?", Jasmine asked with attitude.

"That's my man's wife. Calm down.", I said walking toward Pedro and Bingo who were across the room. I greeted Bingo and Pedro as Ace, Star and Rim walked in. Carmen was in the opposite corner talking to her brother Enrique. All the biggest hustlers in the city were there to celebrate my birthday and I was feeling on top of the world. I had the keys to the city. The thing I didn't know was a party like this was a federal agent's wet dream.

Jasmine got the best radio D.J. from the area and he played all my favorites. By the time he played *I Got it Made by Special Ed,* I was way past my limit. I had already drunk about 6 Hennessey and ginger ales. I got up and sang the song word for word as if it was a video shoot. Everybody laughed and took pictures of me rapping and flashing stacks of money, two things that were completely out of my character.

I purposely made eye contact with Carmen all night and she smiled and stared back whenever possible. Carmen and Pedro were the type of couple that you saw and assumed the man had to have money to keep a wife that looked like she did. The whole time I was staring at Carmen, Flaco was watching Jasmine. I noticed Jasmine and Flaco dancing, but I was too drunk and too busy watching Carmen to say anything. As the party ended, I snatched Jasmine's arm to let her know I was mad.

We got in the car "Happy birthday honey. How'd you like your party?"

"How'd you like your dance with Flaco?", I asked back.

"What? Boy, please! We were just dancing".

"How you get the party in here?", I asked referring to Oasis.

"Manny, that's how. Ask him if you don't believe me!", she screamed. I didn't say a word. When we got home and in the bed I didn't touch Jasmine, as much as I wanted to, I just turned over and went to sleep.

The next night I got drunk again, this time wit my nigga's. We were hanging out on 33rd Street drinking a gallon of Henny and smoking blunts like cigarettes. I stepped in the alley between Building B and Building C to take a piss. I heard tires screech and heard some mumbling before hearing a voice scream "Get down". I went to the back and grabbed the tech. The wall was straight ahead, so I couldn't peek; I stuck my head out and shot the first face I didn't recognize. (Blat, blat) I never saw so many shells come out a gun at once. I hit my first target and then turned and sprayed the black van they were driving. I saw Ace and Rim run into the building and two others grabbed the wounded man and pulled him in as it spun off. I continued firing into the van, although I don't think I hit anyone else. My adrenaline was flowing. I ran and stashed the gun in an apartment in Building A. I washed my hands and arms to remove any gunpowder residue. I waited in the building for 15 minutes but police never came, so I went back out.

By the time I came out, my pager was ringing with Ace's home number. I knew he was okay, so I went home.

When I pulled to my apartment, Rim and Ace were standing outside of Ace's crib. "Man that shit was crazy, yo. Who you think that was?" Rim asked.

"I don't know, could have been them Centerville nigga's. They known for stickin' nigga's", I answered.

"They had Philly tags, but it was probably them North Camden nigga's from Kalic's gang", Ace added.

"I don't know, but that shit was crazy. You hit that nigga right in the chest!"

"He hit him in the neck!" Ace said, cutting Rim off.

I was feeling high from more than the weed. I felt untouchable. I had shot someone and I knew I could do it again. We talked about the situation about 100 more times before I finally went in the house. I knew Jasmine would flip if I told her, so I decided not to. I just went to sleep without touching her again.

As the summer moved on, more and more stickups and shootouts took place on 33rd Street. A little after July 4th, Mathew McDowell came to me with some useful information.

"The State Police are investigating Building C in the Woodrow Wilson Apartments".

"They haven't identified anyone except two trappers. Your best bet is to shut down and let them swallow the sword."

I knew the trapper's he was talking about. One was Roberto. The other was a young Puerto Rican kid who lived in the building.

"Why am I paying you, If you can't stop the raid", I asked annoyed by what I had just heard.

"Listen, I can give you city protection. With the State Troopers and the Feds, you're on your own."

"You're lucky I was able to warn you about this." he said.

"Right, you right. So, what do they have?" I asked.

"They think the buildings are 3 different operations, and they're not too concerned about the weed or the powder."

"They want to get the crack off the street." he answered. "It's best they don't find out all 3 buildings are run by the same person", he said before leaving.

I took McDowell's advice and for the next two weeks we only sold powder and weed in retail quantity. We also got a house on 34th Street and began stashing drugs there. We hired a runner to bring bundles from 34th to 33rd and do the opposite with the money. This was so a trapper could only be caught with G pack or $1,000 cash. The runner used a moped to get back and forth from 33rd to 34th. I also paid 2 lawyers in advance; one who could represent me against the state on a homicide and another who could represent me in a federal drug case.

By early August, McDowell was coming to get his money right from the apartments.

"Where's Gato? Tell him Mathew McDowell is here. Officer Mathew McDowell." he said in a slurred voice.

"Where is he? I'm not leaving until he gets here." McDowell demanded. I checked my pager and called back. It was the phone number we had at the stash house. "Yo, what's up?" I asked.

"Yo some cop named Mathew McDowell is down here and he won't leave until you get here. He's scaring the customers." Roberto said.

"Okay, look. Give him $5,000 and tell him to page me, but I'm on my way." I responded.

By the time I got to the apartments McDowell was gone, but I realized I had a problem on my hands.

The next day, McDowell called me and apologized, although he downplayed the seriousness of the situation. He told me that during a North Camden raid he pocketed a few guns and some heroin. I was only interested in the guns, so we arranged a meeting and I received 2 revolvers and a sawed off shotgun.

Later that same night, state police raided Building C, which had been back open for almost a month. They arrested 6 people, 4 fiends, a trapper and a lookout, who was later released. They found 4 guns and 32 bags of crack cocaine, not exactly the big bust they were expecting. The trapper was bailed out from the county jail the next day for $2,500 on drug charges, the gun charges were dismissed. We opened up shop the very next morning. I figured they needed time to plan a raid and there was no way they would raid the same spot two days in a row. The first day we reopened everybody was on edge, but by day two, it was business as usual.

After the raid, Ace and I realized that our only income could be stopped easily, so we began to sell more weight. What we didn't know at the time was selling weight is what was getting us hot. The Feds and the state boys were only after wholesale sellers, largely because they didn't know that sets were so organized and lucrative. In the late 80's and early 90's you could make millions of dollars in Camden undetected as long as you weren't supplying other dealers. That's exactly why Flaco had been making millions since '88; besides his immediate circle, nobody could get weight from him. Over the next few weeks we took 33rd to new heights. Rim and Ace were making money like never before and they were happy to let me lead, although me and Ace were equal partners.

Things at home were going even better than things in the streets. Two weeks before Jasmine was supposed to go back to Del State she told me she was pregnant. We both knew it would happen sooner or later since I hadn't been pulling out or using condoms. I didn't want her to drop out of school, so she transferred to Rutgers right in Camden. The transition would be a good one for all of us. I was young, rich and in love. What could be better?

Rim and Ace weren't in serious relationships but they both had kids, and I was ready to join the fraternity of fatherhood. The first person I told the good news to was Abuela and she was so excited. She liked Jasmine and was glad that I got a girl who was about something. Pop pop and Ramos schooled me on fatherhood and the fickleness of pregnant women. I assured them Jasmine was unlike the average girl. They just laughed.

My mom even called to congratulate me. She said she would be there when the baby came. By this time, my mother and Uncle Marc had developed a superior attitude and I didn't look forward to her visits like I did when I was a kid. She had only been back to Camden 3 or 4 times since she left. Still, nothing could ruin my day. I was a father to be.

The next few weeks I stayed at the crib a lot. 33rd was doing great and I didn't have to be outside to make the money. I went shopping for all types of baby shit, even though Jasmine wasn't due until early April. Rim was handling all the transporting, using heavyset women in their 40's to drive the coke back from N.Y. Ace and Rim were also networking and fronting dealers on other blocks a quarter kilo at a time. Most of the dudes they dealt with were people they knew from school, the youth house, family or through a bitch. I wasn't fronting anybody shit. I didn't want to be put in a position where I would have to kill somebody for owing me money, so I avoided those types of situations. Rim was building a strong relationship in N.Y. with Sheppy, since he was still handling the money part of the transactions. While everybody was out making connections I was in the house, even when Jasmine was in school, I was at home watching T.V. I had become a millionaire couch potato.

11

Cold World

"Yo this my man, Ace and this my man, Gato. This Jude. Sheppy's people from N.Y." The first thing I thought when Rim introduced us was that Sheppy was planning to take over. Either that, or he wanted to know where we were moving all this coke. Rim bringing a N.Y. nigga here, made no sense.

Jude was a dark half Haitian, half Dominican nigga. He was about 6'3 and looked more Haitian than Dominican. He was average size with a sneaky look to him. "What? You down here chillin' for the day?" I asked Jude.

"Nah, I'm gonna be here a while." he answered nonchalantly. Rim could see I was not approving of the situation and quickly clarified things.

"He's gone be workin' wit me on that new thing over on 39th I was telling you about." Rim said while drinking a pint of Hennessey. 39th Street was only 3 blocks from Pennsauken. It was one of the spots that Rim was financing on the side, and I had nothing to do with it. The introduction took place on 33rd Street in front of Woodrow Wilson Apartments, so Rim felt it necessary to clarify Jude's presence.

The last time I let outsiders in; I got 2 trusted soldiers in Rim and T-Money. Even though I personally disliked T-Money, he did lead Ace to the connect that helped get me my million. When I thought of that, I began to relax and reconsider the cynicism I had concerning Jude, at least for a little while.

We had tightened security and had two known shooters on the payroll because of the continuing war between Kalic and 32nd Street. Our location often put us in the line of fire. The winter months gave way to more murder and mayhem, so everyone was on alert. We kept the shooters around as a precaution. When I got a chance to ask Ace what he thought about Jude, he told me a little more detail about the New Yorker. He said Jude was on the run and was going to be down here hustling on 39th Street. He was Sheppy's nephew by marriage and was used as muscle in N.Y.

There are two types of nigga's on the run out of town. Nigga's running from a punk bid who can't be trusted because if they scared to do a little time in their hood, they will definitely tell, to avoid jail in another hood. Then there's the nigga running from a stretch. He can't be trusted either, because he already has a stretch to do if caught, and probably doesn't mind running another 15 concurrent for laying somebody down. Either way, Jude could not be trusted.

The next day, Ace and I sat Rim down and told him to keep Jude out of all affairs involving 33rd Street. It was bad enough he probably already knew how much we were copping from

Sheppy. Rim agreed and said Jude was an ally not a threat but I wasn't convinced.

"He can be trusted more than the cops you deal with.", Rim said sarcastically during our sit down.

"That's my problem to deal with, and Jude's yours." I answered.

Mathew McDowell was still coming by for his $5,000 a week. Although, now it felt more like a shakedown than a business relationship. I hadn't seen Jeremy Harris, but he was still in the loop making deliveries for Flaco and protecting the alley. It was a week before Thanksgiving and the streets had been getting more violent every month, although the money never slowed up. Jasmine was hearing what was going on in the street, so she sometimes tried to get me to stop hustling, but she was always supportive of me. By this time, my car wash was up and running, and I was making legal money, but quitting wasn't even a consideration.

Jude and Rim starting making moves on 39th Street, and before long they were moving about 3 kilos a week. Rim was still making our monthly runs to N.Y. to see Sheppy, so he and Jude would get coke for 39th at that time. This made the trip even more dangerous because of the amount of coke they were bringing back. Everybody had their strengths. Rim was definitely a transporter. He never complained about the trips and always got that work back. Even though Rim was running 39th, he never stopped handling his responsibilities on 33rd, and that's all that mattered to me.

On Thanksgiving, I spent the day with Jasmine and her family in Lawnside. Her whole family was there and they made me feel real at home. Nobody put me on the spot about where I work or what school I go to or all the usual questions. They knew I owned a carwash and they didn't prejudge me as a young drug dealer. The food made my time with Jasmine even more pleasant. They served all the traditional things like Turkey, Macaroni and cheese, and greens but they substituted pork for fried fish and fried chicken.

Her family taught me what Kwanza really was, and about Juneteenth, which was black American's Independence Day. I learned more there than I did my whole time in history class at Woodrow Wilson high school. By the end of the evening I had made up my mind I was going to get my G.E.D. I wasn't going to tell Jasmine, but I was going to get it before my son or daughter was born.

Later that night, I decided to go out with Manny. We were supposed to meet at Flaco's bar, Oasis, but I took a detour through Cramer Hill. I'm not really sure what made me ride that way but I was so glad I did. As I rode down River Road approaching 27th Street I saw 4 beautiful women getting into a pearl white Jaguar. I slowed down and realized it was Carmen Montoya and three of her friends. I stopped and parked about a half block down from the Jag. I was driving my Benz and as I got out of the car they were pulling off, but came to a complete stop as they got in front of me.

"Hi, Simon", a voice slurred as the back seat passenger window rolled down. "Y'all look crowded in that back seat. Need a ride", I asked flirting with Carmen and her friend.

"You don't want us to ride. You want *me* to ride, don't you Simon?", Carmen said seductively. I was stunned my dream was coming true, but this was a trick question. If I said something out of line, or she wanted to confess, it could get me killed, or what if one of her friends told Pedro. I couldn't take the chance.

"Nah, I'm just seeing if y'all need a ride", I said with a smile.

"Nah, you want some of that grown woman pussy", the driver said laughing.

"I'm too fast for Simon. He can't keep up with me", Carmen said as the Jag pulled off. I didn't know what she meant but I hopped in the Benz and started following her as she sped up River Road. I followed as she made a hard ass left turn onto East State Street. She hit another sharp turn and this one was too much for me. I spun out and smashed into a phone pole. The side of my car was smashed up but it was drivable. Carmen got out and laughed, before saying, I don't like black anyway. I like white. She then got in her car and drove off. I drove my car a block from the club and went in to have a drink.

As I walked through the parking lot, I saw the Jag. I knew Carmen would be there because it was a holiday and everybody was out. When I walked in, the bar was packed but Manny spotted me and ordered me a Hennessey and Heineken. I drank my shot and began exchanging greetings with everybody. I was casually looking around hoping to spot Carmen. Manny walked over and I told him about Carmen and my accident. Manny laughed and told me I needed to leave that alone; it was dangerous and she was probably just playing games with me anyway. He also confirmed what I thought. That white Jag was Carmen's.

Manny and I stayed at the bar drinking for another hour, before I decided to leave. When I got out front, Pedro and Flaco were talking to Carmen and her 3 friends.

"Simon what happened too your car", Flaco asked.

"Crashed on some drunk shit. I don't like black anyway; I think I'll buy a white one.", I said as Pedro and Flaco laughed. Carmen just smiled and right then I knew what I had to do, tomorrow.

The next morning I woke up early and left the house while Jasmine was still asleep. I took my Benz to the body shop to get fixed and then took a cab to FC Kerbeck, the luxury car lot in Palmyra where I bought all my cars. Flaco and D.J. got all their cars there too and we had a connect who had a don't ask don't tell policy. Plus, he didn't report the sales to the IRS. I needed a white luxury car and I saw it when I walked in the door, a 750IL series BMW with a V-12 engine. It was perfect. I bought the car on the spot and drove back to the hood with temp tags.

Before going to 33rd or the projects, I went to Cramer Hill. I didn't expect to see Carmen, but I figured she would hear about the car if I came through. So, I rode down River Road from Palmyra, through Pennsauken, into Camden. It was Black

Friday and the streets were crowded. It was now a little past noon. I rode past Pedro and Bingo's store and past Flaco's Cramer Hill bar but I didn't see Carmen. When I got to the light by Ablett Village I saw the White Jag ride down East State Street toward North Camden. I immediately turned right and followed, not knowing who was inside. I was now following a car that might or might not be Carmen's, into North Camden.

North Camden was separated from East Camden by a little bridge. It was it's own little world. The neighborhood is almost a peninsula and is isolated from the rest of the city. As I crossed the bridge, I immediately thought about Kalic. I was riding in a brand new BMW with only a .38. I didn't know what to expect since I hadn't been to North Camden in years. As I rode up State Street, I noticed lookouts with earpieces, like the secret service wore. Each time I stopped at a light, people were staring in my car. Mean mugging.

The Jag made a right down 5th Street, which was home to one of the biggest heroin spots in the city. I reluctantly followed and noticed that it pulled over at Erie Street. I slowed down and got next to the Jag. I saw that the same chic was driving as the night before. As she got out of the car, I rolled down my window and said, "Tell your girl I got a white 735, since she likes white."

She was stunned. She just covered her mouth and said, "Oh shit". She walked around the car, as if inspecting, and saw the temp tags, which erased any doubt about the car being mine.

"Where she at?" I asked, breaking her trance.

"She inside I'm 'bout to get her.", she said walking into a house on the block.

The driver, whose name I still didn't know, was almost as beautiful as Carmen. She had a golden complexion, was about 5'5 with light brown eyes and long, brown, curly hair. She wasn't thick like I like my women, but she had a model like face.

"You got big balls coming here", I heard a voice say to my right. When I turned, I saw Carmen coming outside in a tight sweat suit smoking a cigarette. I hated cigarettes but she made smoking look sexy.

"Why? Is this where Pedro lives?", I asked nervously.

"No, and anyway, stop worrying about Pedro. He's a pussy. My brother Enrique is the only reason he is even accepted by D.J. and Flaco."

"When I met him, he was selling car stereo's.", she said laughing. She walked right over to the car and got in.

"So, where we going?", she said exhaling on her bogie.

"How about Puerto Rico?", I said.

"I want somebody to fuck, not love, and my brother is Enrique Cintron so monetary gifts don't impress me. I got my own".

"Well, what about the application for somebody to fuck? Can I fill one out?", I asked. (Laughing)

"You're crazy. Call me tomorrow night around ten when Pedro leaves.", she said handing me her number on a pack of matches.

I took 3rd Street home through South Camden. It was definitely the long way, but I wouldn't have to ride past the intimidating security of 's army. Once I got back out East, I rode past 39th and saw Jude and 2 other nigga's who I didn't know. They had to be N.Y. nigga's, I thought. I didn't stop, and next rode past 33rd. I pulled over and hollered at the trappers, but Rim and Ace weren't there. My final destination was my hood, McGuire Projects. I pulled up and Manny was outside with Muscleclo and a few others.

"Damn cuss, them alphabet boys gone be on you soon.", Manny said with everyone else agreeing. I had no clue who the alphabet boys were, but I fronted like I did.

"Nah I'm good." I said while making a mental note to ask Manny, when we were alone, what the hell the alphabet boys were.

"I can't front though this shit is dope", Muscleclo said. Muscleclo was a man of few words so hearing him give my car a compliment meant something. Now there was only one person left to show my car, Jasmine!

"A car! "A car!" We're 'bout to have a new baby in a couple months and you go buy a new car?", Jasmine screamed. "Sometimes the shit you do ... I just don't understand the concept of three cars and living in an apartment. Can you explain that to me?" I had no answers for Jasmine. I felt like a fool. The next day I sold my Benz, which was still in the shop, to Rim.

I planned to use the money as a down payment on a house, a great Christmas gift for Jasmine. After getting the money from Rim I went to register for night school and then went to see D.J. I checked on the carwash and my finances. I had run through some serious money, but the car wash had turned into a solid investment. I talked to D.J. about other possible investments and a good place to buy my first house. D.J. said I should look in Burlington County and gave me the name of a good realtor from the area. He also provided me with company tax filings for *FastWash*, which were exaggerated, to say the least. I now was legally going to be making 6 figures, my first year in business. I could afford a home almost anywhere.

I got a couple of listings for Burlington County and headed to the hood. I still had a ten o'clock telephone appointment with Carmen that I wouldn't miss for the world. I knew the real estate books would keep Jasmine busy while I was out. I rode past 33rd and things were business as usual. I then drove past 39th and saw Jude, Rim and the N.Y. nigga's. I stopped to talk for a minute; I really didn't want to talk as much as I wanted to check out the nigga's from N.Y.

"Yo this my man, Gato I was telling you about", Rim said as I got out of the car. "This is Mickey and Ty." Rim said, as we all exchanged pounds. Mickey and Ty were clearly brothers but I couldn't tell what their nationality was. Rim didn't explain what they were doing and I didn't ask. After all, this was his block and it was really none of my business, although as I would later find out, everybody didn't feel the same way.

"Good look on that car, my nigga. They said it will be ready in 4 days. I can't wait!", Rim said.

"No doubt, you know you my nigga, I'm 'bout to ride out the projects. What you doin'", I asked?

"I aint doin' shit". Fuck it. I'll ride out there with you. Jude, I'll get with you later. Beep me", Rim said.

Jude said "Alright.", before Rim and I slid off in the BMW.

When we got to the projects there was a nice crowd gathered around a crap game. Rim and I made our way to where Ace and Manny were standing. As soon as I got next to Manny, I asked him "What the fuck are the alphabet boys?". "What?", Manny asked confused.

"The other day you said the alphabet boys would be on me. What's that", I asked?

"Oh, you know the Feds FBI, DEA, ATF. They all letters, so nigga's call them the alphabet boys", Manny said. "That 39th Street thing nigga's aint feeling that."

"Them N.Y. nigga's is causing a lot of talk. I even heard Kalic wanted to get at them", Manny said.

The name cut the air like a knife. It was one thing to hear about beefing with 32nd, but for him to beef with my crew was cause for immediate concern.

"How he know they from N.Y.", I asked naively?

"Come on, nigga, this the hood aint no secrets in the hood", Manny answered while passing me a blunt. Rim was right there and even though Manny was talking to me I know Rim heard what he said.

"So that's all the details you heard?", I asked Manny.

"I mean Kalic aint alone. Nigga's aint feelin' that N.Y. shit. Man this is South Jersey, not South Carolina. Aint no New

York nigga's eaten out here! Y'all should've known better than that."

I could tell the comments were directed at Rim. Manny was my family, but Rim was in my team and I couldn't let anything happened to him. He wasn't from my hood, and I could feel the tension, so we left after my brief conversation with Manny.

After we left the projects, Rim decided to take Jude off the block. "At least give him a behind the scenes job, so nigga's don't see him", I said. Rim agreed it was the smart thing to do. Rim wasn't a pussy, but if a situation could be avoided, he was willing to make the sacrifice. Ace paged me with the code to meet on 33rd, so Rim and I met him there. Ace didn't like people telling Rim how to run his spot, even though he agreed, N.Y. nigga's had no business hustling in Jersey.

After a few blunts I noticed it was 10:10 and decided to call Carmen. I used a phone in one of the apartments in Building B; this way even if Pedro was home, the call couldn't be traced to me. *(Phone ringing)*

"Hello." a sexy Spanish voice said.

"May I speak to Mrs. Montoya please?", I asked.

"This is her. May I ask whose calling?"

"Gato. I mean, Simon". (*Laughing*)

"Simon why do you sound like a bill collector?", Carmen laughed.

"I just…"

"Never mind that.", Carmen said, cutting me off, "Where are you?"

"I'm out East." I answered.

"Well, meet me at the speed line station in Collingswood, I'll park my car there", she said.

When I got to the parking lot, I rolled up as usual, and put on the new Brand Nubians tape *One For All*. I smoked the whole blunt watching train after train pull in and leave the station. I started to wish I had a cell phone after glancing at my watch and realizing it was 11:38. I dozed off and when I woke up it was 12:19. I started the car and drove toward East Camden. When I hit Federal Street near 24th I saw flashing lights and yellow police tape. It was only one block from the Oasis and the streets were filled with parked cars and bystanders. I double parked by a rusty navy blue Buick, got out my car and walked toward the yellow tape. The body was covered with a sheet and two detectives were kneeling next to it. The sheet was blood soaked and one detective was digging' in the man's pockets to find identification. The other detective pulled the sheet; far enough back to expose the hole where the victims face use to be. "Can anybody identify this man", the detective asked sarcastically. "Nobody seen shit neither, right", the second detective said. "He has ID", the first detective shouted to the other. "It's a Jude Clarviount from the Bronx, N.Y. My mouth dropped, I immediately stepped back to my car but not before noticing Carmen's white Jag parked in the parking lot of Oasis. My first thought was to go in there and curse her out but that would be a death wish. Instead I went to the crib and paged Rim and Ace.

While I waited for Ace and Rim to call I thought about how fast life can change. *(Knocking sound on door)* "Who is it", I asked. "It's me", Ace answered. Ace and Rim both decided to come over rather than call me back. I opened the door and Rim had a Mac-11 in his hand. Ace had his regular a .45 colt semi-automatic. "So I guess ya'll heard what happened", I asked. "Heard we was there", Rim answered. "Yea, well what really happened", I asked? "We were chilling in front the club and these bitches pulled up in a burgundy Camry". "So we kicking it they asking Jude his name, so he walks over to the car and out of no where a nigga pop up in the backseat and shoot that nigga wit a shotty right in the face". "He aint even roll down the window, he just shoot through the glass", Rim added. "That shit was crazy the car speed off, bitches in front the club was screaming and everything". "It was mad people out", Ace said. "Well I know one thing we need a new connect", I said. "Cause I damn sure and fucking wit Sheppy no more and we still gotta pay this nigga his money". "So who gonna take that money to him", I asked. "Matter fact, who gone tell him his nephew is dead". I was asking questions but we all knew the answer it was Rim's job.

12

Start of the Ending

Ace and I were by the alley waiting for Rim to get back from the police station. It was the night after Jude was murdered and homicide detectives had just picked up Rim for questioning. Three hours later Rim pulled up in the back seat of a green taxi. "What happened what they ask you", Ace asked Rim. "They asked me how I knew Jude and what was he doing in Camden", Rim replied. "What you say," I asked. "I told them I had just met him, and that he moved here with family about 2 weeks ago." "Then homicide detectives from the Bronx came in", "The Bronx", Ace interjected. "Yeah", Rim continued, "They was showing me pictures asking me did I know who Mickey and Ty were". "Let me guess they was wanted on a body", I asked sarcastically. "Yea a couple", Rim answered. "So what else they say, did they mention me", Ace asked. "No they asked who else was there, I said a couple people but I didn't give any names". "You need to call Sheppy and tell him and see, if you can send the money to him", I said. "We should just say fuck Sheppy, and tell him Jude took the money", Ace said. "Then he'll definitely think we killed Jude", Rim replied.

"Nah, we gone give that nigga his money, but we need to find out where Mickey and Ty are ...they don't know where you live do they, I asked Rim? Rim was silent for 10 real seconds before saying "yea they been there once or twice". Rim still lived in the hood on 29th Street, I told him maybe he should get a hotel for a couple days but he said he was good. We then went to FedEx and sent an over night package with 2 hollow books each containing $165,000 in large bills to Sheppy's Restaurant in Washington Heights.

That night I went home by 9:00 to chill with Jasmine. We were going to start viewing houses on Saturday and we had it narrowed down to 3 all in the low 200 thousand range. I was going to start school on Monday and I was a couple of months away from fatherhood, so my life was hectic without the added stress of the streets. I tried to leave the streets in the streets and Jasmine and I rarely discussed that part of my life. By 11:00 Jasmine was asleep and I was up smoking a blunt and watching the Arsenio Hall show. I watched the show and then went to sleep. At 3:48 I got a call on the house phone I had just bought a week before. Only a couple of people had the number.

"Hello", I answered in a cracked voice. "This...this is Me-ka.... Rim's girl, I don't know. I didn't know"

"Calm down. What's going on? Where's Rim?", I asked.

"I don't know. Somebody, some nigga's ran up in our house."

"Where are you right now?", I asked her.

"I'm in Stockton Station apartments, by the gate, going to Westfield Acres."

"Okay, stay there. I'll be there in 5 minutes."

By now Jasmine was sitting up asking me what's going on. I answered her,

"I gotta go get Rim's girl, something happened to Rim, but its all good, I'll be back in an hour go to sleep. I grabbed the Tech-9 and the .38; I always carried and tucked them under my hoodie so Jasmine couldn't see. Then I left in the truck.

When I got to the Acres by the gate going into Stockton Station I saw Meka. She was in a T-shirt and boxer shorts. She had a .380 in her hand and she was shaking from the cold night air.

"Get in", I said, opening the door for her. "Now what the fuck happened?" I asked while driving out of the Acres.

"I heard a bang on my door. Then I heard nigga's coming in. I tried to wake Rim, but he was sleeping too hard, so I grabbed his gun".

"I heard the nigga's running up the stairs, so I started shooting down the steps until the gun ran out of bullets. Then I jumped out the bedroom window and ran and called police and told them somebody broke in."

"Did you tell them your name?"

"No, I just said I heard shots, and gave them the address", she said. "Good Im gonna take you to see my lawyer in the morning.

For now, you got somewhere you can stay?" I asked.

"Yea, my grandma's house in Pollack", she answered.

I took Meka to a house on Whitman Street and told her to call me at 9:00 am. On my way back home I rode by 29th

Street and the cops had it blocked off. A few neighbors had gathered out front and one old man told me they brought out 2 bodies but he didn't know who. I prayed one of the bodies wasn't Rim.

Jasmine was home awake when I got there. I told her everything was okay and she went back to sleep, but I couldn't. Nine o'clock couldn't come fast enough. At 8:30 I called my lawyer and explained the situation. He told me to have Meka meet him out front of the Police Station. When Meka called I setup the meeting. By 11:30 my lawyer called back and told me Meka would not be charged in the murders of Tyrone Crawford of New York or Randy Irvin Myers of Camden, New Jersey. I almost dropped the phone, I couldn't believe it, Rim was dead. *(Hello.... Hello... Simon... Simon you there)* the Jewish voice on the phone said.

"Yea, where's Meka?", I asked.

"I dropped her off at the crime scene, so she could get her things."

"So, what exactly happened?", I asked.

"Well, Malcolm Riley and Tyrone Crawford did a home invasion at the home of Randy Myers. In the process, Meka Franks shot Mr. Crawford 3 times, once fatally".

"They think Malcolm Riley used Crawford's body as a human shield once he was dead".

"Once Meka stopped shooting Riley came upstairs only to find Randy Myers still sleeping. There he shot him twice in the face at point blank range. They already have Riley in custody, so Meka should be okay!"

"Yea, she'll be okay. Thanks Mr. Goldberg", I said to my lawyer.

"Don't mention it Simon", he said before hanging up. I figured Rim being shot in the face was in retaliation for Jude's murder, since he also was shot in the face. I also knew Rim had nothing to do with Jude's murder, but perception is a motherfucker.

That Saturday, Jasmine and I went to a few open houses, as planned. I felt the need to move, now more than ever before. Jasmine didn't know exactly what was going on, but she knew I hung with Rim and that he had been murdered. I downplayed the situation as a random home invasion, but Jasmine wasn't convinced.

After seeing houses in Lumberton and Maple Shade, we went to see a four bedroom in Moorestown. The house was about $120,000 more than the others, but had multiple features. The house had 4 bedrooms, 2 1/2 bathrooms, a large backyard, a fireplace, a two-car garage, and a balcony in the master bedroom. The living room floor was hard wood. There was a foyer and a rec room with a half bathroom, then three steps leading to the kitchen and living room. The dining room was located behind the kitchen, which was also eat-in size. The bedrooms were up another set of stairs, located in the hallway by the kitchen. The first bedroom was immediately to the right of the staircase; it was medium sized with two windows. Directly across from the first room, on the left side was another mid-sized room with exactly the same dimensions. Straight back, from the top of the staircase, was a full bathroom with a shower and separate bathtub and twin sinks. There were mirrors on the door as well as two wall mirrors. The master bedroom was on the right side of the bathroom. It featured a useable fireplace, a walk in closet, a balcony and 2 other windows as well as a full bathroom. The smallest bedroom was in between the master and the first bedroom. It only had one window and a small closet. The house also had an attic the size of a bedroom. The only thing stopping the attic from being a bedroom was the low ceiling. There was a finished basement and a full porch in the backyard. The two-car garage even had an upstairs that could be used for storage. We both agreed this was the house for us.

On Monday, Rim's funeral was packed. Nigga's from Westfield Acres, McGuire Projects, 24th, 39th, and 33rd all showed up. D.J., Flaco and all the big boys came through to pay their respects. There were a few tense moments and police presence was heavy. Rim's girl got into a scuffle with his sister over money and the Benz Rim had bought from me. Star and her family were there but Jasmine stayed home.

After the funeral we went to Flaco's club Euphoria in Cramer Hill. Euphoria was a little more upscale than Oasis, and it attracted a different clientele. All the women in the club were dressed to impress and the men all wore slacks. Ace and I were still in our black suits, so we satisfied the dress code. The bar was crowded for a Monday afternoon. A group of women sat at a table in the back ordering drinks and smoking cigarettes. I noticed one of the women as the one who was driving Carmen's Jag the night I crashed. I thought about going over to say, "Hi", but I decided to send a round of drinks to the table first. I watched as the waiter pointed me out to the women, then I turned and waved. I immediately got a smile from Carmen's friend. She then got up and approached me at the bar.

"Hi, Simon", she said.

"I never did get your name," I answered.

"What do you want to call me", she answered jokingly. I laughed partly because it was funny and partly because I didn't have a fast enough comeback.

"How about...Camden's finest", I finally replied.

"Wow, took you a minute to think of that one", she said.

"It fits perfect though", I said. She blushed and right then I knew I could fuck her if I wanted to. I ended up ordering more rounds until the whole bar was drunk, on me. I even ran out of cash and ran a $2,100 tab. Camden's finest was definitely feeling me. Ace had also run out of money, and there was no way I could go home to get any. I called Manny and he brought me $3,500.

"Wassup? You trying to get something to eat, Camden's finest", I asked.

She laughed before answering, "Dana, My name is Dana, and yea I could use a bite to eat". It felt late but it was only 7:00.

"One last round", I said. One round turned into 6 or 7 and our bite to eat came courtesy of the kitchen right in the bar. We finally left around 8:00, and I was well past my limit.

"Here you drive", I said handing Dana the keys.

"You trust me driving your BMW?", she asked.

"Yea, I seen your skills the night I was following ya'll."

"Oh yea, you crashed. You aint allowed to drive me", she said laughing with her hand out for the keys. The thing I didn't realize was Dana was just as fucked up as me, if not more. We were headed to the Hilton on Rt. 70 in Cherry Hill. The swerving didn't get us pulled over in Camden, but Cherry Hill was another story. The cop was parked in a lot of a closed grocery store.

"Damn 5-0 was over there squatting in the cut".

"Where, I don't see any cops. Oh shit, they behind us", Dana said. "He's pulling us over. What should I do", she asked.

"What you mean, what should you do? Pull over!" I said. The gun was in a built in stash box and Cherry Hill cops weren't up on those, so we were good.

"License and Registration please", the first cop said.

"What's the...Problem officer", Dana asked in a slurred voice.

"Ma'am could you please step out of the car", the cop asked. After putting Dana in cuffs and in the back of the patrol car, he came back to me.

"Are you able to drive sir", he asked.

"Yea, I'm straight, where you taking her?"

"She'll be taken to the station and processed, then to the county jail on 2 outstanding warrants from Collingswood and a DUI". I went back to the city and went to A&A's bail bondsman. I paid the $1,200 bond and left an extra $50 so she could catch the cab home.

By Christmas, Jasmine and I were in our new house. Nobody knew where we lived except Sonny, Abuela and Jasmine's mom. Jasmine was 7 months pregnant, so we turned the room closest to us into a nursery. Jasmine's sister Darlene also moved in with us, to finish her last two years of high school. Darlene and Jasmine had the same dad, a guy named Fred Wise. He was from Trenton and he and his wife were both on drugs. Jasmine knew Moorestown's schools were better than Trenton's, and the change in scenery would be good for Darlene. Jasmine decorated the whole house in 3 days, the bill was close to $40,000, and I didn't care, as long as she was happy. Darlene had turned out to be a blessing in disguise, as she occupied Jasmine's time, while I ran the streets.

My home life was great, but business had suffered since Jude's murder. Ace and I were dealing with Enrique Cintron and Ace's uncle Bingo. It wasn't as cheap as Sheppy, but it was local. The real problem was our inside man, Thomas McDowell, had died of a heart attack. Paying McDowell $5,000 a week sometimes seemed like extortion, but once he died, I realized how much protection he really provided.

City cops were locking up our trapper's left and right, and the state troopers were rumored to be watching our operation. Right before New Years the feud between 32nd and Kalic's crew heated up, and that also played a part in crippling our business. It was winter in the hood. The streets were unplowed and full of grayish snow and homeless people bundled up in old clothes. It was a drastic contrast of the Moorestown neighborhood I lived in. It was a very violent year for Camden. In the city of 80,000 people, there were 60 murders. The last one coming at 11:48 on December 31st right in the Projects.

I stayed home and brought in the New Year with Jasmine. We drank sparkling cider and ate a midnight meal of baked fish and rice. Before 1:00, Jasmine was asleep and I drove the Bemmer to the hood. I drove to Oasis and the parking lot was filled. The usual cars were all in attendance. I walked into the club wearing Jeans and a polo shirt with a blunt in my ear. I said, "What's up" to Ace, Manny, and Flaco. I also exchanged greetings with Enrique and Bingo. I over heard Bingo say Pedro and Carmen were in Columbia for the holiday. I looked around the party but I wasn't in the mood to be around all those people, so I went out front to smoke my weed. I decided to ride and smoke and ended up shooting to Euphoria, Flaco's other club.

The club was a lot less crowded and I really wasn't in the mood to be bothered by anyone. When I walked in I saw D.J. and the mayor, Jorge Lopez, talking with 2 ladies. One was Dana, and when she noticed me she immediately walked over to me.

"Oh my God! Thank you so much! That was so embarrass-ing.", she said.

"You aint gotta be embarrassed. I'm from the hood. Shit happens." I answered. "So, what you getting into later? Can I get my rain check?" she asked.

"Yea just let me get a couple drinks and I'm ready. What you drinkin'?" I asked her.

"I'll take a Hennessey and Coke", she said before joining me at the bar. I was surprised how she left D.J. and the mayor to come talk to me. Dana and I sat at the bar laughing and drinking for about thirty minutes. I heard D.J. and Jorge Lopez talking to someone, but I never turned to see who. When I finally turned around I noticed Pedro and Carmen chatting with the mayor.

"Yo, Carmen's here!" I said to Dana.

"So, she's married. I aint worried about her", Dana said as we got up to leave.

Carmen gave us a funny look as we walked past, I spoke to D.J. and Pedro and Dana tried to say, "Hi" to Carmen although Carmen gave her the cold shoulder.

"Where we going?" Dana asked as we sat in the parking lot letting the car warm up.

"Philly, I figured you don't have no warrants over there".

"Ha, ha! You got jokes nigga?", she asked.

"I'm just fucking with you. Here roll this up.", I answered handing her a blunt and a bag of weed. We sparked the blunt as soon as we paid the toll, and smoked until we got to the Marriot at 12th and Market Streets. The lobby looked like a palace. By the way Dana looked around, I could tell she had never been anywhere like this before. I paid for the room in cash and we took the elevator to the 7th floor.

Once in the room, we smoked another blunt and drank from the mini bar. It was almost 4:00 am when Dana finally said, "Get Naked!" Once I did she began sucking the life out of me. In 5 minutes I had cum all over her face and she enjoyed every bit of it. She was a freak licking it off my dick and playing with herself. By the time I got hard again she had already had an orgasm and was talking dirty. I knew I couldn't play any games

156

so I went in like I was fresh home. I started fucking her as hard as I could. She was moaning and scratching my back like crazy, and then she started biting me. We fucked for about 25 minutes until I was about to nut. "Oh, cum in me baby. I want to feel you cum in me.", she said. She didn't have to ask twice. I nutted right inside her. After I finished and pulled out, she started sucking me again, straight out the pussy, no wipe off or anything. I didn't even eat the pussy. What did I do to deserve this treatment? Maybe it was bailing her out of jail, or maybe she was just a super freak!

The next morning I woke up to more pussy. We fucked all the way till check out time. I took a shower and dropped her off at home in Cramer Hill. She still lived with her mother but didn't have any kids. For a 25 year-old woman in my hood, that's rare. On the way home I stopped by my Abuela's house and got some chips from Atlantic City that I had in my room. I put them in my pocket and went home. When I walked in I told Jasmine I had been in A.C. I didn't have to show her the chips; I knew she would run my pockets when I got in the shower. I took a shower as a cover up and she did just as I thought.

"You lucky I found these chips because if I would have found out you was lying', I was gonna to kill you", she said sounding almost serious.

"Don't talk like that, and anyway, what you doing in my pockets?" I asked, pretending to be annoyed. She just smiled and walked out of the bathroom.

In the shower I thought about Rim and how life on the streets would be without him. The block was hotter than ever.

Plus, I had lavish spending habits. This led me to contemplate a new way to make money. Ace was financially doing worse than me. Things were only getting worse and on January 4th things came to a crash.

The raid was at 8:00 pm on all 3 buildings. 20 state and local police locked up 6 trappers and lockouts. Two baggers and a runner were also arrested, totaling 9 people. The raid produced 27 sandwich bags, each containing 100-nickel bags of crack, 15 sandwich bags with 25 bags of powder, and 30 sandwich bags with 100-nickel bags of weed. After the raid, undercover officers posed as dealers and arrested 67 customers. They gave the customers a chance to tell any info they knew and they would be released on the spot. One of these tips lead to the raid of one of our stash houses which was holding 3 1/2 kilo's and 3 guns. I was sure my name had popped up in the investigation, although there was no warrant issued for me or Ace.

With Rim dead and Jasmine due any day, a raid was the last thing I needed. We still had 7 pounds of weed stashed in an apartment that wasn't raided, but I wasn't dumb enough to go get it. Instead I stayed in the house for the last 7 days of Jasmine's pregnancy.

13

Back 2 the Basics

By March of '91 I was ready to come out of my shell. I had been in the house for almost 2 1/2 months and I was ready to get back to business. My money was getting low and Jasmine was ready to start working. My son, Simon Gonzales, III, was about to start daycare, and the house would be empty. Ace was working a job in construction for DJ's company and Rim was gone. I knew I could get Ace back down with me, but I would definitely have to rebuild the team.

The first person I recruited was Lou. He was dark-skinned with a baldhead and was a sharp boxer. He sparred at my uncle's gym, and after Jose Martinez left the gym, he was the best there. Martinez was already providing muscle for D.J., so I grabbed the second best thing.

Although Martinez was a better boxer, Lou was different, more street. He had a strong reputation as someone who didn't take any shit. He killed his stepfather at 13, for beating on his little brother. His time in Jamesburg added to his rep, and he came home a little smarter and a lot stronger. After being home for only 6 months, he was arrested for battery, after he punched a man and broke his eye socket for disrespecting his cousin. He was sent to Yardville for 18 months and had been home for a little over a year. He was willing to ride for his family, which was important. He had a reputation and demanded respect, he was perfect.

My second choice was Lil Larry. His father big Larry was one of the biggest heroin dealers Camden ever saw. People respected Lil Larry, because of who his dad was, but he also proved he knew how to get money on his own. Ace and I rounded things up. I still had my businesses, which weren't paying all my bills, but I had close to 2 million saved with D.J. I decided to open back up on 33rd, would be the best idea. Lil Larry was from Fairview and Lou was from Parkside, so it wasn't as easy to open a spot on 33rd, as it had been when Rim was alive. Most of the trappers we used on 33rd in the past were out on bail but it would be too risky to use them while their cases were still pending.

Lil Larry suggested that we use his workers from Fairview but I was against this idea. If there ever were a power struggle, Larry's workers would be loyal to him and I would be out numbered. I needed fresh workers who understood that I was the one and only boss. I decided to use some of Manny's workers from the alley. Manny had so many workers that some would only be used during the weekends. I gave those workers a chance to make money during the week on 33rd, and return to the alley on the weekend. This was only a temporary solution, and I was still in need of good workers. I finally turned to the one place I knew I could get young loyal trappers, Woodrow Wilson High School.

On a nice spring day, Woodrow Wilson has two kinds of students, the ones that go to school to learn and the ones that act like they're going to school to learn. I was looking for the second kind of student, the kind of student that cuts class to smoke weed in the park or hang at the pizza store down the block. I found three smoking a blunt in Dudley Grange Park.

"Yo, what y'all nigga's doing?" I yelled to them from the Federal street side of the park.

"I'll tell you what you doing. Shit. You want to keep doing shit or you want to get money?", I asked flashing a stack of cash.

"I want to get money the dark-skinned one said, followed by the other two light- skinned kids. The two light-skinned boys were definitely brothers and all three looked no more than 15. It was obvious, the dark-skinned boy was the decision maker in the crew, so he was going to be my head trapper. He just didn't know it yet.

I took the brothers Jason and Jerome, and their dark-skinned friend Donnie, to Dave and Busters in Philly. I gave them each a hundred to eat and play games with. After we left Philly, I gave them each a couple hundred dollars and my beeper number, and told them to page me in the morning. The next morning Donnie paged me at 8:20. I told him to meet me in the same park as the day before, at 9:00. When I got to the park Donnie was there in a fresh new jumper and some Tims. He told me that Jerome and Jason were scared but he wanted to get money.

"Look I know you not just givin' me free money, and I don't like owing' nigga's so what I gotta do for this bread?", Donnie asked straight forward. Before I could answer, he handed me $600, the money I gave Jerome and Jason saying,

"I told them if they wasn't coming to give the money back."

I knew right away Donnie was going to be thorough.

We drove to Woodrow Wilson Apartments on 33rd and Westfield. The apartments were separated from the high school by Dudley Grange Park so it would be easy for Donnie to walk there.

"I want you to trap for me over here" I said to Donnie pointing to Building C.

"You want me to work the morning shift", he asked.

"Nah, it's getting close to summer so you can work 3-11, can you stay out till 11?" I asked.

"Yea, I aint got no curfew", he answered.

"Good, all you got to do is pass off bags. The runner takes the money and tells you how many. Your only job is to give the customer their product got it", I asked. "Sounds easy, how much I get paid?", Donnie asked.

"$1,000 a week every Friday and a half ounce of coke every Sunday and Sundays is freelance day, so you can sell your own shit out here", I said.

"When do I start", Donnie asked.

"How 'bout today?", I asked.

"See you at 3:00", he said stepping toward the park, "Ill walk back to school."

Later that day, we opened up shop for the first time since the raid. We only used Buildings B and C and sold powder and crack. I had plans to open Building a back up as soon as I got more trappers. Lil Larry was going to manage the set and Lou would provide muscle. I used my same lookout and runners, as before since all they got for their charges was probation. Ace was supposed to be there as well, but never showed up. Ace had become less and less dependable lately. I started with 5 kilo's. We cooked three keys to four and bagged the other two as powder. I got the coke from Bingo for $19,000 a piece, which was a good price locally. We put cameras, like the Feds use, in our lookout apartments to monitor stickup kids and police activity in the area. When D.J. learned of my re-opening, he asked if he could get in. I felt partially obligated to let him get money with me since he always allowed me to make money, even as a kid. I told him we would sell his coke on Tuesday's and Wednesdays, I would let Lil Larry have Monday's and I would get Thursday's, Friday's and Saturday's. Sunday's was the freelance days for trappers, lookouts and baggers to sell their shit, which of course, they had to buy from me, Lil Larry or Ace, if he ever showed up. After the first hour things were running smooth, so I left.

Before I went home, I went out to Cramer Hill to grab a couple of straps from Dana's house. I was now fucking her on the regular and had paid for her to get an apartment a couple of blocks from her parents' house. We had an understanding. She could fuck who she wanted, just not at the apartment. I had a key, but I didn't do the drop in thing.

It was a two bedroom and I had a room where I would stash shit, mostly guns. I paid the rent. She kept the place clean and cooked, whenever I came by. I also had unlimited access to her mouth and pussy which was the best benefit of all. When I got to the apartment Dana was in the living room with Carmen and another chic named Lisa. I paused when I saw Carmen. I hadn't seen her since the first night I fucked Dana. The room fell silent. "Wassup Carmen, Liz. What up Dana", I said.

"Hey babe, you want something to eat?", she replied.

"Nah, I'm in an' out. I gotta make a run".

"Are you coming back?", she asked.

"Just page me." I answered, not sure if she wanted me to come back or not. "Okay.", she answered. Dana was a rare kind of woman. The kind that was willing to put her life on hold at anytime for me even though she knew I had a girl. She would've been the perfect wife for any man; instead she was my number 2.

I went into my room and grabbed a duffel bag and put two nines and a tech in the bag. I had just got 4 new guns from Dre, an SK, an AK; a sawed off shotty and a tech. Dre was a Camden nigga who moved to NC back in the day. Every couple of months he would come bring a shipment of guns, usually big guns. I decided to stock some for the summer. 1990 was a wild year in Camden, and '91 had started off the same way. I took the bags to 33rd and gave them to Lou. He was in charge of enforcement and he knew what to do with them.

After leaving Woodrow Wilson Apartments, I rode around for a while. Crack had changed the city in a negative way.

Being a drug dealer in Camden was more dangerous than ever. I had a couple of soldiers, but what I really needed to do was start rolling with Manny and Flaco again. Bringing D.J. in as a partner in Woodrow Wilson was the first step in re-aligning myself with the rest of the organization. It wasn't that I had stopped fucking with them nigga's. Its just you tend to hang with whoever you're getting money with. I stopped by the alley; at least 20 fiends were waiting to be served. Manny wasn't out, and one of the trappers said he hadn't seen Manny. I looked at the steady stream of customers; 33rd Street had a flow, but nothing like the alley.

Over the next few weeks, I began to hang with Manny and Flaco more and more. On one weekend, in June, we all went to see Brand Nubian at the Armory in Philly. The whole organization was there, Flaco, Manny, Blockz, Muscleclo, Enrique and even Raoul Quivoures, who I hadn't seen in a while. I brought Ace and Lou with me, and Lil Larry and Donnie ran the set. In all, we were like 30 deep, not to mention all the other Camden nigga's there. D.J. was there with Jose Martinez, the boxer who he used as muscle. For some reason I never trusted Jose, and I felt everybody else trusted him too much. Kalic and his crew were there and I got a bad feeling when I saw them, but we had just as many goons and damn near everybody was strapped. Brand Nubian were five percenters so where most of the nigga's from Trenton so, they were in the spot deep, along with Philly.

The show was crazy. Brand Nubian ran through all their hits and even did Slow Down twice. Bitches were everywhere, and we were shining because all of us had on big chains. After the show, everybody was hanging in front of the armory when somebody snatched a chain. The nigga whose chain got snatched turned out to be a God Body from Trenton, and the nigga that took it was from North Camden. Before long, the God's had formed and shots rang out. 3 people got hit, a nigga, a bouncer and a chic. They were all from Philly. Nobody was sure if Trenton or Camden nigga's did the shooting, but nigga's from Philly didn't care. In their eyes, they had beef with nigga's from Jersey.

Knowing Camden had beef with Trenton and Philly made me not want to club in Philly anymore, so we started going to Mahorn's. Mahorn's was a nightclub in Cherry Hill owned by NBA star, Rick Mahorn. It was in Jersey, 5 minutes from Camden, so we ran the spot. Over the summer this became one of our favorite hangout spots. We would chill with all the 76ers and all the stars that came to town and we would spend just as much money if not more at the bar. We were hood celebrities. D.J. and Flaco were on a first name basis with the top entertainers from the area.

In late June, we all took a trip to Cancun there were 19 of us. We took trappers and everything. We were gone for 7 days and Flaco rented the alley to Blockz for $25,000 while we were gone. I left the block to Lil Larry for free, but he had to sell my coke on Friday and Saturday. Donnie was able to get Monday in DJ's absence. Donnie had been working out perfectly as a trapper. He was taking his pay and buying coke and, along with the 14 grams he got every Sunday, he was putting together a nice stash. When I told him of the trip to Cancun he jumped on the chance to have the whole block for a day. He could easily sell a brick and make $15,000 profit for one day's work.

The trip to Cancun was the first time I had been out of town with my nigga's. We stayed at the Grand Oasis in 10 different rooms Ace and I shared one. We rented scooters for the week and hit the island. The bars and strip clubs were the craziest I had ever seen. I paid for pussy, got drunk and ate like a king, the normal things you do on vacation. The only complaint I had with Cancun was the weed it was garbage. After the ounce I came with ran out, I had to buy weed locally, and everywhere I went they had garbage. I was mad but that wasn't enough to ruin our trip. Manny had a room by himself and fucked the same girl every night. "I thought you were going to bring her back to Jersey", I teased him. We partied like rock stars for a week and then we came back to the concrete jungle called Camden.

Everything was running smooth when we got back from Mexico. I went to talk to Lil Larry and he told me there were no problems in Woodrow Wilson or in the alley, but a shooting that happened on High Street could possibly affect all of East Camden. Rasheed from North Camden was shot and killed coming from a relative's house on 28th & High Street. He was down with Kalic and there would definitely be hell to pay. The word was out that if Kalic didn't have the name of the shooter within 48 hours, his gang would randomly kill people in East Camden. Rasheed was murdered on Friday, and the message was given on Saturday. It was now Sunday, and we were 24 hours away from the outcome. I decided to be smart and only have 1 & 1/2 shifts on Monday. By 8:00 pm all my trappers were off the streets.

I knew Kalic was going to do whatever it took to prove his point. The first murder occurred at 9:45 p.m. on Monday, June 3, 1991. The man was a well-known ex-hustler in East Camden. He was shot 2 blocks from my grandparents' home on Baird Boulevard. The next murder occurred at 9:59 p.m. on 27th and Westfield. The target was a 22 year-old man sitting in a parked car. He was hit multiple times in the face, at close range. At 10:10 p.m. a 26 year-old father of three was standing on Westfield Avenue in front of the Acres when he was shot once in the chest. He died instantly. The last shooting happened at 10:17 on 28th and Federal Streets. A man was shot in the side, while riding a bicycle. He then, tried to run into the street, where a car hit him. After being hit by the car, he was still living, and tried again to run. This time he ran into an alley, before being fatally shot in the back of the head and neck.

On the streets, word was out that Kalic's soldiers had killed the four people in retaliation for Rasheed's murder. The police on the other hand had no witnesses or suspects. The hood was littered with cops for the next three days. News crews and community leaders were all over East Camden giving interviews and holding peace rallies. I opened shop again on Wednesday, although the media swarm continued throughout the week.

That weekend, I ran into Manny on Federal Street and followed him back to McGuire. "Man, it's hectic out here right now with these police."

"Man, ya'll nigga's look like ya'll aint miss a beat", I replied to Manny, as a steady stream of fiends copped in the alley across the street.

"Yea, you know how that be. Muthafuckas gotta get high", Manny said with a smile.

"We closed down for a day, but then I was right back open", I told Manny.

"They got it hot as hell out here and I don't even know who killed that nigga Rasheed", Manny said coughing on the blunt he had just sparked.

"Me neither, but I heard he got set up by his cousin's baby dad."

"Word. I used to go to school with his cousin. You talking 'bout light-skin Michele right?" Manny asked.

"Yea, they said her baby dad was there when Rasheed came through, and he called them nigga's from 32nd and told them, and they squatted on him. And after he left, they killed him, like a block away from Michele's crib." I answered.

"Well, rumor or no rumor Michele's baby dad is a dead man walking", Manny said laughing.

After kicking it with Manny for about an hour or so, I went to Heavy Metal Gym to see D.J. D.J. was now a full-fledged businessman and was never seen at a drug corner. He was still seeing profits from a lot of different drug corners, as well as, laundering money for me, Flaco, Blockz and the rest of the top members of the organization. D.J. was in his office talking to Jose Martinez.

Martinez had started training at Heavy Metal when D.J. bought it. He sold steroids to all the body builders and cops that wanted them. "What's up, D.J.? What up, Jose?" I said as I walked into the office.

"Gato, my main man. How's things going", D.J. asked.

"Everything is dobby considering all the dumb shit that's going on," I answered.

"Yea, Kalic and them want to murder, murder, murder. What ever happened to making money? That's why I left North Camden, you know I'm from North Camden, right Gato", D.J. asked.

"Yea, I think I heard Flaco say that before", I responded.

"Yea, Flaco and I, we both from North Camden, but we been out here in East Camden getting money for years now".

"Kalic's been around for a while. His soldiers, they young but Kalic, he's been the same since I known him. Kill. Kill. Kill.", D.J. said.

"Gato, you need to be more incognito and stop being in the streets so much, that's why you have a set manager", D.J. said, schooling me.

"*FastWash* is doing pretty good. What do you think about opening another one, maybe in Delran or Burlington?", I asked.

"Let's do it", he responded.

"It's just an idea right now, but I wanted your opinion", I told D.J.

"Great idea. Anything legal is a good idea, as long as it makes some kind of profit." I stayed a little longer and talked

170

to D.J. about everything from 33rd Street, to the latest episode of In Living Color. After about an hour in the gym, I drove home to see my son and my girl.

D.J. was right and over the next couple of months I tried to stop hanging on the set so much. Jasmine was taking summer classes, and her sister Darlene went back to Trenton for the summer, so I did all types of things to occupy my time. I started going to Garden State Race track with D.J. every Sunday, and on Saturdays I would take my trappers to the massage spot in Chinatown and then out to eat. Staying off the corner helped me be less visible, but being flashy was my biggest problem.

That summer I bought the Jeep Grand Cherokee, a larger version of the popular, Jeep Cherokee. The Grand Cherokee wasn't due out in North America until 1993 but the People from FC Kerbeck were able to order me one from Austria. The Jeep was the hottest truck in the hood at the time. Although there were some nigga's in Camden with more money than me, almost no one was on my level when it came to styling'.

The one exception was Blockz from Parkside. Blockz was the only top member in our Organization that was 100% Black. He owned a promotion company that often bought rappers to perform at hole in the wall clubs in Camden and Philly. He was on a first name basis with plenty of athletes and entertainers. In the summer of '91 he was driving a black, '92, four door Jeep Cherokee with gold rims.

It was the middle of the day and I knew Blockz would be out on Haddon by the Donut Queen. I had Ace riding shotgun in my cherry red Grand Cherokee as I crossed Baird Boulevard Bridge from East Camden to Parkside. I came down Kaighn and made the Left onto Haddon Ave. Blockz and his crew stood in front of Donut Queen watching, amazed as I rode by. I rode around Parkside and Pollack for about 20 minutes before shooting back to East Camden. As we got back out East, Ace was looking at me smiling.

"What?", I asked.

"You the man, yo! I mean you just got it, that thing that all the great ones got. You got it!" The crazy part was I knew exactly what he was talking about but I didn't say a word.

My home life was good and I had Dana on a leash. Business was great and the beef between 32nd Street and Kalic's crew from North Camden had calmed down, life was good. Things were going so good I would frequently let Lil Larry, Ace or even Donnie have the set for the day. One night in August I went to Oasis by myself in the Grand Cherokee.

When I pulled up I was feeling myself extra hard. I had the kind of confidence only a millionaire can have. I walked in and noticed Carmen in the corner drinking and talking to Lisa. I walked to the bar and gave the bartender $2,000 to have an open bar for an hour and drinks for me for the rest of the night. I started out drinking Hennessey and then switched to Remy. After about 5 drinks Carmen walked over, "I know you still wanna fuck me", she whispered. Just talking to Carmen in public was dangerous. Plus I didn't know if Lisa would run back and tell Dana, so I answered carefully.

"You sure you aint got that backwards? If I'm not mistaken, you walked over here".

She was shocked, I wasn't the same shy young boy from before, and she liked it. "Okay so you're right, I do want to fuck you!" she said.

"Meet me at McDonald's on Route 130 in 20 minutes", I responded.

I continued drinking for another 10 or 15 minutes before heading to McDonald's. When I got to McDonald's, Carmen's car was parked in the back of the parking lot. I pulled next to her car and she got out and hopped in my passenger seat. Carmen explained that she had to be home by the time the clubs closed, so we stayed local. She got back in her car and followed me to an hourly rate motel in Cinnaminson. I checked in with no ID and parked my truck in the back. After all the years of waiting I finally had her. This whole thing was like an adventure to her and I was now in the driver seat.

Carmen was not as loose as Dana or Jasmine. Once I had her fully naked I started rubbing all over her perfect body. I licked her from toe to pussy and made her cum a couple of times. Carmen wasn't use to this treatment and was going crazy the whole time. She had her own condoms and gave me one; I put it on and went all the way inside of her. She lay on her back while I held one of her legs straight in the air and put my entire dick in her. It was more than she could take and she pulled me close as I moved around inside of her without pulling it out. She scratched my back and sucked on my neck like we had been fucking for years. Carmen came at least three more times. In fact, I never made a woman cum so easily in my life.

When we finished she laid in my arms for 20 minutes telling me how her husband never made her feel like that, and that she had just had the best sex of her life. I tried to hit it again, but she said she wanted to leave the memory just as it was.

After laying up, she got in the shower and headed back to Camden. I stayed in the bed a while longer. When I did get up I looked in the mirror and had hickies all over my neck, and scratches on my back. I was scared, how the hell could I explain this to Jasmine. I got in my car and drove straight to Atlantic City I would come up with a plan later, for now I just couldn't go home.

14

Kalic's Demise

13 ARRESTS IN CAMDEN'S BIG GANG. THE CREW ARE SUSPECTED IN 8 KILLINGS. THEIR ALLEGED LEADERS, KALIC, AND A 51 YEAR OLD GRANDMOTHER, WERE AMONG THOSE APPREHENDED.

"Did you see this?" Jasmine said waking me up. I read the paper slowly. Kalic and 11 of his soldiers had been hit with numerous charges from drug distribution to murder. Four of the eight murders they were indicted for were the random killings in East Camden that had the hood hot in '91. Another murder was Little Mark. It was October 22, 1992 and the war on the streets of East Camden was finally over.

I woke up and got dressed and drove straight to North Camden. The streets were filled with people. Some were happy, some were sad, but most people were just relieved. The police presence was there, as well as camera crews and reporters. For the past two years prior to the raid, North Camden had been a war zone. Besides being the location of some of the most dangerous heroin spots in the country, North Camden was also home to a vicious gang of killers. Life out North stopped at nightfall. New Jersey Transit sent its buses on a different route after 5:00 pm, so drivers wouldn't have to travel through the area. Children couldn't play outside in the evening. The gang had sucked the life out of the neighborhood. So, to police this was a major bust, and for America's worst city it was major news.

After riding through some of the streets, I would have never considered riding through just a couple days earlier; I went to Dana's crib in Cramer Hill. Cramer Hill was in between East and North Camden. When I got there, Lisa was there. I didn't trust Lisa because she knew too much about Carmen and she was also Dana's close friend. Lisa was the type of person to sell out to the highest bidder, so she was not to be trusted. Even though Carmen told her we were just flirting and nothing happened, Lisa didn't believe her and swore we met up after seeing us both leave the club around the same time.

I wasn't so much worried about losing Carmen, as I was about Lisa telling Carmen's husband, Pedro. Pedro was a very powerful man; every time I slept with his wife, I was playing Russian roulette. Carmen was a very sensible person and although she loved having sex with me she was in no way going to jeopardize her marriage for our fling. We saw each other from time to time, but not on a regular basis.

I spoke to Lisa, and then asked Dana if I could talk to her in the room. She had on the booty shorts that she sleeps in, so I knew she wasn't wearing panties. I slid down her shorts and started hitting it from the back, on the dresser. "What was that for", Dana asked. "I've been wanting some of my pussy since I

176

woke up" I answered. Dana just smiled. After the quickie, I left and went to the gym to see D.J.

When I got there, D.J. was out getting lunch. I waited for him in his office; he was expecting me, and he never forgot an appointment. I respected D.J. the same way I did Sonny and Uncle Ramos. He was a successful businessman that operated like a low-key mob boss. Besides the car wash we co-owned, D.J. owned a auto parts store, Heavy Metal gym, a furniture and electronics store, and a car detail shop. He also co-owned a business with Flaco and Blockz. His businesses combined, reported a gross income of seven million dollars a year. This figure was purposely inflated, which allowed him to launder his drug money. He had been doing this since 1982 and never had a drug charge. Essentially, all his money was legit. My thoughts were cut off when D.J. and Jose Martinez walked into the room with bags from the Puerto Rican Restaurant on 36th Street.

"Gato! My man, what's going on? How's everything? Good, I hope", DJ, asked. "Yeah everything's great."

"This kid here. He's one of the best fucking hustler's in Camden."

"I've known him all his life. He was bred to be a hustler, his Pop Pop is Sonny Robinson", he said.

"No shit? That's Sonny's grandson?", Jose answered.

"You know my grandpa?" I asked Jose surprised.

"Nah, I don't actually know him, but everybody knows *of* him. He's an old-school legend", he responded.

"Yea, I know his whole family. His Uncle Ramos, his father. His father was the smoothest dressed cat in Camden. He was a pimp, a good one", D.J. said with a gaze in his eye, as if he was reminiscing.

"Blockz told me he saw you, Gato. He said you had a new customized Jeep or some shit", D.J. said snapping back to the present.

"Yea, well it's not custom. It just didn't come out in the states yet," I answered. D.J. shook his head with a slight smirk before replying,

"Being a drug dealer will get you rich, but living like a drug dealer will get you killed, or prison time".

"Now think about what I said, Gato. Being a drug dealer will get you rich, but living like a drug dealer will get you killed, or prison time. Do you understand that?" he asked. I slowly nodded my head yes.

"Do you really? Because we had this conversation before, about being low key and it worked for about a month. Now you're getting cars that aren't even out in the U.S!" D.J. said firmly.

"Y'all old heads kill me. I remember '87 when you was pullin' up in the '88 Benz 190. You and Flaco are the reason why I am the way I am".

"Just don't forget what it's like to be 19 with money", I continued.

"I just want to help you avoid the pitfalls I've seen so many others fall into."

"I've been doing this a long time Gato, a long time. I'm a true rags to riches story. I'm from the dirt", D.J. insisted. "My mom, she had 12 kids in a two bedroom apartment, no husband to help. At 9, I moved out and stayed with different family members and friends, so she didn't have to feed me."

"Sometimes I would go see her, and she would ask me, "You hungry?"

My stomach would be growling. I always said, "No", because I didn't want to take nothin' from my brothers and sisters.

I got a job that summer. 9 years old makin' cheese steaks, selling newspapers whatever. I did that until 10th grade. Then I dropped out and started working full time as a painter. Can you believe it? A fucking painter", D.J. said, as Jose and I laughed. "Then I started selling wooden car steering wheels..." I bust out laughing cutting D.J. off in mid sentence.

"You laugh, but in 1978 wooden steering wheels was the shit, they cost $50 in the D.R. and they sold for $200-$250 over here. Making those trips is how I started selling cocaine. Nobody sold cocaine back then. It was heroin, refer, that's it. It was a rich man's drug. It cost $40 or $50,000 a key back then.

I started small, bringing back a quarter key on commercial airlines, nothing sophisticated. By '82, I moved from North Camden to East Camden, right in McGuire housing Projects. I was making money, but Hector Quinones, Robert Saca, dudes like that, they was on top. Me and dudes like Albert Soldevilla, we was on the come up, but you see where he is now, right? He going to prison just like Hector and Robert. You no why, they all lived like drug dealers, instead of businessman. I'm respected, I eat lunch with the mayor, I live like a businessman. That's why I last."

After talking to D.J. I rode around for a minute, thinking about what he said. I heard about Hector Quinones. He was caught with 670 kilo's in '85. My uncle Ramos knew him. Roberto went to jail around '87, after putting a hit on an undercover cop. The attempt was a failure. While Roberto was in jail, his wife and 2 sons had a plot to kill the assistant D.A. An informant notified police of the plan and the three were arrested. As for Albert Soldevilla, he was just arrested in '92 for trying to buy 70 kilo's from an undercover. I understood how D.J. was different from them, and I decided to be a businessman instead of a drug dealer.

When I finally parked, I went to Oasis to holler at Flaco and Manny. "Gato, what's up?" Flaco said. Then to the barmaid, "Get him a drink."

"What's up cousin? You see that paper today?" Manny asked.

"Yea, that shit crazy. I knew it was them nigga's doing all the killing last June", I said sipping my Corona.

"Yea, well, they 'bout to get a long time for what? Which one of them had a million dollars?", Flaco asked.

"Maybe 5-0 will calm down out here now", Manny said.

"Yea, perfect timing too. It's winter. This is my season, no distractions straight getting that bank", I said before being interrupted by Manny.

"No distractions, except Christmas nigga. You got kids now."

"Kid, nigga kid. *You* got kids. I have *a child*." I replied with a laugh. I finished my beer and bullshitted with Manny a little while longer before heading back home.

I thought with Kalic in jail, the streets would be more peaceful, but I couldn't have been more wrong. On Mischief Night, over 100 fires were set in the city. Everything from vacant homes and buildings, to cars and storefronts were set ablaze, and Camden was declared a state of emergency. The end of the year was approaching, and once again, Camden was about to set a record for murders. A neighborhood kid's body was found on the roof of East Camden Middle School and the media and the police began to swarm again. The murder of a father in front of his two sons, and the murder of a boy by two men in ninja suits, made the streets just as hot as when Kalic was home.

Around this time people started calling Camden CMD, which stood for Cash, Murder, Drugs or Crack, Marijuana, Dope depending on who you asked. The one good thing about Camden was the violence and murders didn't stop the white people from the suburbs from coming to get their drugs. The alley was making more money than ever, and on 33rd we were also making a killing. Ace seemed to be back to normal and was sitting on at least a million dollars for the first time. My home life was also great. My son was now walking and talking and Jasmine was finishing up her junior year at Rutgers. Camden was filled with violence, but for some reason I thought I was immune.

The news of Camden's 51st murder was a total shock to me. I knew T-Money had been home for about a month but I still hadn't seen him. Ace had visited him a couple of times and gave him some cash to get on his feet. T-Money took the cash and bought some heroin to sell. With North Camden being hot, opening a dope spot in East Camden made perfect sense. Things worked out and T-Money was given more dope, this time on consignment. T-Money's girl apparently, took the money he made from the dope and ran off to Delaware. T-Money's headless body was found in Crestberry Apartments in the city's Fairview section. His head was later discovered in a trash bin in the back of the complex.

Although I never really liked T-Money, his death was hard on me. After all, his connect made me rich, and Ace was still good friends with him. And Jasmine. How was I going to tell Jasmine? She always downplayed their relationship as nothing serious, but she had known him since she was young and I knew this would be hard on her, as well. That night I took Jasmine out and we got drunk together. She cried on my shoulder and I comforted her without getting jealous. I almost cried myself, not so much for T-Money as for my city, and myself. I was from a place where murder and crack sales were a part of everyday life.

When the funeral came around, I decided not to go. I stopped by the viewing and left some flowers, but I would have felt funny sitting in the funeral with my girl crying over her old boyfriend. Besides that, Jasmine and Star were still close and I knew Jasmine would want to be with her and her family. Star took her cousins death the hardest. Loosing Rim and now T-Money had changed her outlook on life. She shared her new views with Jasmine and in about 5 hours she single handedly wrecked my life. When Jasmine got home, she told me what Star had convinced her of. She told Jasmine that death was around the corner for any hustler, and that for her sake, and the sake of my son, she should convince me to quit like she did Ace.

"What you mean like she did Ace", I asked.

"You heard me. Ace said he quit and that he was going to tell you face to face tomorrow", Jasmine answered smiling.

"Whatever. That nigga aint quit. Matter of fact, fuck! If he quit, he wanna go broke, that's on him. I aint quitting, not yet, quit for what? Man that nigga crazy if he said that", I replied, mad now, because I knew Jasmine was telling the truth.

"What if I said, if you don't quit, I'm leaving? Then what would you say", she asked in a serious tone.

"Leaving, leaving to go where? Back to the projects?"

"If I had to", she replied.

"You would be real dumb to leave Moorestown for the projects"; I answered before leaving the house. As I drove to Camden, I thought about what Jasmine said and I knew she wasn't bluffing. I also knew there was no way I was going to stop selling drugs.

I couldn't understand why Ace would quit in the middle of his best run. He was saving more money than ever before, and he was finally getting respect as a big boy hustler. When I met up with Ace, he told me his plan.

"So you done", I asked Ace.

"Man, I aint quitting shit. I just told Star that", Ace said noticing the displeased look on my face.

"So, now you going to be running around hiding that you hustle", I asked. "We suppose to be hiding this shit."

"This shit aint legal. We suppose to hide, and our girls aint suppose to know as much as they know", Ace continued.

"They don't need to know our business for a bunch of reasons I don't need to explain to you", he said. This was like a school lesson, a warning for me to get my business a little tighter. Ace was absolutely right. I thought he really wanted to quit but he was more focused than I had seen him in years.

Over the next couple of weeks, Ace and Star both went back to their normal state of mind, Jasmine didn't bend so easily. Her nagging ways were fucking with my business and my mood. I began spending more and more time with Dana. One night in early December, Dana and me were up drinking a gallon of Hennessey.

"Do you ever feel bad about fucking me?", Dana asked. "Well you shouldn't", she said answering her own question.

"Because Jasmine was fucking T-Money, from the time he came home, until he died". Her words cut me like a sword. I jumped right up and put on my coat.

"You going to go run right to her. You're such a sucker", Dana said as I walked out. I knew Dana was right, but I couldn't stop myself. I got to Moorestown in 8 minutes, but I only remember brief parts of the ride. The Hennessey had me seeing in triple and I was going in the house to confront all 3 Jasmine's on this T-Money situation.

When I stumbled into the crib, Jasmine was in the kitchen. The next couple of minutes were a blur but I do remember here admitting to running into T-Money at Pennsauken Mart. I had never hit a woman before, but I remember her screaming and the cops coming. I woke up in Burlington County Jail on a domestic disturbance charge. In their jail, you could only bail out during business hours, so I was stuck until Monday morning. I was locked down in one cell with a Burlington nigga named Streets. He was a wild young nigga in for some bullshit driving violations. When I bailed out on Monday, I posted bail for Streets, but I left before he actually got out.

Manny came to get me and told me that Jasmine had taken all my things, including my BMW and my Jeep Grand Cherokee to my grandparent's house. I knew I didn't want to stay at my grandparent's house, so I crashed at one of the apartments D.J. had in the city. I didn't tell Dana I moved, because I knew she would want me to stay with her, so I kept it to myself. I also made sure I didn't go to her house any more than usual.

I thought Jasmine would crack by Christmas. I spent thousands of dollars on gifts for her and my son. On Christmas Eve, I went to my house with a red knapsack full of gifts, like Santa Claus. When I got there, Jasmine was happy to see me, but said this didn't change things. We stayed up making cookies and doing all that Christmas shit for my son. After lil' Simon finally went to sleep, Jasmine brought me a blanket to sleep on the couch. "You wanted to see your son open his gifts, that's fine, but that don't got nothing to do with us sleeping in the same bed", she said, before going into her room and closing the door.

I laid there for no more than 10 minutes when my pager went off. It was Ace, telling me his Uncle Bingo had been found sitting in a parked car on Line Street with 5 bullets in his head and neck and he was in critical condition. I got right up and drove to Cooper Hospital. When I got there, I was surprised to see Keisha, Jasmines old roommate from Willingboro. She was sitting in the waiting room, with about 6 other people, and they were all crying uncontrollable. "What's going on Keisha", I said to her, as she looked up, surprised to see me.

"My sister. They killed her, right in front of my house", the words sent a chill up my spine. I was used to murder and mayhem in Camden, but for a 17 year-old girl to be stabbed to death in Willingboro was unheard of. I hugged Keisha and tried to console her. I saw Ace and Pedro at the end off the hall, so I made my way down there. When I got to the end of the hall, Ace was shaking his head and Pedro was sitting silently looking at the floor. I knew the look it had become all too familiar. Bingo was dead.

I stayed at the hospital for a couple more minutes before returning home to Jasmine and my son. I woke Jasmine up and told her what happened. She felt bad for Keisha, who she hadn't spoken to in a couple of years. She called her and offered her condolences. We then stayed up talking all night before waking Simon up at 6:00 a.m. to open his gifts. We spent the whole day together as a family. It was great. Jasmine and I ended our feud, but she wasn't ready for me to move back in, so I stayed at my side apartment.

The next day, I met with the whole Organization; Blockz, Manny, D.J., Flaco, Ace, Muscleclo, Luis Noel, Enrique Cintron and even Raoul, who I still despised for killing Butter. The meeting was called for one reason only, to find out who killed Bingo. Bingo worked directly for Pedro, so catching his killer was a priority. It was revealed that Bingo had a customer named Ishh who lived on Saunders Street, a block from where Bingo was shot. It was also said that Bingo was with a woman minutes before he was killed.

186

Those were our only clues so we started there. Muscleclo's job was to put pressure on anybody we thought knew something. He had a fierce reputation in the streets and nobody fucked with him. Lou was my muscle, so I put him on the job as well as Jose Martinez who worked for D.J. Between the three of them, we would come up with either some answers or some bodies, and either way, Pedro would be happy. Seeing how fast D.J. was to react for Pedro made me realize how stupid I was for fucking Carmen. One word to the wrong person about our affair, and I would be killed, probably by my own crew.

The news came quickly, Rose Marie Diggs was the woman last seen with Bingo. Rose Marie was married with 3 kids, but she was also fucking Gunz, a nigga from Line Street, known for stickups. Muscleclo and Lou put pressure on nigga's from Line Street about the murder and Gunz name came up. Rose Marie lived in an apartment on Mitchell Street in East Camden. It was December 30 when two masked men broke into her house, shot and killed her, and wounded Arthur Moore A/K/A Gunz. Gunz was shot twice in the side and chest and was in serious condition at Cooper. A single shot to the face killed Rose Marie. Once the murder was carried out, the situation was never discussed again. I wasn't sure who actually committed the murders, and I didn't ask. Even if Lou, who worked for me, was one of the triggerman it wasn't my place to ask and to be honest, I didn't want to know.

15

1993

1993 started of with a bang actually, 3 bangs. Three shoot-ings and 3 murders. Camden nigga's didn't take off for holi-days. A gang, from The Centerville section of the city, called Eight Ball was blamed for the shootings on New Years Day. A double murder on Louis Street and another on 7th and Ferry brought the body count to 3 for the year plus the three non-fatal shootings in the city. It was January 4th. Protesters demonstrat-ed on the steps of city hall, holding tombstones with the names of murder victims. 33rd was as hot as I had ever seen it, but at the same time, we were making more money than ever. To D.J., this meant never stopping, just running until we hit a brick wall. I finally discovered Ace was sniffing powder and smoking wocky. Wocky was mint leaves soaked in embalming fluid. This made him less reliable and he had stopped being involved with the daily operations of the set, although he still was getting paid.

My first bad break came when Lil Larry was arrested after police watched him put a duffel bag in his trunk and then followed him and pulled him over. Once they came up with a reason to search the vehicle, they found 2 Ziploc bags with 250 grams apiece of crack. They also found a bag with 1,000 grams of powder, a nine-millimeter and $13,000 cash. He was taken to the station where he was interrogated for 10 hours before being able to use the phone. They were threatening to charge him with being the leader of a narcotics operation, which could get him 25 years state time. When he was finally taken to the county jail, after refusing to cooperate, his bail was set at 1 million dollars cash or bond. Even with the 10%, it would cost $100,000 to get Lil Larry out of jail. I went to D.J. and Ace and told them the news. I let them know that for $33,000 apiece we could get Lil Larry out. In a serious face, Ace told me, "I don't got it".

"What the fuck you mean, you aint got it? This nigga knows a lot. We need to get him out," I answered.

"Like I said, I don't got it right now", Ace responded. Ace was high and he was pissing me off, so I asked D.J.

"Gato, I think it's best we just let Lil Larry be, he should have his own bail money anyway. The best thing for us to do is just distance ourselves from him", D.J. replied.

I was shocked. This was how D.J. acted toward T-Money and now Lil' Larry. What if it had been me sitting in the cell! I left feeling like I was alone in this game. I called Albert Andrews from A&A's bail bondsman; I had used him to get Dana out of jail before. I told him that I needed to bail somebody out on a million dollar bail without signing any papers. He agreed and I took him a shoebox containing 1000 $100 dollar bills. Albert signed for the bail himself and Lil Larry was home only 2 days after being arrested. Albert took this risk because as long as Lil Larry went to court the $100,000 was A&A's to keep. What I didn't know was, at the police station the cops threatened to take Albert's bondsman's license if he didn't give a name of who had really posted the bail. They didn't believe he posted it, but said they would let him keep the bond money if he gave up a name. If he didn't they would revoke the bond, keep the money and report him which would lead to an investigation of all his past bonds. Of course, this was all bullshit that cops didn't have the power to do, but keeping the money and avoiding an audit was too much of an incentive for Albert. So, he folded and gave up my name. I was now under investigation. The only problem was, I didn't know it.

State and local authorities were now watching my movements. My first run-in was on 33rd, right in front of Woodrow Wilson Apartments. I was outside smoking a blunt when police cars pulled up. There were at least 6 people outside, but they seemed to be focused on me. "Let me see your ID", the state trooper asked, in a threatening voice, with one hand on his gun handle. The troopers had come to the city to help with the takedown of Kalic's gang, and they've been in Camden ever since. I showed the officer my ID and asked, "What's the pr...."

"Shut the fuck up! I'll ask the questions", the trooper said cutting me off in mid sentence.

"What the fuck you doing out here? This is a long way from Moorestown Mr. Gonzales", the trooper asked.

"He came to see me", the voice of a young girl said. The trooper looked at the girl and then at my ID before responding,

190

"You shouldn't be hanging outside Camden's a dangerous place. Stay out of trouble", he then handed me my ID and the cars pulled off.

The girl that helped me was named Margaret, and she was the definition of a hood rat. Her life consisted of smoking wocky and trying to come up anyway possible. She was fly though. She kept her nails and toes done and was always up on the latest fashions. Her kids were less fortunate, until their paternal grandmother stepped in and took them. Margaret now rarely saw her children; she was all of 17 years old. State troopers killed her baby dad the year before, inside a Chinese restaurant. She lived alone in a one-bedroom apartment right on the set.

"Good looking out. You saved me", I said handing her 3 $100 bills.

"No problem, and thanks for the money. Shit, you keep treating me like this I'm a have to give you a key", she said smiling still standing in her doorway.

"Yea, $300 that's what a key cost", I answered.

"Money will get you some pussy, but only pipe work can get you a key", she said as she turned and walked into the house leaving her front door wide open. In my head I thought *"This bitch just know I'm coming in there"*. After all she was 17 and had fucked at least 20 different killers and hustlers that I knew about. She was a hood rat that didn't even have her own kids. She had no job, and fucked and sucked for a living. I was a fucking millionaire. Why would I fuck her? I wondered all these things, as I walked into the apartment and shut the door behind me.

As I sat on the couch drinking a Clearly Canadian, Margaret got on her knees and unzipped my pants. She pulled my dick out and started giving me the best head I ever had in my life. She sucked just the head and then mixed it up with some deep throat. She had her own rhythm it was crazy. The whole time she was sucking my dick, she was playing with herself. I took my pants all the way off and could feel her pussy juice on my leg, she was wet as hell. She was talking dirty like "Cum in my mouth, Gato. Cum in my mouth". Right when I was about to cum, she stopped and started sucking my balls and jerking my dick. I nutted straight up in the air, she sat up and looked me in the face and said, "What? You thought I was going to let you nut in my mouth? You can't get that yet". She then wiped all the cum off with her hands and sucked it off her fingers. It wasn't the point off my cum being in her mouth, it was just her holding something back and this bitch was only 17! After sucking her fingers dry she started rubbing my dick on her pussy. It was so wet I felt like I was going to cum right then, before my dick even got hard. My shit got rock hard again, instantly. She started riding me hard as hell, backwards. She was damn near jumping on my dick. She started shaking and I could fell her cumming on me. The pussy got wetter and wetter and she was screaming, "I can feel it in my stomach!" She then told me she was cumming again, before telling me, "Hit it from the back Gato, hit it from the back". Then in one motion she hooked my back with her right arm, and used her left to place me on the floor, where she pulled me so I could hit it from the back without my dick coming out. I started off slow because I knew I was close to cumming but she kept yelling "Harder, harder! Oohh yea, like that Gato. Right there".

"I'm 'bout to cum again Gato", she yelled. Little did she know I was seconds away from cumming myself. We were in a race that I was pretty sure I was going to win, even if I didn't want to. I did win, and I came right inside her. As I finished cumming she started yelling again.

This time saying, "Don't stop, I'm cumming baby". I had gone from Gato to baby that fast. This time was the big one, and she started squirting all over the floor.

"Oh shit, um, wow! I needed that", she said pushing my dick out her with her pussy muscles.

"Don't worry, I'm on the pill. I see you got that, after-nut look, on your face".

"You know, nigga's get that look, after they nut in something they aint got no business cumming in".

"But, that *during* the nut look, that says a thousand words", she said pointing to a mirror that I hadn't noticed hanging directly across from us.

"I knew you came before me nigga, but you better not have stopped. Shit my money nigga coming over tonight and he got a little dick", she said getting up and walking towards her hallway.

"Lock that door on your way out, and hurry up. That nigga be trying pop up all early sometimes."

I couldn't believe she was, this blatantly, a whore. I couldn't believe that I just hit it raw. I *really* couldn't believe I wanted to hit it again.

Lil Larry was a real nigga, and even though I trusted him, D.J. would have no parts in doing business with him. I began taking on more of the daily responsibilities of the set. This made it easy for the police to watch me since the whole apartment complex was under surveillance. Margaret lived in apartment 3C, so she had a clear view of the block from her living room window. I began spending more and more time at her apartment. I started paying her rent and got a key and charged it all to the cost of doing business. Me having a key didn't slow Margaret down one bit. Plenty of nights, I would come to an empty apartment at 2 and 3 'o'clock in the morning. Most times, I would leave and never mention to her that I had come by. The more I told myself I didn't like this bitch the more I realized I did.

Lou and Donnie were still around and a couple of new young trappers were also down with the team. By spring of '93 the cops would come like 6 or 7 deep and clear out the block. They would then bring in undercovers, posing as hustlers. They would then serve 100's of customers and arrest them for intent to purchase CDS. They would take all the people they arrested to a holding area, usually a school, and process them there. They would then offer anybody with information about our organization a free walk. No testifying, no prosecutor just a backroom discussion that would forever remain confidential. From these sting operations, state investigators were able to learn which drugs were sold in which buildings, who the trappers were, who the muscle was, and who the "big boys" were. They began tailing our cars and staking out our homes.

The first time I realized I might be being followed, I was in East State Village with Margaret. I took her there to get a couple of bags of wocky. I call them bags but it was actually sold in wax paper. After getting the wocky, we left out of East State. By the time we got back to 33rd, Margaret's friend who lived in East State called and said the spot was raided right after we left. I felt lucky not to get caught up in the raid, but I still had no idea it had anything to do with me. Later that night, her friend called back and said after police raided they kept asking, "What was Gato doing here, but nobody knew who Gato was".

This is how I knew I was being followed, but for what? I was scared to tell D.J. what happened, so I didn't. I called Ace and asked if he had noticed anything unusual. He said he hadn't, but he had been hanging in Parkside lately so he wasn't even on their radar. I felt like being at Margaret's was making me hot, so I went to Dana's. I had been treating Dana bad lately, and for no reason. She was the one person who had my back no matter what. I wanted to do something special for her so; I brought a black bag filled with money to her house.

"Here", I said as I walked in the door and threw the bag on her lap.

"What's this", she asked.

"Um about $88,000", I answered.

"What? You want me to do hold it", she asked with a confused look in her face. "You can hold it, spend it, invest it, just please don't burn it", I said laughing. "Stop playing, nigga", she said throwing the bag back to me.

"It's not a game, but if you give it back again, I'm keeping it", I said throwing the bag back with a little more force this time.

"So, you just going to give me $80,000 for nothing", she asked still confused. "Not for nothin' for loyalty, you've been good to me, I just wanted to say thank you".

"Okay, what the fuck is going on? You're scaring me. Why you talking like you dyin' or something?" she asked with a frightened look in her face.

"Relax, I replied, nothing's wrong. I'm just appreciating people while their still here to appreciate, or while I'm still here, to appreciate them".

"Simon, I don't know what's wrong with you, but I'm not good to you because you have money, I do it cause I love you!"

"Let's go to the movies or something", I said.

"Me and you? A date? Wow, now I know something's wrong. But fuck it, I'll take it while it lasts."

The next day, I continued giving out money, $150,000 to my grandparents and $50,000 to Uncle Ramos. I felt like it would be better to spread a little money around, just in case I went to jail. After handing out money I went to Moorestown to Jasmine's house. I stayed and played with my son all day. Jasmine, like Dana, noticed a change in me. I kept all the details of the police investigation to myself. I still wasn't sure why, or to what extent the police were actually watching me.

I finally decided to check with Jeremy Harris. I went to see D.J. and told him I needed to get in contact with Harris. Jeremy wasn't as valuable as he used to be. Everybody in Camden knew he was crooked, and he wasn't able to access the same info, he once could. He was now freely robbing drug dealers all across the city and he was probably as hot as me. I went to the gym to meet Harris and ask him if there was an investigation into me or 33rd Street. He told me there was no city investigation, but that the "State Boys", did what they wanted and rarely collaborated with city cops. This eased my stress, just a little bit, but I knew I had to shake the troopers.

My next move would be simple, move Margaret from Woodrow Wilson Apartments on 33rd Street, to a house on 34th. This way I could be close to the set without being visible. It would also keep me from their surveillance photos that were obviously being taken on 33rd. I took my Grand Cherokee and traded it for the brand new Lexus GS 300. I switched my address to my grandparent's house and registered the car there. The cops hadn't seen my Beamer so I traded it in for an updated model. I moved Jasmine and my son to a condo in Mount Laurel and put our Moorestown home on the market. By June I had been off the radar for nearly 2 months. All my cars were switched and I got rid of my apartment and got one in Uncle Ramos name in Lindenwold. I was being real cautious and probably had the state trooper's cage rattled. I still ran the set but with all the convincing I tried to do, I still couldn't get Margaret to move. She was the type of bitch who liked being in the mix, so moving off the set was not an option to her. I still came to her house, but I never drove. I always took a cab.

Everywhere I laid my head, and all my cars were now off the radar. Donnie was running the set and I did nothing more than pick up and drop off money. Lou was handling more drug deliveries, and I was almost totally removed from the drug game like D.J. The one thing I still did was re-up; I mean after all who else could I send to get 5-10 kilos of cocaine without worrying. Jasmine and I had a good relationship, even though we weren't together. I helped take care of my son, and I still hit it from time to time. Everything was gravy, I had shook the state troopers and lived to see another day.

The new rap group Onyx came to Mahorn's nightclub to perform in June of '93. Since it was a couple of days before my 20th birthday, I decided to go. Half the crowd had baldheads, imitating the group. The songs they performed, Throw Ya Guns in the Air, Slam, and Bacdafucup, were definitely riot starting songs. And although we anticipated something popping off, the show was a peaceful success. I felt funny being at the club without Manny, who was doing a 364 in the county jail for gun possession. Everybody from the hood was there. Even Star and some of her friends showed up. Right before I left the club, I ran into Keisha. The last time I saw Keisha was at the hospital when her sister died. That was an inappropriate time to ask for her number, but tonight was fate.

"How you doing Simon", Keisha said in a slurred voice.

"I'm good. Long time no see. How you been", I answered.

"I've been okay", she said sipping on a vodka and cranberry.

"So, you coming with me tonight?" I asked.

"Coming with you where?"

"My house, your house, Marriot? You know, wherever", I answered.

"Hold on, let me get my coat and tell my girl", she responded. For a second, I thought about the last time I fucked Keisha, how she was bleeding all over the place. How I called her a nasty bitch and kicked her out. But hey, if she didn't bring it up, then why should I?

The next morning I woke up in my apartment with Keisha lying next to me. We were both drunk the night before, and after getting to my house we both passed out in the bed without fucking. When Keisha woke up about 10 minutes after me she went crazy.

"Oh my God! Where am I at? Oh shit, no! No! Did we fuck last night", she asked dead serious.

"Nah, why you bugging", I responded.

"Because I'm not suppose to be here. Jasmine's my friend, I know I did her wrong before, but she helped me through a rough time with my sister and she didn't have to". Not after what I did to her", she continued. "I gotta get dressed, I got to get outta here", she said as she franticly put on her clothes.

"So, you mean you came here, spent the night, and now I'm not gettin' no pussy? No wake up head? No nothin'?" I asked.

She just gave me a, "Nigga, please!" look and kept getting dressed.

After she was fully dressed, we walked out the crib, not noticing the car that had been parked down the street from my house the whole night. The car started and sped up towards us.

(Tire screeching sound) It wasn't the cops it was Jasmine. She hopped out of the car with tears in her eyes and my son fast asleep in the back seat.

"Her! It had to be her", she said crying. I was speechless. Keisha tried to explain, but Jasmine cut her off with a right hook and a left one, Keisha, who was bigger than Jasmine went to the ground. After that, Jasmine demolished her, punching and kicking her in the face, all while yelling, "This is how you pay me back bitch!" In no time, the police were there. After taking everybody's information they let Jasmine go and gave Keisha a ride to the speed line. The cops then laughed at me and told me, "You better learn how to control your bitches", before leaving. Even though I wasn't with Jasmine, I knew I had just disrespected her and I felt terrible about it.

By the end of the summer, in my mind I shook the State Boys, and I was free to go about my business. Jasmine and I had somewhat repaired our relationship and were back on speaking terms. Lil Larry had accepted a plea of 4 with a 2 and gave up no names. As far as the court was concerned, 33rd Street was his drug operation. My life was back on track and I planned to do it real big this time.

16

Pussy Kills

I stood on the side of the Cherry Hill Women's Center nervously smoking a Black & Mild. The protesters stood in the front, holding signs that said "Life starts at conception". Margaret was inside crying, but she knew what had to be done. She was already 3 months pregnant and it took me 2 months and $25,000 to convince her to get rid of the baby. Margaret probably didn't even want a baby, but she was a great actor. To make sure she actually got the abortion I had to go with her. The fucked up thing about the situation was, it might not even have been my baby, but I certainly couldn't take the chance of finding out. She came outside an hour later walking slow with the face of a killer. She got in the car and slammed the door and began crying.

I thought to myself, "This bitch is good", as I drove down Kings Highway toward Route 70.

"You alright", I asked.

"I just killed my baby! No, I'm not alright", she fired back. I said nothing. When we got to her house, she walked in and went to her room and laid down. She was taking this acting job to a new level. Maybe she really was upset; I mean even whores have feelings, right? At any rate, my problems were over. Or, so I thought.

Even though Margaret was a known hood rat, there were plenty of nigga's jealous of my position. Since I didn't hang in the streets that much, I missed a lot of block talk. The word was, that might have been Art's baby, and he wasn't happy that I forced her to get an abortion. The thing was, I wouldn't have cared if she had a baby by Art, but there was a 50% chance the baby was mine, and I wasn't willing to gamble with those odds. Art on the other hand, was wide open and definitely wanted me out of the way. Nigga's getting killed over pussy was nothing new, and Art loved this bitch, so I decided to let him have her. The abortion was over and I was going to be out of Margaret's life for good.

Meanwhile, things on 33rd had returned to normal. Money was flowing, crack heads were coming in abundance and stick up kids were plotting. About 2 weeks before Thanksgiving, 2 nigga's came to rob the set. They pulled up in a black Buick and a passenger hopped out of the car and acted like he was copping. He told Donnie he wanted a bundle. When Mousey, our runner was summoned, the passenger pulled a gun. He took the bundle Donnie had, and a couple of dollars from Mousey. It would have been a smooth robbery, but he was greedy. He tried to walk Mousy to the stash. As he walked with his gun to Mousey's side, shots went off. It was Lou coming from the opposite side of the building.

Lou not only shot the passenger, but also started letting off at the car, where the driver was still waiting. The passenger made it back to the car and the black Buick skated off. The police flew from 34th Street and began pursuing the Buick. In all the commotion, Mousey was hit once in the leg and Lou was able to get out of the area. By 6 'o'clock, the shooting was on the news. The chase lasted over 20 minutes, from Camden to Egg Harbor Twp. It finally ended when the Buick spun out of control, and hit a telephone pole. The two passengers fled on foot, leaving a third passenger in the car. When police got to the car they found the backseat passenger, a 15 month-old baby, unharmed. The cops also found two loaded nine millimeters under the passenger seat. The passenger was caught after a brief foot chase, and the baby turned out to be his son. The car had 3 bullet holes in it, and police said they were also looking for the shooter from 33rd Street. The driver was found at Absegami Veterinary Hospital just outside of Atlantic City, with a bullet in the shoulder.

The so-called investigation into the shooting was all media hype. As far as police were concerned, they had the criminals and the child was unharmed so the case was closed. The very next day, we were back open and it was business as usual. Juggling three chicks was crazy. There was the one that loved me, the one I loved, and the one I loved to fuck. Dana, the one that loved me, turned out to be smarter than I thought. She took the money I gave her an opened a Multi-cultural Hair Salon on Westfield Avenue in Pennsauken. There were Dominican chicks giving doobies, African chicks braiding and even a gay white dude who dude who had a fake French sounding accent. It had been 5 months since I gave her that money and in that time she had made a real come up. She was happier than I ever saw her before. She called me less and less, and I began to feel her gradually pull away from me. A couple of days before Thanksgiving, I decided to drop in on her in the shop, *International Beauty*. I parked on a side street and knocked on the back door, which lead directly to her office.

"What's up, stranger? Long time, no see", I said, as she opened the door and welcomed me in.

"Yea, you know I've been real busy lately, running the shop and everything."

"But, I'm actually glad you came by, because I need to talk to you", she continued. "I'm moving out the apartment. You've been paying my rent for years and you got me the shop and now it's time I stand on my own two. I'm also going to start making monthly payments to you, to repay this loan".

"Loan, I never said nothing 'bout no loan. That's a gift, but this sounds like a break-up speech", I replied.

"Break-up? How can I break up with somebody else's man?"

"Who? I'm single," I answered. Yea, we'll Jasmine came in here yesterday to get her hair done and she was talking about how your mom and Uncle Marc are coming from California to your house for Thanksgiving Dinner."

"She wants to look good because both of your families will be there".

"Do you know how that made me feel, hearing that?" she asked.

"We've had a fucking relationship for three years now, we both know it's not going anywhere", she said with tears in her eyes.

"You're right. You deserve better I wish you the best", I said whipping her tears. "You don't have to move out the apartment though, you can just pay your own rent", I said bringing a smile to her face.

"No, now that part had more to do with me getting out of Camden. I'm trying to get a condo in Palmyra. I just bought a Camry. So, I'm good"; she said trying to convince herself, as well as me.

"Business, condo and a car with no kids. Your stock is high. Somebody gone snatch you up. A nice professional nigga. You gone have to stop smoking weed though, them professional nigga's don't play that", I said as we both laughed.

"If you need anything I'm always here", I said as we hugged.

"Go home to your girl. She loves you. Be good to her", she replied as I walked out the back door.

The next couple of days leading to Thanksgiving, I stayed at the new condo in Mount Laurel with Jasmine and my son. The time was great, and I realized how much I missed my family. On Thanksgiving, we went to the annual game between Woodrow Wilson High School in East Camden and Camden High in Parkside. After the game, we had dinner with at least 20 friends and family members. It was good to see my mom. The last time I saw her was around the time my son was born. Pop Pop and Abuela were there with Jasmine's mom and sister. Even Star and Ace came. Everybody stayed over late and we watched the Miami Dolphins beat the Cowboys 16-14. After everybody left, I stayed home with Jasmine, instead of going out to the bar like I usually did on holidays. The next morning on Black Friday we got up early and went to New York to do our Christmas shopping. Toys R Us on 34th Street was the biggest toy store I had ever saw and we were overwhelmed with the amount of toys they had available. We stayed in the city for a few hours and spent almost $7,000 on toys and clothes for our son. Afterwards we had lunch at Tad's steaks before coming back to Jersey.

Once the holiday weekend was over I went back to work. Ace was back in the loop and told me he wanted to go uptown to holler at Sheppy. I knew this was risky, but Ace's thinking was Jude and Rim were both dead so we should be able to move on and continue business. After talking the idea over with D.J., we decided to send Lou and Jose Martinez with Ace to Sheppy's restaurant to talk about the possibility of us doing business again. The meeting turned out to be a success. Sheppy said he knew Jude was an asshole and even advised Rim not to bring him to Camden. He never held any ill will towards us and was happy to renew our relationship. Ace told me the price would be $16,000. He said neither Lou nor Jose knew this information. I could have told D.J. the number was $17,000 but I kept it real with him. The first run was to take place in two days and would be a million dollar deal. 63 Kilo's would cost me, Ace and D.J $336,000 cash apiece, no consignment. D.J. wanted to send Lou and Jose again with Ace to pick up the coke. I wasn't really comfortable with Jose as a transporter. He was a muscle dude that sold steroids to people at the gym but he was no street dude. Cocaine was a long way from steroids and I felt Jose was out of his league. D.J. had as much to loose as me so I trusted his judgment and went along with the plan.

Ace came back in the Lincoln we always rented from Luis Noel with two chicks and 63 bricks. Lou and Jose arrived a couple minutes later in a rented Toyota Camry. We met at *FastWash* the car detail spot I co-owned with D.J. As we pulled out the duffel bags Ace said in amazement

"You ever think about this in terms of grams, I mean a lot of nigga's our age are buying 28, or maybe only 14 grams, this is 63,000 grams my nigga, 63,000!" "Yea, that is crazy now that you say that shit", I replied.

"Where you putting all this shit, I know you aint taking it home", Ace asked.

"Nah, I'll probably take some to Cramer Hill, I still got the keys to Dana's old apartment and the rent is paid for the year." As D.J. walked inside the car wash section where we gathered to unload the Lincoln he had a devilish grin on his face.

"How much we selling ounces for", Ace asked.

"Ounces, ounces Flaco gets 100 keys and he sells all that shit hand to hand that's why he's fucking rich", D.J. answered.

"What we waiting for let's start cooking and bagging this shit, all of it." D.J. continued "I mean my 21 I want all 21 of mine cooked and bagged up as nickels tell those bitches that were driving to get started Gato you cook I want 300 extra on every key", D.J. then turned and walked out. In my head I thought

"Damn I should have charged him $17,000, talking to me and Ace like he's crazy" Ace drove the girls and some of the coke to the stash house on 34th street. As I cooked up I had the girls bag up some powder. I figured now was as good a time as ever to open Building B back up with a powder flow. We

stayed there for almost seven hours cooking and bagging almost 10 bricks between 8 people. After finishing, Ace and I went to Corrine's Place for some Turkey Wings and Beef Ribs. We decided to hang out a while and went to Crystals a bar in South Camden. While there, Ace got into a little argument with some nigga, over some dumb shit. After that we left realizing it was getting late and we were out of pocket with no strap.

The new coke was raw, and in no time 33rd Street was back to looking like an outdoor flea market with lines stretching at least a block. The powder flow really took off like never before. We were the second busiest powder cocaine block in Camden behind the alley. After seeing how the spot took off, I decided to bring the weed back to Building A which would bring in an additional $30,000 - $40,000 a week. It also added to the traffic especially on the weekends. All our customers were familiar with our trappers. They were instructed never to try and cop something if they didn't recognize any of the people on the set. This came in handy on December 2, when police did another reverse sting. This time they only arrested 13 people; one of them was our lookout that was charged with obstruction for letting customers know that the dudes on the set were cops. The cops were growing restless; they could never arrest anybody high enough to shut down the whole operation. They decided to try a new tactic. They would park on 35th and Westfield and on Dudley and Westfield. Through surveillance, they would be notified of cars coming from Woodrow Wilson Apartments on 33rd street. They then selectively pulled the cars over. If you were white you were getting pulled over period. If you looked like you weren't from

Camden, you were getting pulled over. Once pulled over the people usually had their rights violated and were searched or harassed. Once they found drugs they would try and make you admit you got them from 33rd. This strategy was working and might have threatened our business if it hadn't had been for Ryan Crawford. Ryan was a white boy from Cherry Hill who was a faithful customer and the son of a federal judge. After being harassed, threatened and searched, the police found nothing and Ryan told his dad. After this incident the police stopped their procedure. Ryan never stopped coming to cop and actual told one of our trappers about what happened. Ryan said he always put his weed in his ass before pulling off from the spot. He said they were asking why he had come from those apartments and where were the drugs. Once he was let go he called his dad, who immediately called to find out who was in charge of the operation. By the morning the harassment stopped.

What Ryan Crawford did was good and bad for us. It helped protect our customers, which was good for business. The bad part was State and local authorities now wanted us more than ever. The investigation directly into me, which had been going on since Lil' Larry was bailed out, was also being intensified. Had the Feds conducted the investigation into me, I would have been in custody on money laundering charges. The state and Camden police were looking to take me down with drugs period. I knew the set was hot, but I didn't believe I was personally under surveillance, so I continued to sell drugs.

The Thanksgiving and Christmas holidays seem to blend together, and for hustlers it's a great time of year. The A

Building stayed flooded with college kids and high schoolers buying weed. The powder flow also increased as rich white guys wanted to party between Thanksgiving and New Years more than other times of year. Crack on the other hand made the holidays the most dangerous time of the year in the city. Robberies occurred in December at least twice as often as other months. A man was shot on Westfield Ave. while trying to catch the bus to the Cherry Hill Mall. After being shot in the stomach he was robbed of $400. This happening on 34th and Federal brought more heat to the already hot block. Home Invasions and break-in's were also a part of Christmas in the city. I spent a lot of time in the crib during December. I wasn't hiding just spending time with Jasmine and my son. We made cookies, decorated the tree and all the things my grandparents did with me when I was a kid.

On Christmas Eve, Ace and I went out again, this time we went to Flaco's bar Oasis right in East Camden. When we got there, I noticed the same nigga Ace was arguing with in Crystals. We decided to leave the bar and wait in our car for the nigga to leave. We sat in the car for almost 2 hours before the nigga left out with one other person. We waited for them to get in the car before pulling on the side of them. Ace rolled down his window and fired at least six or seven shots directly in the car. We drove off slow as if nothing happened. We drove to my grandparents' house where I stashed the gun, before dropping Ace off and going home. When I got there Lil' Simon and Jasmine were asleep on the living room couch. I brought Jasmine's gifts from the car and then laid down next to my family and waited for Santa Clause.

Lil' Simon woke us up right around six o'clock in the morning. He was excited to see all the gifts under the tree. We opened his gifts and took pictures for our family. Jasmine opened her gift and loved it. It was a diamond studded tennis bracelet and matching necklace. The necklace had a charm with a picture of me, Jasmine and Lil' Simon. Jasmine was almost in tears she loved the gift. I also was surprised to find a gold bracelet and Rolex with sapphire stones under the tree for me. After opening all our gifts Lil' Simon and Jasmine went in the kitchen to eat breakfast. I went out front and brought in the newspaper. As I read through the paper I came to the city crime report section. The headline of one story read "*2 men fight for their lives after being shot early Christmas morning*". I started to call Ace, but I didn't it was Christmas day and I didn't want my street life to disrupt my family. I stayed in the house watching movies for the rest of the day before going to Jasmine's mom's house for diner.

The next night I was in the Projects getting drunk with Manny, who had just come home. We rode around a while and ended up at a bar on 34th and Federal, across the street from Woodrow Wilson Apartments. After drinking about 6 shots I noticed Margaret come in with another chic. I didn't know the girl Margaret was with but she jumped right on Manny's dick. I played the cut while Manny laughed and bought drinks for the two. After half hour Many came to me and said "What's up cousin they trying to fuck, you going to take one for the team?" Even though I said I wasn't going to fuck Margaret any more she was looking extra good. I was drunk as hell so I went along with the idea, which was my first mistake. My second mistake was going to Margaret's crib instead of the motel. The four of us sat in Margaret's house smoking wet. It was the first time I ever tried it and, they only convinced me because I was drunk. That ended up being my third mistake. After two blunts of wocky, Margaret and I went in her room and had the great sex we normally do. This time I made sure I wore a condom, so I woke up with no regrets. As I laid in the bed butt naked Margaret, who was also naked, sat on my lap. Her pussy was still wet and my dick was rubbing against it. I knew I didn't have any more condoms and I knew what was going to happen next. And that ended up being my fourth mistake.

"Get up I'm 'bout to cum", I said to her.

"You don't want me to get up nigga, you like cumming in this pussy, don't you", she answered. I could have definitely pushed her off, but it did feel good. Afterwards, I knew I had made another big mistake.

"Don't worry I'm back on the pill nigga"; she said smiling before getting up and walking around the room naked.

I got up and got dressed and went in the living room where Manny was waiting. "You ready", he asked.

"Yea, we can be out", I answered.

"So when you coming back", Margaret asked.

"I'll be back", I said without giving specifics. As Manny and I left, I noticed Gary, who was Art's brother. I knew he would hear about me being there and it could be a problem. But fuck it; no nigga was going to stop me from doing what I wanted. Manny and I decided to go to a breakfast spot on Haddon Ave in Parkside. While we were there Dana walked in with another nigga. It was kind of awkward seeing her with

212

another man for the first time. He was a clean-cut dude who didn't look broke, but he definitely wasn't a hustler. They both spoke to Manny and I, but in a way that a stranger would speak to you, just being polite. I tried not to look, but I couldn't keep my eyes off the pair. They ordered their food to go and left out. Dana looked happier than I had ever seen her. And no matter how much it hurt to see her with somebody else, I was happy that she was happy.

1993 ended the same way it started with a bang. 3 murders in 4 days from December 26th to the 30th, all with no suspects or clues. As far as my drama with Art, it got worse since I had started fucking Margaret again. We had an argument that lead to a fistfight, and me pounding him out. Although rare, fair fights did still happen in the hood. This one was right in front of Building A and everybody was there. I thought the ass whopping would put a stop to the bullshit, but I still had to be careful. Art loved Margaret and pussy kills.

17

Nine Lives

By spring of 1994 I was having my best run in the streets. Pedro had matched Sheppy's price so we were now getting coke for $16,000 right in Camden. It came 100 kilo's at a time, 50 for us and 50 for the alley. Every time we went to meet Pedro, I got nervous thinking about how I had slept with his wife Carmen, although the secret never surfaced. The police had calmed down in East Camden, and were again focusing on North, because some of Kalic's soldiers had made bail and were being linked to a triple murder in Cramer Hill. Another one of his goons even broke out of the county jail, although he was caught a few hours later in Philly. All that was good news for me, it meant things were quiet on the home front. On 33rd, we were back to three eight-hour shifts and on a good day we were bringing in at least $25,000 a shift. The alley was doing even more than that. Ace was again getting money and running wreck lace. He was never around and really did nothing but invest and collect.

In Late May 5 federal agents, 5 state troopers, 5 sheriffs, and 5 local police were recruited to form two special units. One would attempt to solve unsolved murders in the city, they were nicknamed the "MS", which stood for Murder Squad. The other group would focus on non-fatal shootings in the city and they were dubbed "SS", which stood for Shooting Squad. The agency's headquarters was a trailer right on 7th and State Street. The corner, used to be one of the busiest heroin spots in North Camden. Through Mayor Jorge Lopez, D.J. learned one of the cases the two squads received was a double shooting that occurred in the parking lot of Flaco's nightclub. The case became of special interest because both the "Shooting Squad", and the "Murder Squad", got the file since one victim recovered and one was fatally wounded. The shooting took place on Christmas Eve, but neither D.J. nor Flaco had any knowledge of the shooting. Lucky for us Jorge, said there were no witnesses and the dude that was still living had no clue who shot him and why he was shot. We were in the clear, and we never told D.J. or anybody else about what happened, not even Manny.

Art was still around but he hadn't been a problem except for the occasional ice grill. I was back to fucking Margaret full time and she was on my dick harder than ever. She cut the rest off her nigga's off even her moneyman. This turned out to be a bad thing for me, as she now became a second girlfriend. Other than Jasmine she would flip at the sight of me talking to another female. It was actually harder handling Margaret than Jasmine because Margaret was a hood chic. She was always on the scene and heard all the gossip in the hood. If I fucked a new chic she would hear about it and immediately confront me, anywhere. Once I was in the Spanish restaurant on 36th Street with Didi, when Margaret walked in. She started throwing napkin holders at me and Didi before finally attacking her. Didi was from the hood, but she wasn't a hood chic. She was mild mannered and usually was never seen outside hanging out. Since middle school, I had only seen her a handful of times mostly in traffic or coming in and out her house. She was hesitant to fuck with me because as she said "I had too many bitches!" Getting her ass kicked in the Spanish store certainly wasn't going to help my cause. But Didi was beautiful and I needed her on my team at any cost.

The price turned out to be a five-day, four-night getaway in Jamaica. I showed up to Didi's door a week after the fight with the tickets in hand. She was mad, but there was no way she was turning down this trip. I told Jasmine I was going to the D.R on business and she believed me, so everything was set. I took Didi to Philly to go shopping and she spent $3,500. At the time I still hadn't had sex with her and I was waiting to see what she was working with. Didi was half black and half Vietnamese with a Spanish name. She was short about 5'1 with hair to the middle of her back. She was one of those chicks that wasn't outright thick, but was thick for her size. She had olive skin and talked with a slight oriental accent. The night before we left we stayed at the airport Marriot. She allowed me to strip her butt naked and eat the pussy like a four course meal. After cumming in my face numerous times, she told me I would have to wait till we got out of the country to get some pussy. I thought she was playing, but she turned and went to sleep and I was forced to go in the bathroom and beat my dick, which had been hard for over an hour.

216

The next morning I woke up, kind of salty about not getting any pussy the night before. We had an early flight and neither of us said much while waiting in the airport.

"What you mad you aint get no pussy last night", she asked with a smile. Didi was laughing, but I was dead serious and she was real close to being left in Philly, although she didn't know it. We got on the plane and I laid back to go to sleep.

"Do you mind if I lay on your lap", she asked in a sweet voice. "Go head", I answered still mad about not getting no pussy. About 20 minutes went by and I had dozed off, when I felt a tuck on my pants. I was awakened to the great feeling of a wet mouth. With a cover over her head Didi went for broke and sucked my dick, even better than Margaret did. She finished and never lifted her head from under the blanket. I leaned back and smiled this was going to be a good trip after all.

"We are just approaching International waters and are estimated to land in Montego Bay Jamaica in approximately 20 minutes", the pilot said on the loud speaker waking me up from my power nap. Didi was looking at me with a devilish grin and asked me

"Do you know what the mile high club is?"

"Nah, what's that some frequent flyer shit", I asked really naive to the saying. "No silly", Didi said laughing. "Remember I said you can't get no pussy till we get out the country", she asked.

"Yea".

"Well we're in international waters", Didi said sucking her pointer finger seductively, while walking to the bathroom. Without hesitation I jumped up and followed her in the bathroom. When I walked in she was butt naked and asked me "How do you want it"!

"From the back", I answered. She turned and I put it in, unlike when I fucked Margaret I wasn't worried about hitting it raw, shit a baby with Didi wouldn't be so bad anyway. I mean overall Jasmine might of had her beat because of the body, but Didi had the face of a supermodel. I nutted in about 3 minutes and blamed it on the high altitude. Didi just laughed

"The altitude right, don't worry will get it right in Jamaica even if it takes four days of trying", she answered.

The majority of the vacation was spent fucking. Not just in the room either, Didi was a risk taker. She wanted to fuck on the balcony so everybody could see. She was a sex addict; I couldn't understand how she held out that first night at the Marriot. It didn't even matter now; I had her right where I wanted her.

The day before we left, we had a long talk on the bed while smoking a blunt.

"So when you going to break up with your girl." she asked calmly like we had already discussed the matter.

"What, what the fuck you talkin' 'bout? Margaret? That aint my girl." I answered.

"I know I aint talking about that bitch, I mean Jasmine". I sat for a second looking puzzled without answering.

"Listen", she said while looking at herself naked in the mirror, "Do you see me? I'm no side bitch; you got two choices when we get home."

"Leave your girl, or we just had a great time in Jamaica, and we will leave it here". I waited for her to say she was just playing but she looked serious.

"So let me get this straight, if I don't leave my girl I can't get no more pussy", I asked?

"No, I said if you don't leave your girl we will leave it here. That means whenever you want some pussy, you got to bring me to Jamaica!"

"So, I gotta spend money to hit it?"

"It's not the money, it's the attention". I'm number one in Jamaica, so it's all-good. The minute I become number two, I'm done". I won't be one of those bitches who spend the prime years of her life being somebody's secret. I'm too fly for that." The fucked up part was, she was right.

When we landed in Philly we got our bags and I got her a cab. "Alright I'm gonna call you later", I said.

"Only if your single or you got some plane tickets", she said while closing her door without as much as a smile.

My Jeep was parked at the airport, so I drove to Mt. Laurel to spend time with my family. On the way there, I had bought a couple of souvenirs from the Dominican shop in Cramer Hill. I could give them to Jasmine and tell her I got them on my trip. I always covered my tracks. Jasmine was so happy to see me. My son was with her mom and she was home, busy planning my 21st birthday. As she told me the details, I realized what I had, a beautiful 23 year-old college graduate who had become the best mother, girlfriend and schoolteacher in the world. There was no way I was going to leave her, not even for Didi.

We had been together on and off for 7 years now and we knew each other inside out.

My birthday fell on a Tuesday, so Jasmine decided to have the party on that Friday June 18th. The party was going to be at Club Escape in South Camden. D.J. Juice from Trenton was doing the music and the host was Roz from Urban Expressions, a local video show. There was also going to be professional dancers and a live performance by Biggie Smalls. The event was set to go down in a week and I couldn't wait.

The next day Manny, Ace and I went to Newark to get outfits for the party. We shopped at Universal's and Dr. Jay's on Market Street and ate at Blimpie's inside the train station. Every car that rode by was playing Redman's new song Rockafella. We decided to try and find some weed on 21st Street because we heard Redman mention it on a song. When we got there sure enough they had weed so we grabbed a few bags and then jumped back on the parkway and headed home. We listened to a best of Jersey tape we bought in Newark. It had everything from Redman and Naughty to YZ and Poor Righteous Teachers on it. We smoked about 3 blunts on the hour and 20 minute ride back to the hood.

When we got there the sirens and ambulances lit up the street. A 17-year old boy broke in his girlfriend's apartment and threatened her with a gun. When he left, she herd two shots and called the police. When the police arrived the 17 year-old boy was laying in a pool of blood with two shots to his back. When they uncovered the body it was Jerome, one of the twins I had tried to recruit a few years back. He had since found his way into the streets and now had become another unsolved murder in Camden. After hearing the scoop, we went to McGuire and sat across from the alley we grew up playing in.

"Remember that was just a alley where we smoked cigarettes", I said to Ace with a smile. "Hell Yea, matter fact that's our shit, Manny tell Flaco we want in.", Ace said with a laugh. I remember when I first moved to East Camden and you introduced me to Flaco and D.J. Shit, that's probably the most important moment of my life".

"That shit definitely changed my life for the better", Manny said hitting the blunt. "Nah, how 'bout how we had the weed spot right over there. That was the shit. That's how you met Jasmine", Ace continued. "There are a lot of memories in these projects".

"Yea, a lot of ghosts too", I said out loud. In my head I was thinking of all the bad times, about Butter, Rim and even T-Money. Then I thought about Roberto Saca and all the fallen kingpins. My train of thought was interrupted by the blunt being passed back around.

"Yea, the good old days", I said half sarcastically.

The night of the party, I got dressed at home with Jasmine. She was wearing a fitted sweat suit and some white sneakers. She had on a tight shirt underneath and left her jacket open so she could show her hearing bone chain. She had big titties so the chain just rested on them. The pants fit so well that her ass looked even bigger than usual. Her hair was pulled back tight in a long ponytail. I was wearing a pair of Nautica jeans and a Nautica three button shirt with some white classics. I had on a pair of shades, and the gold and sapphire bracelet and Rolex Jasmine had bought me for Christmas. We rode in a stretch limo and cruised the city, drinking and smoking before arriving at the club around 11:20.

Biggie was due to perform around midnight so I planned to hit the bar and get some more drinks. When we walked in it was all eyes on us. There were definitely plenty of bitches mad I came with Jasmine. The club was packed. A couple of players from the Sixers and Eagles were there along with the ghetto celebrities. Blockz was there with all his Parkside nigga's and Flaco, D.J., Pedro, Raoul Quivoures and all the other big boys from the city were there. Everybody in the club was a baller, or with one. In a club full of millionaire's I made sure I kept Jasmine right by my side. Dana and Carmen were both there but I didn't give anybody airplay when Jasmine was around. By 11:45, I was fucked up and ready to hear Biggie, like the rest off the club. It started to get a little rowdy and in the mix of all the commotion two nigga's from Centerville snatched the chain off a Sixers rookie. The player had an entourage and a fight broke out. Police were called to clear the brawl. After restoring order the cops discovered that the fire permit was expired and shut down the spot. Just as police were evacuating the building Biggie and his team were pulling up in a fleet of limousines. The driver who picked Biggie up also worked for the club. He took Big to the club owner's house to get paid. When Big got to the house in Pollack, he was told that the owner wasn't there, so he left. The angry club goers that followed him didn't. Instead they drug the man that answered the door out of the house and punch, kicked and robbed him. So much for my party.

Jasmine and I decided to ride in the limo to Atlantic City. We stayed in the Taj Mahal and lost every dollar we took. Jasmine was so drunk that she threw up on me while sucking my dick in the back of the limo. I just whipped it off and hit it from the back we were both piss drunk still fucking when the driver got to the crib. He must have heard us because he sat out front of our house for 20 minutes while we finished fucking. When we were done he escorted us out the car to our door.

"Come back tomorrow for a tip. We lost all my money in A.C", I slurred before slamming the door in his face.

When I woke up, it was almost 5 o'clock the next evening. Jasmine had gone to Trenton for her sister's graduation party. So, I got dressed and went to the hood. My party was the talk of the town. All the chicks were talking about how many ballers were there. Margaret was clearly mad when I saw her come out of her apartment. "I heard you and your bitch, I mean girl, had a good old time last night." she said in an angry voice. "Well happy belated birthday, I guess I get the day after".

"Here you go with your shit. You know that's my girl. You know the situation. If you can't handle that let me know", I said feeling mad about how she always talked about Jasmine.

"Don't talk like that Gato, you know I play my position, but it hurts sometimes, I do have feelings."

"I know, well lets get something to eat." I answered.

"Okay, do you got any weed?" She asked.

"Nah, we can run out to Parkside and get some." We drove together in my Bemmer to Parkside. We got some soul food from Corrine's and then got our weed and came back to 33rd Street. When we got there I could feel something in the air. I didn't know what it was, but I felt kind of funny. I grabbed the nine that I kept in my stash spot and took the food in the crib. We ate and smoked a couple of blunts and walked to the liquor store up the block before coming back to her place. We started drinking and smoked a couple of more blunts and next thing you know it was midnight and we were both fucked up.

We went to the bedroom and she sucked the life outta me. I tried to hit it by my dick, wouldn't get back hard so I did the next best thing. "Take the bullets out that gun and fuck me with it!" she screamed as she came from me eating the pussy. I wasn't sure what to think, but I did it anyway. I uncocked my gun and took the clip out, then started putting the barrel up her pussy. The more she moaned the harder I pushed the gun in her. After 3 minutes she came again, this time all on the barrel of my Ruger. By now my dick was rock hard and I told her to turn over and let me put my gun in from the back. She laughed before turning around and putting her face in the pillow and her ass in the air. We started that way and ended with her on the floor, leaning over the foot of the bed. I was standing up and pounding that pussy. I started with a condom, but by round 2 I was hitting it raw, and not even thinking of pulling out. That damn Hennessey! I'm not sure how we stopped; we just both kind of passed out butt naked and drunk.

Around1:00 a.m. there was a thud and then I heard more noise; two men had kicked in the door to the apartment. As I scrambled to find the clip to the gun, Margaret tried to get out the window. The two men appeared in the bedroom and opened fire. I was hit in the arm and the chest and Margaret was hit in the back. She was hit with a .22 and me with a .45. The shooters never ransacked the crib or nothing, just kicked in the door and started shooting. After they left, Margaret and I staggered out of the apartment and made it up 33rd to Westfield Avenue. A man riding by stopped and took us to Cooper Hospital. I lost a lot of blood and was seriously injured. I was placed in critical condition and Margaret was listed as fair. Some witness said a man in all black and a man in a UNLV jacket ran through Dudley Park after the shooting. I was in surgery for 7 hours and then sedated for another 2 days. When I woke up I heard more bad news. Police had searched the apartment and found my 9. I was being held on gun charges.

When I tried calling home to tell Jasmine, she already knew. In fact she had been to the hospital and they asked her was she a friend of Margaret's also. They also told her, the details about us being naked when we were brought in. She wished me well in my recovery, but said our relationship was over. I was too weak to try and argue, so I temporarily accepted her decision. Later that day a state investigator came in smiling.

"It should only be a matter of time before we have the shooters in custody, because we have them running away on camera. We got a lot of things on camera, Gato", he said as he smiled even more than before. "That's why it's my pleasure to place you under arrest on the charges of being the leader of a narcotics trafficking network, also known as the New Jersey Kingpin statute. You've been running a million dollar set on 33rd Street; well, your run is over my friend. It took a long time. We've been on you since '93, but it's all over now", he said with a grin.

I was stunned, I thought he was there to ask questions about the shootings or the gun they found, and instead he dropped a bomb.

18

Pick 12

It had been a month since I got shot and I had recently been transferred to Camden County Jail. The jail was packed. Nigga's from all parts of the city were they're waiting to be sentenced or bailed out. When I got there Donnie, who had just turned 18 and Lou, were already there. The state troopers had raided various cribs in Woodrow Wilson Apartments and found a tech, two nines and a .38 along with 4 kilo's of powder, a key and a half of crack, scales, money counters and empties. They even charged us for the baking soda. They raided my house in Mt. Laurel and confiscated my safe. They asked Jasmine if the house was hers and she said yes, but that the safe was mine. That was a smart move, because if the safe had drugs or guns in it she would've been charged. Instead she was allowed to keep the condo and they took the safe, which contained more than 2 million in cash. Besides that the house was clean.

My bail was revoked and Jasmine put a block on the phone so collect calls weren't accepted at my house. The first visit I got was from Margaret. She had fully recovered from her gunshot wound and told me word on the street was Art and his brother did it. I told her to go see D.J. and get me some money so I could get commissary. My lawyer was already paid for and I needed him to put in a motion for me to get a bail. After all, I did have proof of income through my company FastWash. Margaret told me she missed me and would wait for me no matter what. I didn't believe her, but it sounded good. Plus, neither one of us knew exactly how long that wait would be. Margaret came back to see me the next day, as she did every-day for the first couple of weeks I was there. She was having a hard time finding D.J. and Ace had not been seen in the hood since the night I was shot. It was bad enough being in this hellhole, but being here with no money was the pits. Donnie and Lou could easily trade off some info for a reduction in time and that was my greatest fear.

Kalic and some of his soldiers were still in the county wait-ing to go to trial, although a couple of them had agreed to cooperate and were taken to Burlington and Cumberland County Jails. Snitching was not an option for me. Authorities had no idea about D.J. at the time, so I was the top of the food chain. My first court appearance was a reality check. I knew I was in trouble but the 15 years they offered me had me stunned. "15 Fucking years for selling drugs I mines well have killed somebody." I said to my cellmate once I returned to the county. Only a few weeks later Donnie, Lou and I were all indicted. I still wasn't sure why Ace wasn't, but word was that he was working for DJ's construction company. After a couple of weeks went by Jasmine finally came to see me. She told me that she had gone to the gym and saw D.J. He told her that he didn't have shit for me and for me to tough it out. He told her that he had papers proving FastWash was 100% his business and he didn't owe me a dime. She said he gave her a $20 bill to give me. Jasmine blacked out on him but he paid no attention. That news was more shocking than the15 years the state had just offered me.

"How much money of yours did he have", Jasmine asked.

"Millions", I replied while shaking my head and leaving the visit early.

That night I thought about killing D.J. I wanted to murder the man myself. I would not get the chance for a long time. I wanted to see him face to face to see what his explanation would be. I mean I've known the man all my life. He was like a father figure and he fucked me. He fucked me good! The next couple of months I went through the bullshit motions and status conferences in court where nothing gets done. Finally in January of '95 my trial was put on the schedule for March 17th. I was ready to go and find out my fate. Two weeks before my trial was to begin, Ace was arrested on drug distribution charges. They waited for him to get back in the game and then they snagged him. His charges weren't as bad as mine, but he was added to my indictment as a co-defendant. This put another delay in my trial. I never saw Ace when he got to the county because unlike me, he got a bail. Donnie and Lou had also bailed out since our initial arrest and I was in jail by myself.

While waiting for a new date for my trial, I got the worst news ever. My Abuela had died. It was sudden and unexpected but Delilah Robinson was gone. I wasn't allowed to attend the funeral, so I had to view my grandmother for the last time, while in shackles. I couldn't be around anybody so I saw the body alone with two Correction officers by my side. It was the lowest point in my life. They allowed me 5 minutes with the woman that raised me. Then they sent me back to my 6 by 9 cell. I was a wreck. The day after the funeral, Sonny came to visit me. He told me he was selling the house and him and Uncle Ramos were moving to California. The news was shocking; he said there's no longer anything in Camden for him with Abuela dead and me in jail. At that moment, I knew it was me against the world.

My trial began in August of 1995. And after 6 days of testimony, evidence by the prosecution and a great argument by my lawyer I was found guilty. The word "guilty" echoed in my head after the judge said it. Everything got slow and it felt as though I was in a movie. As the bailiff led me out of the courtroom, I noticed Jasmine, Dana and Margaret all there in different parts of the courtroom. All of them were crying. My son wasn't there. I still hadn't seen him since I left the hospital. My sentencing date was set for October 1st. After I was convicted Donnie and Lou copped out to 12 years apiece. They would both be eligible for parole after 4 years in prison.

Meanwhile, back on the streets, the Organization was getting bigger than ever. Jose Martinez began transporting cocaine from a connect he had in Miami back to Camden. Muscleclo was back in the hood running the alley with Flaco. Manny was still doing him, and Blockz was still getting money and had the whole Parkside on smash. Ace was still home. He got tighter with D.J. and now was one of his closest associates.

The world as I knew it was upside down, but everybody else was still eating. Even Dana had opened her second beauty shop in the area and Jasmine got a teaching job at a prestigious High School in Cherry Hill. As for me, I was finished.

A week before I was sentenced, FBI agent Bobby Myers came to see me about possibly cooperating with a federal probe into D.J. He told me that DJ's run was coming to an end, and to save myself. The FBI is always fishing for shit, so I told him to kiss my ass. Apparently, Myers also approached Ace about snitching also, but I had no knowledge of their meeting. Ace was still on the streets at the time so he told D.J. about the agent. For some reason Ace thought that the offer would look too tempting to me and I probably would snitch. What none of us knew was that during one of his trips to Miami, Jose Martinez was busted with a couple of kilos and agreed to wear a wire. This is what started the investigation into D.J. The next week I was sentenced to 25 years in state prison, still standing tall.

It was almost a year later when I heard that Ace had copped out to 12 years, like Donnie and Lou. All of us were sent to different jails. Donnie went to Yardville and Lou was sent to South Woods. Ace was sent to Bordentown and, as for me, I went to a place called Trenton State Prison. It was the worst jail in New Jersey. The average inmate in Trenton had 20 years, and I was one of the youngest nigga's up there. I still hadn't told anybody about the FBI agent and I still didn't know that he had also contacted Ace. It was nearing summer and the prison felt like a concentration camp. You have to be constantly alert in here; I was locked up with New Jersey's worst criminals. The Iceman and the child molester that inspired Megan's Law, they were both here with me. And what did I do except provide a service? The good thing was that once my status went down, I could be transferred to another prison. Also, I had no back number so there was no mandatory amount of time I had to do, so I could come home in as soon as 10 years.

My cellmate Chucky was an older dude, around 50. He was in for murdering two heroin dealers during a bad drug deal in Newark. This was the last stop for him. Life with no parole meant he'd be dieing right here in this cell. He was always upbeat and had a positive spin for any negative situation you were facing. The first couple of months up state he really helped me out with getting adjusted and learning the rules of the prison. The prison had rules, but so did the prisoners. The prisoner's rules are the ones that I needed to be learning because they can get you killed.

I had learned to make my hut as comfortable as possible. Jasmine had sold all the cars in my name and gutted me for most of the money. With the couple of dollars I did get, I was able to buy a T.V. and a radio and they were my most valued possessions along with a picture of my son. From time to time she would bring my son to see me. Writing letters to him and Margaret and occasionally Dana were some of the best parts of my day. The others were watching Martin or listening to the old-school lunch hour. Songs from the late 80's always made me reminisce about the times when hustling was fun. It does start out fun, until it becomes a job. Once it becomes a job then it's a struggle and by then you're usually caught up. The struggle was going to have me spending the rest of my 20's and 30's and possibly some of my 40's in prison or on parole.

On March 9th, 1997 I woke up and turned on the news and saw the story about Big being killed in L.A. I thought back to how we had met that night in Camden and how I had smoked out with his crew in South Camden. The whole day I listened to Biggie on the radio and thought about how 2 of the greatest rappers of the era had just died so young. I liked some of the newer rappers but Nas, Snoop, Biggie and Tupac were definitely my favorites.

By June I had been in prison for 3 years, I had already been denied my final appeal and it was set in stone that I would be here for at least 7 more. I had made a couple of friends and even had a CO who lived in Camden and brought me a Post newspaper everyday. On the morning of June 3rd, the headline read "Camden Drug Kingpin Arrested".

Kevin "Blockz" Bright was arrested after police charged him with being a drug kingpin in Camden's Parkside neighborhood.

"You know him youngin", my celli asked.

"Yea, this is one of the nigga's...I mean people that use to run with me." Chucky was originally from North Carolina and he hated the word nigger, no matter who said it or how it was said, so I respected that.

"Not that guy that took your money?" he asked. "Nah, not him. That's D.J., but they must be getting close to him."

"If he's as smart as I think he is, then he already quit."

"You givin' that man too much respect after what he done did to you", Chucky said.

"I give credit where it's due, and he is smart. I was dumb for trusting him."

"No, you was dumb because you stopped selling weed and started selling that crack. I aint never seen nobody in here for selling weed." Chucky said laughing. "Aw, don't get mad now. Somebody with life can joke with you about 25. Shit, you don't even got a back number. To me that's short, I been down here since '77. I aint never even seen crack, except on T.V. and shit. I just know ever since about '87, '88, I've been seeing a lot of young black and Hispanic brothers coming down here for that shit with an asshole full of time. Your boy Blockz, he'll be done here in a couple of years. Shit, by then your status will have dropped and you'll probably be somewhere a little more comfortable."

Another New Year went by and it was now only 2 years from the millennium. It was a cold morning in late February when I got the news. Not from my lawyer but in the Post like everybody else.

"13 CHARGED AS LEADERS OF CAMDEN D.R.UG RING \ ONE OFFICIAL CALLED IT "THE BIGGEST D.R.UG TAKEDOWN IN OUR MEMORY." TWO D.R.UG CORNERS WERE THE TARGET.

During early morning raids yesterday in Camden and surrounding areas 10 of the 13 defendants charged with running a sophisticated drug operation were rounded up by federal agents. The defendants: Darren "D.J." Johnston 38, Samuel "Flaco" Torres 35, Manuel "Muscleclo" Vargas 31, Luis Noel 41, Raoul Quivoures 27, Enrique Cintron 42, Pedro Montoya 37, Carmen Montoya 30, Jose Martinez 30, and Manny Gonzales 27. Three other defendants were already in custody on

234

state drug charges they are Kevin "Blockz" Bailey 31, Simon "Gato" Gonzales 24, and Ace Young 25."

"Hey Chucky, what the fuck does this mean? Aint this double jeopardy or something?"

"How can they charge me with the same thing twice?" I asked naive to the ways of the federal government.

"They the Feds. They do what the fuck they want."

"The good thing is, they'll probably run your sentence concurrent so you probably won't get any extra time".

"The bad news is, if they give you a concurrent 25 year sentence, you have to do 85% of the time they give you, so that's about 17 years." I was sick all over. I couldn't believe this was happening again, now I had to play the waiting game again.

The wait didn't take half as long as I thought. Later that day, FBI agent Bobby Myers came to get me, along with two U.S. Marshals and an assistant federal prosecutor. They took me to a little building right on the border of Cramer Hill and Pennsauken. When I got inside, there were two big boards with pictures of all the defendants, our cars, girlfriends and homes. Bobby Myers was smiling. "I told you this day would come and it's finally here. Now before you tell me to kiss your ass again, I have a few things you need to listen to." He pressed play on a reel-to-reel looking recorder. I recognized the voice. It was Ace. "D.J. a agent asked me about you. I didn't tell him nothin' but I think we need to be worried about Gato. He'll rat on everybody. He'll even rat his own cousin out. Jasmine called me and said you owe Gato money and that he knows a lot about you. I think that they'll both snitch.

"You should recognize this second voice also", Myers said.

"I'll kill her and anybody else that snitches on me. That little guy Donnie, I'll kill him too. Then I'll bury Gato's money in the casket with Jasmine and his son if they betray me."

"Now listen we have 90 hours of taped conversations implicating D.J. Jose Martinez was arrested in 1996. He's been wearing a wire for the past two years gathering useful information. This is your one and only chance. I'll give you exactly 5 minutes to make up your mind, but the decision should be clear. Oh yea, I forgot to tell you, if you testify against D.J. you will be released from prison immediately, but these federal charges you're facing carry a possible life sentence." Myers said.

"So, what, I tell and ya'll drop the fed charges?" I asked.

"No you tell and we dismiss federal and state charges against you and you become a free man", Myers answered. What's to think about? He threatened to kill the mother of your son; he stole millions of dollars from you. I mean this isn't loyalty; it's stupidity." Myers continued.

"If you have all these conversations, why do you need me? I mean, what is it you want to know?" I asked.

"You would have to give a detailed description of your role in the organization, your interactions with D.J. and all the other defendants. Most of them will probably cop out and do the same thing you're doing anyway. If that happens we don't need you and the deal will be taken off the table, so it's now or never." Myers said frankly.

"If I say yes, what happens next", I asked?

236

"You'll be debriefed by this man. His name is Jonathan Fine. He's the U.S district court's assistant prosecutor. Then you'll be moved to another facility until the trial comes around. You take the stand, and explain to the jurors, the kind of money and violence that you and your co defendants were involved in. When you get off the stand you go home. That simple." Myers answered.

"Okay, I'll do it but you have to include Ace in the deal" I said without further hesitation. Great I'll let Jonathan ask you what he needs to know and then we'll take you to Salem County Jail. Your personal items will be there by the morning", Myers said before leaving me with Fine and the 2 U.S. Marshals. The debriefing took almost 5 hours. Fine asked questions about just about every drug dealer I knew. He asked about shooting and unsolved murders, all of which I had no answers for. He told me that Ace was going to be held in Atlantic County Jail. When we finished I was transported to Salem County Jail. When I got in the jail I was on the same wing as a Philadelphia mob boss. He had survived several assassination attempts. We had a lot in common and became acquainted. I would hold cigarettes and other contraband for him. Of course he didn't know why I was there, and there was no way I would tell him the truth.

19

The Trial

By December of '99 the trial of "The Organization" was set to begin. 7 people had copped out so only D.J., Flaco, Muscleclo, Raoul Quivoures, Luis Noel and Carmen Montoya were going to trial. I felt bad that Carmen was caught up in all this, but it was her husband's fault, not mine. When jury selection was set to begin, all the defendants except Muscleclo, and D.J. copped out and the trial was rescheduled. The jury was approved after a couple days of interviews. There were nine women and three men. I was not allowed to be in the courtroom while other defendants were testifying, so I made sure Margaret was there everyday. She would come see me on Saturdays and give me an update.

DJ's trial opened in February of 2000. In opening arguments DJ's lawyer Mark Ashley painted him as a legitimate Camden businessman who rose from poverty to wealth. He was active in the community and paid over a million dollars in taxes a year. Jealousy and testimony by admitted drug dealers were fueling the lies that the trial was based on.

The first witness called to the stand for the prosecution was Tameka White. She was a 27 year-old teller at Summit bank in Collingswood. She testified she never did anything illegal for Johnson, but on numerous occasions she switched big amounts of small bills to larger ones. She also testified he had 2 accounts that received weekly deposits of $11,000 each. She had been out to dinner with Johnson and received roses from him. She considered him an acquaintance. Mark Ashley decided not to cross-examine the teller. Tameka was a soft ball compared to the prosecution's second witness.

Samuel "Flaco" Torres took the stand with a slight smile.

Jonathan Fine: *Please state your name for the record*

Flaco: Samuel *"Flaco" Torres.*

Jonathan Fine: *Tell us how you got your start selling drugs?*

Flaco :*I started in like '84 working for Jorge Lopez.*

The courtroom fell silent. In open court, he had accused the mayor of being a former drug dealer.

Jonathan Fine: *Are you saying that...*

Flaco: *Yea, I'm saying the mayor of Camden is a former drug dealer. A cheap one at that.*

Jonathan Fine: *Care to elaborate?*

Flaco: *He didn't pay well, so I moved to East Camden.*

Jonathan Fine: *Is that where you met Mr. Johnson?*

Flaco: *Nah, I knew him from North Camden, but that's how we started doing business. He started frontin' me kilo's to sell in McGuire and then I opened the alley across the street.*

Jonathan Fine: *What is, "the alley"?*

Flaco: *There was an alley across the street from the projects, and I started selling drugs there.*

Jonathan Fine: *Was Mr. Johnson also financing the cocaine being sold in the alley?*

Flaco: *Yes.*

Jonathan Fine: *Who else worked in the alley?*

Flaco: *Trappers come and go, but Manny Gonzales was the manager; D.J. was the financier. It was my block and Muscleclo was the muscle and part owner. He had connects to unlimited coke in the D.R.*

Jonathan Fine: *So Muscleclo was the supplier?*

Flaco: *He was one of them. There was Pedro. We had connects in Florida, N.Y., D.R.*

Jonathan Fine: Was the alley your only drug corner?

Flaco: *Yes. I sold weight from my used car lot but the alley was my only block. D.J. had something to do with 33rd Street, but I didn't get none of that money.*

Jonathan Fine: *So who ran 33rd Street?*

Flaco: *That was Gato's spot.*

Jonathan Fine: *Can you tell us who Eduardo De Jesus was?*

Flaco: *Well he started out working for us in the alley as muscle. Him and Cuba from the D.R., but they wanted to take over so they became rivals.*

Jonathan Fine: *What do you mean by they wanted to take over?*

Flaco: *they wanted to kill me and have the alley to themselves. I heard rumors of that, so I set up a test.*

Jonathan Fine: A test? What kind of test?

Flaco: *Well, he was here from the D.R. with Cuba. I told him Cuba was plotting to kill me and he had to go. I sent him to take care of it.*

Jonathan Fine: *And by take care of it, you meant you wanted Cuba killed?*

Flaco: *Yes.*

Jonathan Fine: *And what happened?*

Flaco: *I sent two other people with Eduardo and they said he purposely missed Cuba.*

Jonathan Fine: *So, what happened next?*

Flaco: *We decided he had to go.*

Jonathan Fine: *We, meaning whom?*

Flaco: *It was a collective decision between me and Muscleclo.*

Jonathan Fine: *So, who carried out the plot?*

Flaco: *We flipped a coin; Muscleclo won the toss so he was the triggerman.*

Jonathan Fine: *How'd it happen?*

Flaco: We *lured him into one of our stash cribs, Manny grabbed his hands and Muscleclo shot him twice in the head.*

Over a two-day period the questioning went like that. Straight questions and straight answers. Flaco had outlined the whole Organization through his point of view. He gave up names of dirty cops like Jeremy Harris and told about how they were tipped off about raids. He also told of the many businesses owned by members of the organization. But the cross examination by Mark Ashley wouldn't be as sweet.

Mark Ashley: *You testified that it was a joint decision to kill Eduardo De Jesus, but you didn't mention my client's name. Why?*

Flaco: *We felt like he didn't need to be involved in that decision.*

Mark Ashley: *Oh. Okay, I guess you forgot to mention that. You also forgot to mention the part about you kicking Eduardo in the face; is that right?*

Flaco: *He was already dead when I kicked him.*

Mark Ashley: *And where did you get your Doctorate?*

Flaco: *I'm not a doctor, but I know a dead body when I see one.*

Mark Ashley: *Speaking of dead bodies, what happened the night you sent Eduardo to shoot at Cuba?*

Flaco: *I already told you; he missed.*

Mark Ashley: *He missed his target, but he did hit somebody, right?*

Flaco: *Cuba was hit, but not fatally, and a bystander was killed.*

Mark Ashley: I *guess you forgot the minor detail of an innocent life being lost? So, have you been charged in the murder of the bystander?*

Flaco: *No.*

Mark Ashley: *What about the murder of Eduardo?*

Flaco: *No, I didn't kill either one of them.*

Mark Ashley: *Since you sent the shooter, that would be considered felon murder, or at least conspiracy, but yet you haven't been charged with either? I wonder why?*

Flaco: I *guess you have to ask the prosecutor that one.*

Mark Ashley: *Maybe you should ask him since you two have become such good friends lately.*

Flaco just smiled as the people in the courtroom laughed.

Mark Ashley: *Do you have any tattoos?*

Flaco: *Yea, I have 14, but I think I know the one you want to see.* (He stood up and lifted his shirt exposing his stomach where a tattoo read: F--- the FBI)

Mark Ashley: *Don't you want to change that to I love the FBI since it's Valentine's Day?*

Flaco: *Happy Valentine's Day.*

There was a quiet laugh in the courtroom.

Mark Ashley: *Yesterday you talked about how Jorge Vargas tipped off about drug raids. You said you even left Camden for six months in '97. Where did you go?*

Flaco: *Boca Raton, Florida.*

Mark Ashley: *Do you mind translating Boca Raton from Spanish to English?*

Flaco: (smiling) *It means mouth of the rat. So, I guess that makes me a rat.*

Mark Ashley: *How much time were you facing before you decided to cooperate with the FBI... the people you love so much?*

Flaco: *Life, with no parole.*

Mark Ashley: *Well, that's a great incentive to make up a pack of lied. Seems like they should call you Boca Raton instead of Flaco!*

Jonathan Fine: *Objection your honor!*

Mark Ashley: *Withdrawn. I have no further questions for this witness.*

Judge: *The court will adjourn until tomorrow morning at 9:00 a.m.*

After Flaco's testimony the prosecution called a handful of supporting witnesses before getting back to the actual co-defendants. The second co-defendant called to the stand was Blockz. Blockz testimony was used mainly to paint a picture of the lavish lifestyle that was made possible thanks to his drug dealing. He actually had no direct connection to the alley or 33rd Street. He was the flashy member of the Organization so the government used him to show the lifestyle of a big time Camden drug dealer.

Jonathan Fine: *How did you meet Darren Johnson?*

Blockz: *A friend of mine Luis Noel was getting his cocaine from D.J. I met DJ through Luis.*

Jonathan Fine: *He was buying cocaine directly from Mr. Johnson?*

Blockz: *Yes, this was early to mid 80's and D.J. was selling drugs himself. I was still in High School. Later I started using drugs and selling beat bags and no one wanted me around. Eventually, I was sent to jail on distribution charges and then I came home, got clean and started selling drugs for real.*

Jonathan Fine: *When did your business relationship with Mr. Johnson begin?*

Blockz: *About 6 months after I was released from the half-way house. At the time, Luis was my supplier, but his supply couldn't keep up with my demand, so he reintroduced me to D.J.*

Jonathan Fine: *And what happened next?*

Blockz: *D.J. introduced me to Flaco and he became my supplier. He also gave me check stubs to give to my parole officer.*

Jonathan Fine: *So, Mr. Johnson never actually sold you drugs?*

Blockz: *Nah, he just introduced me to everybody. I dealt with Flaco, Muscleclo, or directly with Pedro Montoya. D.J. didn't sell drugs anymore. He financed drug spots and laundered money for hustlers. And also held cash for them.*

Jonathan Fine: *How do you know this?*

Blockz: *He did it for me; he helped me start my entertainment company Invisible Face. The money the Feds found in the safe in his office was mine too.*

Jonathan Fine: *How can you be so sure?*

Blockz: Because *they found $236,000 and that was exactly how much I gave him, plus it was still in the yellow footlocker bag I gave it to him in.*

Jonathan Fine: *Were you the only dealer giving him this kind of cash?*

Blockz: *I don't think so, but I never saw anybody else giving him money.*

Jonathan Fine: How much money were you personally making after linking up with Mr. Johnson and his associates?

Blockz: *I was a millionaire. I don't know how much I made a month, but I know I ran out of places to hide money and that's when I turned to D.J. for help. I was selling weight. I usually made at least $5,000 a kilo, and I sold 4 or 5 of those a week.*

Jonathan Fine: *What were you spending the money on, before turning to Mr. Johnson?*

Blockz: *I had a Land Cruiser, 2 houses in Collingswood. I bought 2 row houses in Parkside and knocked out the wall between them. I converted the whole thing into one house. 5 bedrooms, 3 hot tubs, marble floors, gold trimmed bathrooms and a chandelier. On the outside, except for new windows, I kept it exactly the same. There were two doors, two addresses and it looked no different than any other houses in Parkside. Besides that, I bought a crib in Cherry Hill for my baby mom and I also paid off my grandmother's house. I had a Benz, a Ford Pick up and I traveled to the islands regularly. I even bought a boat!*

Jonathan Fine: You bought a boat?

Blockz: *Yea, I went to price one and the lady said do you know how much these cost and started talking to me like I was broke, so I left and came back with $135,000 cash and bought it. It was a speedboat. That and the mini Palace I had in Parkside got me hot.*

Jonathan Fine: *Who did the work on your house for you?*

Blockz: *A construction company that D.J. and Jorge Lopez co-owned.*

Jonathan Fine: *You were arrested in June of 1997, correct?*

Blockz: *Yea, D.J. got a tip from a customer who had a relative in the department. He said that my house would get raided on June 1st.*

Jonathan Fine: *Did it?*

Blockz: *Nah, but on June 2nd it did.*

Jonathan Fine: *What were you charged with?*

Blockz: *Well, by then, all my houses were clean, but they still charged me with being the leader of a narcotics trafficking network.*

Jonathan Fine: So, when did things go bad between you and *Mr. Johnson?*

Blockz: *Well, in 1994 I was arrested for a gun charge. When I got out Noel fronted me 10 kilo's. When I cooked it up, it didn't come back right.*

Jonathan Fine*: Explain what you mean by, "the drugs didn't come back right".*

Blockz: *Basically, the drugs were bad, so I didn't pay him. Then he gave me another 10 and I didn't pay him for that either. D.J. used to tell me the other guys in the organization didn't like me. He would tell me that Noel and a couple of others wanted to kill me because I wasn't paying them on time. Me and* Muscleclo *even pulled guns on each other before, but I did what I wanted. Even after that, I remained close with DJ. In '97 when I got locked up I told him to take care of my grandma who's in her 90's. That's it. That, and to post my bail if it dropped from the $500,000 it was set at. He didn't do either one. In '98 when ya'll indicted me and said I was facing life, so here I am.*

Judge: *The court is adjourned. We will reconvene Monday morning at 9:00 a.m.*

When I read in the paper that Blockz was finished testifying, I got knots in my stomach. I knew Ace was next, and then me. Manny was supposed to be testifying in state court against Muscleclo on murder charges. In the whole two years that Jose

Martinez was recording conversations, he never once got Muscleclo on tape. He had a great defense in federal court on drug charges, but the state had him by the balls. He was most likely going to accept a guilty plea of 30 to life, state time. On Monday evening, I watched some of the things Ace said on the stand. The next morning, I got the paper as usual; especially curious of what my best friend had to say.

ACE YOUNG TESTIFIES JORGE LOPEZ BOUGHT WHOLESALE AMOUNTS OF COCAINE IN 1989. IN A FEDERAL TRIAL, HE SAID HE SOLD TO CAMDEN'S FUTURE MAYOR. THE MAYOR DENIES THIS.

The second admitted drug dealer testified today that in the late '80's and early 90's he sold drugs to Camden's future mayor, Jorge Lopez. Lopez denies even knowing Young but says he and Darren Johnson were from the same neighborhood. In court today, Young also testified about how he assisted his childhood friend Simon Gonzales, in creating the 33rd street set. Young, Gonzales and another dealer, who is now deceased, formed the set with help from Johnson. He told jurors that Gonzales (known on the streets as Gato) and Johnson had a father and son type of relationship. Young said his friend patterned himself after Johnson. He told the court about trips he personally took to New York and Florida to buy drugs to be sold on 33rd Street. Young said he had even received a 100-kilo shipment in N.Y. by the age of 19. He said his friend Gato could get anything from Johnson. Young described Muscleclo as more of the muscle than a leader, although he did have coke connections. He said Muscleclo carried out the violent acts to competitors and disciplined trappers for being late or disrespectful. He also testified his

248

friend Gato was making between $15,000 and $25,000 a week from the 33rd Street set.

I wondered why Ace had gone into so much detail about me. Was he jealous of me all these years or was he just doing what he had to do to come home? Tomorrow was *my* day, and after hearing everybody else's testimony I didn't know *what* to expect. Margaret came to see me that night, which was unusual. She usually came on the weekends. She told me that my Uncle Ramos had come to court to hear Ace's testimony. She said he showed no emotion on his face. That made me even more nervous. Tomorrow was the big day. I was going to take the stand and do something I never thought I would. The worst part was I had to do it in front of Jasmine, Uncle Ramos and Margaret. D.J. was the one person I couldn't wait to see.

The next day I was taken from Salem County Jail to the U.S. District Court in Downtown Camden. I was wearing my kaki suit from state prison. I took the stand and barely noticed Sonny and Uncle Ramos in the packed courtroom. I briefly made eye contact with D.J., who gave me a slight smirk, but I would have the last laugh.

Jonathan Fine: *State your name for the record.*

Gato: *Simon Gonzales. They call me Gato.*

Jonathan Fine: *Gato. That's Spanish for cat, right? Interesting nickname, how'd you get that?*

Gato: *I survived a couple of shootings, so they say I got nine lives.*

Jonathan Fine: *So, tell us how you met Mr. Darren Johnson.*

Gato: *He was around in my neighborhood when I was young. He was one of the big drug dealers.*

Jonathan Fine: *You were sentenced as a drug kingpin at 21. That's an awfully young age. Would you mind telling us how you got started?*

Gato: *I got started selling weed in McGuire housing Projects. I moved up to crack after getting permission from D.J.*

Jonathan Fine: *Permission, you mean you have to ask to sell drugs?*

Gato: *Yea, well D.J. already ran a drug set in McGuire, so I had to ask to open another one. Mine was in the back close to Admiral Wilson Blvd.*

Jonathan Fine: *Did D.J. finance your operation?*

Gato: *I bought my own work at first, and then he started frontin' me more, once he saw what I could do.*

Jonathan Fine: How did you get from McGuire to 33rd Street?

Gato: *First, we got a spot on Howell Street. We were getting money over there, until I got shot. After that, I went to the burg. When I came home, Ace was hanging with some dudes from the Acres. We started an operation in the Woodrow Wilson Arms Apartments on 33rd Street.*

Jonathan Fine: *Who started this operation?*

Gato: *Me, Ace and two friends. Both of them are dead, and out of respect for their families, I'd rather not mention their names. D.J. partially financed the operation, on and off, for the entire run.*

Jonathan Fine: *In 1996, you refused to cooperate with authorities in an investigation against Mr. Johnson. Why the change of heart?*

Gato: *You're not supposed to tell on people in this business, but I trusted him. Well, you're not supposed to trust anybody in this business either, but I did trust him, and he stole close to 3 million dollars from me. He threatened my son's mother. He has no loyalty to anyone.*

After I testified D.J. looked more shameful than I did. Mark Ashley tried to cross-examine me aggressively but it backfired. I was different from the rest of the defendants. I was a naive kid who was misguided by a monster. Even after that, I was still loyal. I was only sitting in this chair because of what he had done to me. The more he tried to make me out to be a rat the worse he made D.J. look. Finally he stopped trying. As bad as the trial was going for D.J. so far, it got worse on the final three days when Jose Martinez testified. Not so much his testimony, because Mark Ashley reduced him to tears a couple of times. But the 90 hours worth of incriminating conversations he recorded with D.J. He had D.J. on tape bragging about financing the campaign of the mayor and how the mayor's bodyguard, an ex-cop had sold Gato guns before. D.J. discussed possible snitches that needed to be eliminated and how he was shielded from the law by crooked cops.

He even told Martinez, "I'm a legit businessman that pays a million dollars a year in taxes. They're not just going to come pick me up. Somebody's going to have to wear a wire to get me".

251

The person he was talking to turned out to be that someone. The prosecution gave their closing arguments and pointed out that even though only one person was charged with murder the organization was directly or indirectly responsible for 21 murders in the city from 1988-1998. On that note they rested their case. The defense gave a good argument about all the defendants being rats, who wanted to get out a life sentence, and he might have been right. But, it was all-true and the jury believed every word. When the foreman read the verdict D.J. dropped his head as if he was actually surprised. The jury was then asked to vote on seizing his assets. They did, but left his family with $410,000 in liquid assets. Sentencing was set for May 15th.

Nine days after D.J. was found guilty, mayor Jorge Lopez was hit with a 14-count indictment. Most of the charges involved money laundering, misuse of government funds and corruption. None of the counts were for murder or drugs. D.J. saw this as a way out and agreed to testify against the mayor in exchange for consideration during sentencing. His testimony was done in a closed meeting with the U.S. District Attorney. When May 15th rolled around all 13 defendants were in one room for the first time in years. The judge read off the defendants and the time they received.

Carmen Montoya: 84 months
Pedro Montoya: 105 months
Enrique Cintron: 46 months
Manny Gonzales: 148 months
Luis Noel: 84 months
Kevin "Blockz" Baily: 160 months

Raoul Quivoures: 63 months
Samuel "Flaco" Torres: 160 months
Ace Young: released by court
Simon Gonzales: released by court
Manuel "Muscleclo" Vargas: 30 years state time
Darren "D.J." Johnson: 196 months

In the end only two people kept their mouth completely shut Muscleclo and Carmen. Even Carmen's brother Enrique told about how cocaine was dropped in canisters into the Delaware River and retrieved by scuba divers. Juan Martinez was put in a federal witness protection program and, as promised, Ace and I were released on May 15th right after sentencing. I saw Uncle Ramos and Sonny in the courtroom but after signing the release papers and changing clothes, they were nowhere to be found. For now, I had my life back, and that's all that mattered.

When I walked out of the courtroom a free man, for the first time in 6 years, I felt strange. I had places to go, but nowhere that I wanted to go. I had snitched and I was going to be an outcast in the hood. Jasmine had a new boyfriend and was pregnant and I never did catch up to Sonny and Uncle Ramos. Margaret was still doing the same things she was in '94 and to top it off, I was broke. There was only one person I knew could help me, so I stopped a cab "Take me to International Beauty Salon on Westfield Avenue, I'll pay you when we get there", I told the driver. I had a plan, I knew some hustlers in other cities I could restart my career, after all every hood has a couple snitches. The next day I was on the cover of the Post.

Camden Post

May 16, 2000

TRIAL HELPS KINGPIN AND HIS LUITENANT GET A SUSPENDED SENTENCE. SIMON GONZALES AND ACE YOUNG TESTIFIED AGAINST CAMDEN D.R.UG LORDS. THEIR COOPERATION PUT 11 OTHERS BEHIND BARS.

"You see this shit in the Newspaper?" These kids now a days, they always trying to justify snitching. There is absolutely no justification for snitching at all", Jorge Vargas said.

"Look on the bright side, the lawyer we got you said there only going to indict you for corruption, it's a slap on the wrist compared to what could of happened, if they would have found out you where really behind the whole *Organization*." You didn't tell on me or Sonny so we're going to take care of you... the mayor a drug dealer they would have gave you life for sure", Ramos said.

"I guess your right, just make sure my wife gets that money you promised", Jorge said while shaking his head.

"I'm a man of my word, besides I don't want you to start ratting I'm too old to go back to jail", Ramos answered laughing.

"Hey, I'm cut from a different cloth than them dudes I keep my mouth shut I'll be home in about six, while you two old muthafucka's live the good life", Jorge said laughing.

"Well, Jorge it's been good doing business with you but we have a plane to catch", Sonny said as him and Ramos left city hall with one way tickets to California.

Her Little Secret

How far would you go to keep a secret? Lerrez Crawford grew up in one of Camden, New Jersey's worse neighborhoods and was raised by her crack-addicted parents. She never had anyone to tell her to reach for the stars, but somehow after a heinous childhood Lerrez managed to due just that. After her roller coaster ride called life finally smoothed out, Lerrerz found herself traveling to places most people only dream of. After escaping her past life and the city she once called home, Lerrez thought her old identity was buried since she certainly wouldn't be seeing anybody from the projects in her plush Beverly Hills neighborhood. But, it's a small world and things have a way of catching up with you even 3,000 miles away from home as Lerrez finds out. To what extremes is Lerrez willing to go to, to keep.... **Her Little Secret**!

Her Little Secret Coming Soon.
By T. Freeman Jr.

The Sons of Sin

Taino went down for murder at a real young age and missed out on his teenage years. During his years in prison he went through allot of changes, trying to get his mind of the game. He was only 16 when he went to prison for murder, and the game was all he knew. His little cousin Jay and his boy Quan's name have been ringing bells in the streets of North Camden and throughout The New Jersey State Prison system. He hears they are in the streets and heavily involved with the drug game. He talks to Jay from time to time about the dangers of the streets but deep down inside he feels he has one last run in him and that Jay and Quan could be good assets if schooled right. Taino went to jail so young for murder that he never was able to make allot of money during his time in the streets and with his little cousin doing big things he sees an opportunity to make allot of money and then go legit, although he never revealed this to anyone, not even Jay. When Taino finally comes home and aligns himself with Jay and Quan, they start a new movement in the streets and it's called... **The Sons of Sin.**

The Sons of Sin Coming Soon
By Taino De La Ghetto and T. Freeman Jr.

Ghetto Heaven

I was born into a different type of heaven, conceived out of darkness. From a righteous woman from a righteous source a place where I had no choice to go to. From fathers pleasures to a mothers pain to earthly possessions that were by ill gotten means. An angel of light an Angel de Luz who equipped me for pain, pleasure, and abuse. A place where we diligently seek to do no good, where I sat enthralled by the words of the hood. The place I was said to be a state of mind where the intelligent lay dormant while being led by the blind. A devout servant of temptation and lust where having a hard crust was a necessity where the motto was I must get ahead of thee. Pulling back the weak and taking advantage of the meek often laying back in the darkness and counting the rain while the sound is drip drop, drip drop, on the windows of pain. A different type of heaven where pleasures were scarcely spread about, where a smile and a hug were always in drought. Attempts to find happiness often end in futility where loneliness and discomfort where always ahead of me. Pleasurable entities came few at a time, desperation and desolation boosted the crimes, inspiration came from unexpected places in unexpected ways, but sometimes it was enough to get you through the pain and to know this type of heaven is heavenly ordained is enough to drive the average person insane. No matter how insignificant that this may seem it was all that we had by any and all means. My dominant beliefs led me to believe this interpretation was a permanent state that was always irate in a ghetto paradise surrounded by gates. A self-imposed slavery that was a child of ignorance that stunted the growth of my creative intelligence. A proven formula for ultimate demise unless you awaken and shaken and start to realize that this ghetto heaven was a ghetto hell!!

By Taino De La Ghetto
From the forthcoming Poetry Book *Unspoken Words of a Prisoner*

Made in the USA
Lexington, KY
01 September 2012